Just Outside by Stacy Aumonier

Stacy Aumonier was born at Hampstead Road near Regent's Park, London on 31st March 1877.

He came from a family with a strong and sustained tradition in the visual arts; sculptors and painters.

On leaving school it seemed the family tradition would also be his career path. In particular his early talents were that of a landscape painter. He exhibited paintings at the Royal Academy in the early years of the twentieth century.

In 1907 he married the international concert pianist, Gertrude Peppercorn, at West Horsley in Surrey. A year later Aumonier began a career in a second branch of the arts at which he enjoyed a short but outstanding success—as a stage performer writing and performing his own sketches.

The Observer newspaper commented that "...the stage lost in him a real and rare genius, he could walk out alone before any audience, from the simplest to the most sophisticated, and make it laugh or cry at will."

In 1915, Aumonier published a short story 'The Friends' which was well received (and was subsequently voted one of the 15 best stories of 1915 by the Boston Magazine, Transcript).

Despite his age in 1917 at age 40 he was called up for service in World War I. He began as a private in the Army Pay Corps, and then transferred as a draughtsman in the Ministry of National Service.

By now he had four books published—two novels and two books of short stories—and his occupation is recorded with the Army Medical Board as 'author.'

In the mid-1920s, Aumonier received the shattering diagnosis that he had contracted tuberculosis. In the last few years of his life, he would spend long spells in various sanatoria, some better than others.

Shortly before his death, Stacy Aumonier sought treatment in Switzerland, but died of the disease in Clinique La Prairie at Clarens beside Lake Geneva on 21st December 1928. He was 55.

Index of Contents

CHAPTER I - WHICH CONCERNS A PENKNIFE
CHAPTER II - A RUM BUSINESS
CHAPTER III - THE DISENCHANTED DAY
CHAPTER IV - THE JUDGMENT OF EDITH
CHAPTER V - MESSRS. BLINKINSHAW & BEPSTOW
CHAPTER VI - FRANK LEFFBURY
CHAPTER VII - THE DESIGNER
CHAPTER VIII - SELF EXPRESSION
CHAPTER IX - "RACING AWAY INTO THE UNKNOWN"
CHAPTER X - THE BUNGALOW AT BODIESHAM
CHAPTER XI - ARTHUR HAS TWO VISITORS
CHAPTER XII - PARIS AND BACK
CHAPTER XIII - ALICE FLIES A KITE
CHAPTER XIV - A NEW CENTURY DAWNS

CHAPTER XV - THE REFORMER
CHAPTER XVI - LADY MTLLWORTHY'S MUFF
CHAPTER XVII - THE MOUNTAIN PEAK
CHAPTER XVIII - IN SEARCH OF SENTIENT JOYS
CHAPTER XIX - THE FUGITIVE PHILOSOPHER
CHAPTER XX - AN AFFAIR IN'THE OLD GUYS'
CHAPTER XXI - A FIELD OF DAFFODILS
CHAPTER XXII - ALICE HEARS THE NIGHTINGALE
CHAPTER XXIII - LOVE AMONG THE TOMBSTONES
CHAPTER XXIV - TOUCH AND GO
CHAPTER XXV - THE DUST OF THE SEA
CHAPTER XXVI - KICKING THE SHAVINGS UNDER YOUR FEET
CHAPTER XXVII - THE SENSUALIST
CHAPTER XXVIII - ARTHUR WRITES A LETTER
CHAPTER XXIX - MR. LEFFBURY REPUES TO ANOTHER LETTER
STACY AUMONIER – A SHORT BIOGRAPHY
STACY AUMONIER – A CONCISE BIBLIOGRAPHY

CHAPTER I

WHICH CONCERNS A PENKNIFE

The train rumbled dilatorily through the open country. The boy, huddling in the comer of the third-class carriage, stared at the changing series of views framed by the window on his left, with unseeing eyes.

His mind was occupied with other visions, visions of the episodes of his recent experience. They were all very, very vivid, and they left him trembling and unstrung, and his eyes swimming on the borderland of tears.

It is said that when a man falls over a precipice he recalls all the unimportant and some of the important events of his life during the few seconds' flight through the air. In somewhat similar case there were several precipitate moments during this journey when Arthur Gaffyn endured a composite review of all the perverse moods and experiences of his seventeen years of life that had reached their apotheosis in that ill-omened ten minutes in "the Rook's" study.

The climax was unendurable, horrible, and -in some vague way, unfair! It was useless to keep on saying to himself that school was in any case a disgusting place, that the chaps at Cullington were a lot of cads, and that the headmaster—or "the Hook"' as they called him—was a beast He found it easier to convince himself of the truth of the last statement than of the other two. The Book he knew had disliked him from the first, never troubled to try to find out anything in him, had damned him at sight as not a representative specimen of the school "type."

But the school? It was absurd perhaps, but there was an indefinable something about the school, a sort of sentiment which pervaded the place. There were things about it he would never forget, things and boys he knew that he would remember when all other memories were dim.

There was old Seedy Simpson, who had been his chum for two years. He had a curious affection for Seedy. And there was Tony Younger, and Steele, and young Bates; and then there was Curly

Smithers, who had short flaxen hair and a most wonderful infectious laugh. They were all decent chaps, and the memory of them would make him sigh forever and ever.

And there were jolly days, days of sunlight, and "rags" and absurd games, and days when he had distinguished himself in some surprising manner. And there were curious odd moments when the place satisfied him. Just a grin or a look some boy or master would give him, the sun making patterns on the classroom floor, and birds twittering outside the window. There were even moments in chapel—usually the dullest and most boring of places —when the drone of some old hymn would find an emotional response within himself.

And there was cricket which always made an appeal when it was n't rammed down one's throat, and the thrill of a game of fives, which he played well; and there were some glorious bouts of boxing in the gym, at which he was no mean exponent. Indeed, one of the proudest moments of his life had been when Moll, the gym-instructor, had said, "Young Gaffyn is one of the best judges of distance we have."

And now it had all come to this sudden and violent end—dismissed!

The disgrace of it! He tried to persuade himself that it wasn't a disgrace; that it was all due to the Book's prejudice; that the whole thing was ridiculous; that he was not really "the person without moral bias" that the Book had denounced; but the weight of his condemnation depressed him. It was useless to try to console himself with the reflection that nothing within himself had changed, and that incidentally he was now a free spirit, lording it in a railway carriage while the chaps at Cullington were swotting at their Greek prose, or their tiresome permutations and combinations. The terrible and irrevocable fatality could not be denied. He felt himself to be "a thin ghost or disembodied spirit" haunted forever by the Book's portentous threat of doom. It was not so much the Book himself , although he was terrifying enough; it was what the Book represented. He had been denounced by that cold abstract voice that seemed to express the unalterable edict not of a man but of a tradition, centuries and centuries of unswerving faith in certain set forms and conventions,—truth, justice, 'the honor of the school.'" And at his back he had not only the traditions of Cullington but of all other schools, and of all the masters at all the other schools, the church, the king, the judges, the police, the army, the navy, the whole human fabric. Whatever Arthur thought himself, he could not stand up against this. He felt as though the forces of human life had formed a phalanx from which he was shut out.

The train pulled up at a station and some people got out. It started forward again, jerkily, and he beheld an outlying district of congested squalor, where small back gardens and yards made a pathetic attempt to strike a note of gaiety. It was the first objective thing he had observed, and his heart was vaguely stirred by the pathos of it.

"These people, too," he thought, "are outcasts. Perhaps I shall come to this."

But his mind became busy again reviewing the incidents of the crime that had led to his undoing. It had been the custom every year for the Head's wife to take all the boys who sang in the choir for a treat It was a very rum business. They had a brake and drove over to Moblechester, and had tea at the Aquarium. It was a curious building where all sorts of queer things went on. There were crowds of stalls and side-shows, and a man who did silhouette portraits, and there was a large central hall where a concert took place. The tea was prodigiously good, but he thought all the rest of it rather boring. None of his particular friends were in the choir, and he wandered about the building very much alone. It was a heavy, humid sort of day, and the high-spirited fooling that went on among the other boys got on his nerves. After a time he went in to the concert-hall by himself and sat up in a comer. There was a String-quartet playing. He hadn't a program, and he didn't know what it was they played, but after sitting there some time, the music affected him in an unaccountable manner. He felt very much as though he wanted to cry, as though he couldn't stand it. At the same time he had a feeling that he could only describe as being egotistical. He looked round at the other people there, and hated them. He hated their ugly, silly, expressionless faces. He felt tremendously moved, and somehow superior. He wanted to commune with some one, some one who would understand, but there was no one there who would be likely to understand. The only person in sight whom he knew was the Head's wife. She was seated in the front row, looking very bored and important. The situation became intolerable, and he went out. He wandered round the gallery, and a mood of sullen perverseness came over him. He avoided any boys he met from the school and wandered into a cutler's booth. It was a large place elaborately constructed in white wood and metal, with innumerable mirrors. There was an attendant talking to some ladies by the door. He strolled to the end of the shop. There appeared to be millions of glittering metal things. One long counter was covered with penknives. His eyes alighted on a particular penknife in the corner. It was a large knife with mother-of-pearl covering, and it had about eight or ten attachments. One could do nearly everything with it. It was a splendid knife. It would certainly cost over a sovereign. He stood there pondering and gazing at the knife a long time. As the train travelled heavily London-ward, he tried to analyse his own real feelings and motives at the moment when he perpetrated the mad act that had been the cause of his dismissal. It was very difficult, difficult and confusing. It had all been so sudden, an impulse, in fact. He knew that it had suddenly occurred to him how jolly it would be to have the knife, and he knew he had not enough to pay for it. Interwoven with this thought was the reflex of the sullen mood of resentment against his fellow-man on that humid afternoon, and the further encouragement of a small voice that said:

"There are swarms of these here. One won't make any diflference."

And then he had a vision of himself swanking with the knife when he got back to Cullington. The whole thing was instantaneous. He slipped the knife into his pocket, and made for the door.

He had got out into the gallery and then the appalling thing happened. It was so horrible, he struggled not to think of it. But the vision of that moment recurred again, and again, and again. He had not allowed for the mirrors. There was another attendant, a young man with a dark mustache. He would remember that man's face till his dying day. It was a perfect nightmare. He had been caught hold of and taken into an office. The Head's wife had been summoned. Two or three flushed officials talked excitedly. He had nothing to say. He believed he cried in a dry-eyed, ineffectual sort of way. He lost the power of speech and volition. The Head's wife was terrible. She looked at him with those hard, cruel eyes of hers. She must be the most unattractive woman in the world. He remembered noticing the light down on her upper lip and the stiff, silly way she held herself. He remembered her imploring the officials to spare 'the honor of the school,' and the acid tones of her voice as she added:

"If you will be kind enough to leave the punishment of the offender to the Head, I assure you, gentlemen, you shall be satisfied in every way. Every reparation shall be made. It is a serious thing for us for the school."

She had seemed to him at that moment terrifying but unconscionably ridiculous. He could not remember then what the officials had said, or what the Head's wife had said. He seemed to lose all power over his receptive senses, and stood there dumbly, unnerved, like an animal waiting to be slaughtered. He had visions of prison, and he thought to himself:

"It is all over. Everything is finished."

Some one led him down to the brake on which the boys were to return. By a curious chance none of them had witnessed his adventure. He remembered Watkinson of the lower Sixth strolling up and saying:

"Hello, Gaffyn where have you been since tea?"

And himself answering:

"Oh, mucking about."

The return journey in the brake, and the normal condition of things when they got back to school steadied him somewhat He kept asking himself whether the whole thing weren't an hallucination, some mad dream that had come to him while listening to the music. Or even if it were true, whether it would n't blow over, after the imposition of some trifling punishment. He tried desperately to work at his "prep" but the incidents of the afternoon kept interposing themselves between his eyes and the book. It was useless. Suddenly Baynes, the senior prefect, entered the class-room. He looked round and spotted Gaffyn, and then said in a matter-of fact way:

"Gaffyn, the Head wishes to see you in his study after chapel."

Then indeed the nervous impulses of his body rioted exceedingly. He tried to appear casual, as though he knew what it was about, and that it was of no importance. But incidentally he felt physically sick. He answered, "All right" and dared not lift his eyes from the book till the end of "prep."

In chapel the cold greenish light from the gas-brackets made the faces of the boys and masters appear ghoulish and revolting. From his point of vantage in the choir he watched the Book's face. It gave no clue to the sinister proceedings that were to follow. It looked cold and expressionless, less like a rook than like a vulture. He wondered for the first time why he had been called a rook and not a vulture. He was certainly very dark, had raven-black hair turning gray at the temples and a heavy dark mustache. He was very short-sighted and wore thick spectacles. This probably accounted for his always looking down, and indirectly it may have accounted for his walk. He had a most peculiar walk, a sort of pounce from one foot to the other, as though he were not sure of himself beyond a stride. He seemed to poise on one leg, and then dart forward on to the other and poise again. It added to his bird-of-prey appearance.

Not once during the short service did the Rook look up, and not for a moment did Arthur take his eyes off him. Some dreary hymn-tune droned through the chapel, and Mr. Harris up in the organ-loft had pulled out the vox-humama stop, and was giving full play to that peculiar drone of hurdy-gurdy emotionalism which is deemed the right and appropriate atmosphere for breeding a religious spirit in a Christian heart. It was strange but at that moment he felt a recurrence of the sense of egotistical elation which he had experienced at the concert in the afternoon. He thought to himself:

"How silly all this is; silly and sordid and commonplace!"

But immediately the vision of all other chapels, and the tyranny of righteousness (again accompanied by the police, and the judges, and the king, and the army, and the navy) once more combined to depress him. He felt very much alone. If only there were some one, just one other person who would believe in him, help him. He was not wholly bad, he kept saying to himself. Chapel was finished, and the boys were scurrying to their different dormitories. With desperate deliberation he walked up to the Book's study. He knocked on the door, but the master had not yet arrived, so he stood patiently without.

He seemed to wait an interminable period, and then he heard the steady pounce of the Rook coming along the corridor. He stood on one side in the respectful attitude expected of a boy at Cullington College. The Rook walked by him without glancing in his direction. He opened the door and turned on the electric light, and went into the room, followed by Arthur.

He fancied the Book mumbled, "Shut the door." In any case, he did so, and stood in the usual culprit's place facing the desk. In the brief moment while the master was walking to his seat behind the green standard lamp, the whole appearance of the room impressed itself on the boy's mind in an indelible picture. The heavy Victorian furniture and the cold green walls, the photograph of Zermatt between the two windows, several photographs of school and college teams, and, for some reason or other, an enlargement of a portrait of Mr. Balfour framed in oak.

To his dying day he would remember that moment, and the intense silence while his heart was beating against his ribs. He thought the Book was never going to speak; he meant to go on just torturing him with his accusatory silence.

But at last the voice came, like the snapping of a steel spring:

"Well, Gaff, what have you to say?"

Arthur shivered. He believed he murmured limply:

"I don't know, sir."

There was another ghastly pause, and then the Book said:

"You don't know, eh?"

He became aware of the Book looking at him for the first time. His eyes looked enormous through the thick glasses. The tones of his voice changed. He spoke in a thin, melancholy key:

"Do you deny that you took this property from the cutler's shop?"

Arthur answered faintly:

"No, sir."

The Rook took off his spectacles and wiped them. Arthur was aware that he could not see him without his spectacles, but he looked so horrible without them, so like a blind monstrosity, that he secretly prayed that he would put them back again. But he went on rubbing and blinking at the lamp. Suddenly in a loud, stem voice he said:

"Indeed! And may I trouble you to tell me why you took it?"

Arthur shuffled from one foot to the other and coughed. He could not get his voice. At last he managed to stammer:

"I did n't think it would matter very much, sir."

"Oh!"

The head-master of Cullington readjusted his glasses and fixed his eyes on the desk in front of him.

"Really! That's very interesting. You did n't think it would matter very much? You think that deliberate stealing doesn't matter much? You think that honor, and truth, and honesty do not matter very much, eh? You think that the honor of the school does not matter very much?"

Arthur did not answer, and the Rook continued:

"This is not the first time you have been before me, Gaffyn. But it is, I think, the first time you have been before me for stealing. There are many other things against you, but stealing is an offense we do not condone. If you will steal a penknife, you will steal anything else. If you will steal and think it does not matter very much, it means that you will do anything that Satan prompts you to. You are the most dangerous sort of boy to have in a school, in fact the most dangerous element to have in society of any sort, for you have ability and no moral bias."

The Rook paused and fumbled with some papers; then he said icily:

"We do not require such boys at Cullington. You will catch the 2:37 back to London to-morrow. You are dismissed."

Arthur was staggered. He had expected punishment, but it had never occurred to him that it might take this extreme form. He could not for the moment grasp exactly what it signified. Only one thing stood out clearly—freedom! He would be leaving school, getting away from it all. There was no mention of police, or corporal punishment, or anything of that sort. It would be more a sort of mental and moral punishment. He would be bundled off and left to stew in the juice of his own bad conscience, branded forever with the hall-mark of guilt by the school, and all the other schools, by the judges, the police, the army and navy and all the other paraphernalia of an upright people. He would wander about the world a forsworn convict. He was astute enough at that moment to jump to the conclusion that it was the longest-headed, most diabolical punishment of all. And it was all brought about by a pearl-handled penknife. A temptation rose to his lips to mutter, "What a ridiculous fuss to make about a penknife!" but he did not say this; he merely answered: 'Very well, sir.'

The Rook was still staring at his desk, and he heard him say in a matter-of-fact voice:

"We have promised the director of the Aquarium that you shall leave the school to-morrow. I have written to your father explaining the reason. You may go."

As he lay shivering in his bed that night, his mind became acutely concerned with the Book's penultimate sentence, "I have written to your father explaining the reason."

Good Heavens! Was there ever a more deplorable position to be in? His father would have the reason explained to him! He could not by any stretch of the imagination picture how it would affect his father. If his mother had been alive, his dear French mother who had died five years ago, he would have rushed to her and thrown his arms around her neck and sobbed. And she would have sobbed, too. She would have scolded, blamed, stormed, commiserated and hugged him. It would have been a terrible quarter-of-an-hour, and then would have come that sense of peace, and the cosy feeling of starting all over again. And afterwards she would have fought for him cunningly and desperately. She would have routed the judges, and the masters, and the army, and the navy, and all the rest of them. She would have triumphed, and made him triumph. But his poor, ineffectual, highly-strung, sensitive father! How would he take it.

Never, never, never in all their united lives had his father given him anything of intimacy, or any demonstration of affection. Not but what he believed that his father had a real affection for him in his peculiar way, but he simply could not bring himself to show it. When they were together there was always a feeling of intense self-consciousness. He would talk, but always of general and abstract things. If the conversation showed the slightest tendency to veer towards personal matters his father would behave like a frightened rabbit. He would be most garrulous when most nervous. He would dash about for topics to ward off the terrible personal equation.

It must be said for Arthur, whose character has already given evidence of a certain lack of stability, that during that sleepless night, and also during the train journey to town, he was more concerned for his father than for himself. It would simply be torture for his father to get that letter from the Rook 'explaining the reason.'

He was still analysing the probabilities of his father's behaviour, and heaving with the turmoil of his own emotions, when the train slowed down and rumbled across the iron bridge and into the big terminus.

It became necessary then to bestir himself, and rescue his box from the general commotion going on round the luggage-van. He somewhat guiltily ordered a four-wheeled cab. He resented having to do this, because his father would have to pay for it, and his father, he knew, was by no means well off. But there was no alternative; his box was too heavy to carry.

The cab itself had a guilty look, and it meandered off in the direction of Bloomsbury at the pace of a thing that dreads to find the journey accomplished. When they arrived in Eccles Square, he asked the cabman to help him in with the box. The man looked at him with the expression of a person whose most sacred feelings had been violently outraged. But he made no comment and got down from his seat. The journey up those five stone steps to his father's house was accompanied by the most amazing exhibition of physical suffering on the part of the cabman it had ever been Arthur's lot to witness. He gasped and panted wheezed and struggled, so violently that Arthur had visions of his home-coming being marked by the man's dissolution on the hall mat. However, when Mrs. Stabbe, the cook-housekeeper, had come to the rescue, and lifted the box quite easily by herself and put it round the comer, Arthur asked him how much the fare was.

Through the violent derangement of his vocal organs the cabman managed to say, "Three-and-six," and Arthur handed him four shillings.

When the door had slammed, Mrs. Stabbe remarked:

"Lord! Master Arthur, you're just like your father. The fare's only two shillings."

Arthur grinned uncomfortably and said:

"Is the guv'nor in, Mrs. Stabbe?"

"Yes, sir" she answered. "He's in the studio with Mr. McIlrane."

CHAPTER II

Mr. Gaffyn senior was an architect, and he lived alone in this high narrow house in Eccles Square, attended by Mrs. Stabbe and one maid. He conducted his business in a studio at the back, that had formerly been a laboratory built over the garden by the former tenant, who was an analyst. The house was a curious mixture of elegance and shabbiness. There were a few pieces of rare old furniture, a few traces of gentleness and refinement, the faded relicts of a woman's influence, and for the rest, everything was serviceable, fairly comfortable, and very much worn. There was oil-cloth on the upper landings on which the pattern had been completely obliterated, except in corners where people didn't tread, and in many places there were holes right through to the boards. The heavy curtains in the drawing-room seemed to have secreted the grime of Bloomsbury for generations. The ceilings were black, and the paper was hanging in ominous bulges in the hall. On the other hand, there was a splendid modem bathroom, all white tiles and new nickel fittings, probably some innovation insisted on by the late Mrs. Gaffyn. The small breakfast-room at the back had been fitted with new oak panelling, and there were six framed pastels of a very modem genre, signed by J. Guillot. Over the mantelpiece in the drawing-room was a photograph of Arthur's mother holding a baby in her arms. And this baby was not himself. It was his little sister who had died within the year of her birth and who had been the cause of his mother's death. This much he had learned from his Aunt Elizabeth. His mother was the daughter of a famous French baritone, a Monsieur Jules Carbonnet, who created many parts in the operas of Massenet at that time, and who was, moreover, a man much talked about, owing to his somewhat eccentric manners and his florid mode of life. "Florid" was not Aunt Elizabeth's term. She called it "peculiar" and she added by way of parenthesis that she was afraid old Carbonnet was not all he ought to have been. The term "florid" was introduced mentally by Arthur in forming his own deduction of the character of his notorious grandfather.

It appeared that his father met his mother in Paris, where he had been sent when quite a young man by some architectural society to report with two other architects on the result of the labors of Baron Haussmann in restoring the irrepressible city after the Franco-German War. Mr. Gaffyn had been chosen partly because he promised to be one of the coming architects, and partly because he spoke the French language fluently. The exact conditions under which he met Mile. Carbonnet remained obscure. As far as Arthur could remember, the marriage had been entirely successful. They seemed to get on wonderfully together. He remembered his mother's endearing terms. She called Mr. Gaffyn "ma mie" and sometimes "my little one" which, in view of the fact that her husband was six feet two inches, seemed peculiarly piquant to the boy. And Mr. Gaffyn on his part would blush painfully if anyone were present and mutter, "Yes—we—well, m'm, my dear—"and would quickly plunge for some topic of general interest. But he would fidget about, and watch her in a furtive, adoring manner. Arthur could not remember that he ever used a stronger term than "my dear" or that he ever gave her little presents, or made endearing advances. He was just as conventional and self-conscious with her as with other people. But she seemed to understand him, and treated him precisely like a baby.

Arthur was the only child until a certain tragic summer. Between the day of his birth and the birth of his little sister there had been an interval of eleven years.

Arthur could not bring himself to dwell on those terrible days. The anguish of his father seemed to express itself in eccentric movements. For a time he became frankly "a queer character." He never gave any evidence of giving way to grief. He was like a sane man hiding behind the pose of an insane man. When, on the day of his wife's funeral, tearful relatives threatened to throw themselves on his bosom he talked to them about Byzantine architecture.

He wore extravagantly out-of-date clothes, studied Spanish, and physics, and subjects which bordered on the esoteric. He became a profound seeker after qualities. If he secured a commission, he would spend an unconscionable time over his designs. He would go to South Kensington, and spend days considering the section of a certain cornice. He would then set it up with meticulous precision. Suddenly some other idea would come to him and he would tear up this elaborately considered drawing and do something quite different.

Alas I for the early promise of the young architect who went with such excellent credentials to Paris. Very few commissions came his way. People became impatient of all this nervous searching after quality, and this vacillation. They shrugged their shoulders and called him "Poor old Gaffyn." A man of irreproachable taste and great sensitiveness and power of invention, he had all the qualities of a great architect without any of that sense of practical application which will see a thing through. And a strange thing was that, despite his passionate groping for beauty in his work, he seemed to take delight in surrounding himself with ugly and commonplace things in his house, and in being chilling and matter-of-fact in his convention. This was so, in any case, since the death of his wife.

He had an assistant who was a curious counterpart of himself. He was an old-young man named McIlrane. That is to say, he was actually twenty-six years of age, but he might have been anything from thirty-six to forty-six. He was as profound a student as Mr. Gaffyn, and equally as ineffectual. He had a thin aquiline face and wore spectacles, and he imitated Mr. Gaffyn unconsciously. There was surely never a more unpractical couple destined to run a business. The marvel is that drawings were completed at all. They entered big competitions, and talked about some minor point of esthetic interest until it was nearly the day of sending in. As a matter of fact, there is no record of their ever having secured a prize in open combination, or of having been the joint architects of any recognized building, with the exception of one small mausoleum, which a wealthy stock-jobber had erected to the memory of his uncle who was killed in the Zulu War.

But they lived a wonderful life of their own, sublimely oblivious to success or failure. They burned the midnight oil profusely, and were never tired of expounding new theories about architecture or biology, or of experimenting in new media for the expression of their architectural ideas. Mr. Gaffyn would watch McIlrane making a shaded charcoal sketch of a cap. When it was finished, they would pin it up on the wall, and go to the other end of the studio and stand side by side with their heads slightly aslant and criticize it.

"Er—don't you think, perhaps Mr. Gaffyn would say, "th—er—filet of the scroll—er; a little broader, eh?"

And McIlrane would reply:

"Ah! I thought perhaps you'd think so, Mr. Gaffyn. Yes, yes, I am quite sure you're right, though I may have rather emphasized the cast shadow underneath. Perhaps in the model the effect would be broader."

They would make another drawing, and then a clay model of the cap, and worry over it for days, and eventually decide that it was the wrong type of cap altogether. And all this for a job which they stood only the remotest chance of getting! The stock-jobber's mausoleum was indeed a magnum opus—it took seven months to design—but the client was not particularly pleased with it. He did not consider that it was sufficiently suggestive of the Zulu War. And after he had freed himself from his architects, he employed a local brass furnisher to cover it with spears, and assagais, and skulls.

The meeting between Arthur and his father on the day of his return took place in the hall. After the retreat of the cabman, and Mrs. Stabbe's intimation that the master of the house was in the studio, Arthur remarked that he would not disturb him. He would see him later. He then went upstairs and mooned about the different rooms to see if there were any alterations or additions, a vague expectation that was quickly doomed to disappointment After that he unpacked his box in a sketchy way and had a warm bath. This was a luxury he always looked forward to in his father's house, for it was an operation that at school was attended with the greatest degree of discomfort.

He took a long time over the bath and dressed in a leisurely manner, and then strolled down to the dining-room on the ground floor. There was very little there to interest him. The air seemed heavy with stale tobacco smoke, and on the horse-hair settee was a pile of old copies of The Times, and various trade journals. He took an apple out of a bowl on the sideboard and stood munching it in front of the window. After a few moments he heard the studio door open and slam, and his father's footsteps scurrying across the hall.

Arthur's heart was beating rapidly, and he bit desperately at the apple, feeling that in some way the action helped him to control his nervousness. He heard his father fumbling at the hat-stand. He was evidently going oat. He did not know of Arthur's return. Making a great effort to steady himself, he strolled casually across the room and into the hall.

Mr. Gaffyn was in the act of taking an umbrella out of the stand. He looked up quickly and said:

"Oh—er—"

Arthur replied:

''Hello!''

There was a desperately disconcerting pause. He noticed his father fussing about with his gloves and putting some papers down. He made a curious noise in his throat, and at last said:

"Oh, so you've got back, then."

Arthur wriggled against the wall, still munching the apple. He answered:

''Yes, I got a cab from Charing Cross. The man helped me in with the box.''

Mr. Gaffyn again said, "Oh" and blew his nose. He then took his hat down from the peg and remarked jerkily:

"I'm just going out to try and get some decent tracing-paper. This stuff of Boliver's is hopeless; don't take the ink, you know. McIlrane thinks Shaw's is the best.''

It was Arthur's turn to say "Oh" and there was another pause. Neither father nor son looked at each other. Suddenly Mr. Gaffyn said:

"I see you 've got one of those apples. Fred sent them up from Basingstoke—not bad. Codlings, you know. I don't think they're a patch on Blenheim oranges—haven't the flavor."

Arthur leaned against the wall, and screwing up one eye, peered along the line of an oak frame with the other, as though intensely interested to see whether it were true. At the same time he answered:

"Oh, I don't know. I rather like a Codling."

"Oh, they're really all right" answered Mr. Gaffyn; "only they're cookers. We're very busy. We're going in for this new Grimchester Municipal Buildings job. It's a very big thing; working night and day."

Arthur again said "Oh" but in a different key. It was an "oh" that struggled to convey the idea that he was immensely pleased and interested, although as a matter of fact his only feeling was one of intense relief, for he felt convinced from his father's manner that he meant to avoid the tragic subject which was the immediate cause of Arthur's presence in the house. And this, indeed, proved to be the case. Mr. Gaffyn gripped his belongings, and opened the front door. He repeated:

"Yes, it's a very big thing" and he darted out into the street; and never under any circumstances did he ever give any hint, or make any reference to the letter which the Book had sent him "explaining the reason why."

Later in the evening they dined together, an uncomfortable meal of desultory interjections. The safest ground was the health and welfare of various relations and friends. Arthur would say:

"Is Aunt Elizabeth all right?"

And Mr. Gaffyn would reply:

"I'm, yes, fairly so so. She gets touches of this gastric catarrh; doesn't take care of herself."

There would be another pause, and then Mr. Gaffyn would say:

"George Carrowby has got rid of the lease of that house at last."

And Arthur would reply with one of his most sympathetic "ohs," having but a vague idea who George Carrowby was, and certainly never having heard that the said gentleman had a lease he was anxious to dispose of. After a longer interval Arthur would jerk out:

"This pudding's good"

And Mr. Gaffyn would reply:

"Yes, it's better than sometimes. She usually gets it too stodgy."

It was a brief meal, Mr. Gaffyn eating with great rapidity, and fidgeting with his pipe, which he would occasionally take out of his side pocket and place on the cloth, and then replace again. Arthur was too nervous to be interested in anything but the pudding. The cheese had barely made its appearance before Mr. Gaffyn lighted his pipe and said:

"Must just see what McIlrane did about the plan of the ground floor."

And he went quickly out of the room and back to the studio. Later in the evening a friend of his called, a Mr. Cottersby, a local surveyor, and Arthur heard them discussing drainage, and the marvellous results to be achieved by using the new system of reinforced concrete. He listened for some time, and then wandered once more round the house. He discovered a seven-years' old copy of Cassel's Sports and Pastimes, and spent an hour examining the diagrams of gentlemen playing badminton and rackets, and young ladies striking graceful attitudes at archery. This amusement then began to pall, and he crept downstairs again and listened in the hall. The maid, a fat-faced Welsh girl, called Ada, came up from the kitchen with a tray on which was a Tantalus and some glasses. She went into the studio. As the door opened, Arthur heard Mr. Cottersby's voice saying:

"Yates & Platts' estimate was more than seven hundred and fifty lower than the lowest, so old Griggs, the assessor, began to smell a rat. He called a committee meeting,—I happen to know because my partner. Stillway's brother-in-law, was on it,—and he said—"

The door snapped to, and Arthur muttered to himself, "Oh, hell!"

He ate two more of the Codling apples and went upstairs. The gay bathroom once more made an irresistible appeal. He undressed, had another warm bath, and then went to bed.

It would be difficult to know how much of the wretchedness of that night was due to the unreasonable action of eating raw apples, just before a hot bath, and how much was due to the reaction from the strain he had passed through, but he spent a very unhappy night.

A feeling of loneliness and remorse crept over him as he rolled between the sheets. He wondered about the chaps at Covington, and what they were thinking of him. Old Seedy Simpson and Dicky Younger—they would all get to know about it. He was free, a free man to wander the world, and they were slaves, tied hand and foot, but oh! how he envied them! The morning would come. At half-past six the bell would ring and there would be the usual grousing and clatter, and they would have to get up and rush down to chapel and have a cheerless breakfast of thin tea and bread-and-butter, and then be bullied by the masters for not having learned things overnight; but they had something, something that he had lost, that he would never be able to regain. He could get up in the morning any time he liked, nine, or ten, or half -past He could probably have bacon and marmalade for breakfast, and mooch about all day, but there would always be that peculiar fear, something that the Book had branded him with, the mocking condemnation of the whole world; and it was all because of that ridiculous penknife.

It was true the Rook had said, "There are many other things against you" but they were on a different plane to this. Bagging apples twice (one does n't steal apples, one bags them), insubordination several times,—there was that disgusting day when he lost his temper with Elkin, the mathematical master, and told him "he did n't care a damn about his silly theories"—and that other occasion when one spring afternoon he had gone off for a ramble across the country instead of playing cricket. On the way back he had met Rodwell, his form-master, on horseback. And Rodwell had scowled at him and said: "If you were half a man, Gaffyn, you would be playing cricket!"

He didn't know why this remark infuriated him so, but it did. He was keen on cricket, but on that day the country seemed more alluring. There were small fleecy clouds scudding before the light wind. It seemed unreasonable if one could not sometimes enjoy these things all by oneself. He had noted Rodwell's fat back shaking on the horse as he ambled down the hill. He had suddenly run after him, and bawled out in a rude voice:

"I didnt feel in the mood to play cricket!"

There had been a lot of trouble about that, apologies and all that sort of thing. One does not have "moods" in a public school. It is n't done. And if one does, one controls them, and in any case, under no circumstance does one lose one's temper with a master. He lay there palpitating with a sense of outrage at the mere recollection of that incident. After all, why should one have to play cricket? It was understandable that one should have to learn lessons, for if one did not, no one, except perhaps a beastly swot like Baynes, would ever bother to learn anything at all. But a game! He supposed it was all somehow involved in that bigger thing, "form" and what the Rook called "the honor of the school. "The school ought to do well at cricket, of course. It would n't do to get another hiding from Bradwell College, as they had last year; a fearful hiding it was, an innings and over a hundred runs. But still, surely there might be other things. Suppose a chap, for instance, had the instincts of a landscape-painter. Was he never to go about observing things except from cover-point or long leg? Suppose that old boy—what was his name?—Corot!—suppose he had been sent to an English public school. Would he have been considered "half a man" or a person without a sense of "form" because he sloped off one afternoon by himself to look at the windmill at Cheney-Guildhurst silhouetted against the meadows of Wray's Farm, instead of acting as long-stop to Greene, the first eleven fast bowler.

Of course he ought not to have taken the penknife; that was a silly, unpardonable thing. He vowed to himself he would never do anything of that sort again. Not that he felt there was anything fundamentally vile in the action,—he would not have taken it from a poor man, or from anyone if it had made them unhappy,—but it was so obviously likely to lead one into endless trouble and difficulties.

But in the meantime, what was going to become of him? He would have to work, he supposed. He was, in any case, to have left school the following term. He would have to do what his Aunt Elizabeth called, "go out into the world and earn his own living." What did he want to dot Frankly, he had not the faintest idea. In fact, the idea of earning his own living appeared revolting to him. He would like to be a great person suddenly, without all the sordid business of going through the mill. He would like to be a Sir Joshua Reynolds, or a Mr. Gladstone, some one people would talk about in the newspapers, and nudge each other as he passed, and say, "There he is."

There was no reason why he should not attain this eminent position, so why should he feel so wretched? He wanted some one to confide in intensely, some one who would believe in him, who would hug him and torture him at the same time. Who was there who cared for him f He knew that his father did in his rum way, but never, never, never had he given the slightest sign. And for his part, he loved his father passionately. He could not help it. He loved the feeble fuddling way he did things, the something pathetic that seemed to lurk behind his eyes and colour all his movements. He thought of his father's eyes that so seldom looked at him. They were not the eyes of a furtive, dishonest person. They were extraordinarily clear and gentle, like the eyes of a very young girl, and they moved restlessly, as though they covered some sacred thing that was too sensitive to endure the prying intrusion of the outside world. He wondered whether, when the discussion of drainage was finished, his father would lie in bed, as he was doing now, and feel all overflowing with vague, inexpressible feelings that made one want to cry. It was all badly arranged, this world. There were other people. There was Edith, of whom we shall hear later. He detested her cordially. And there was Aunt Elizabeth; she was an awful old fool, but he rather liked her in an unaccountable way. She was his father's sister. And then there was Eleanor. How very strange! Why had he not thought of Eleanor before? Of course there was Eleanor. For years now he had loved Eleanor very dearly. She was his cousin. Aunt Elizabeth's daughter. How often had he not lain awake at night at school, and thought of her lustrous eyes. She had wonderful eyes. They seemed all misty and comforting. The rest of her face was obscure, a sort of dim halo of olive skin and fair, brown hair, just an atmosphere for the beautiful eyes to rest in. It seemed strange that during these hapless days, and this unendurable night, he had not remembered before the beautiful eyes of Eleanor, that it had only just occurred to him what a good idea it would be i to marry her. And then she would hug him, and torture, him, and he would be wretched again, and then would come that wonderful, comforting sense of peace.

"It's an awful rum business" he thought, and dwelling upon the divagations of this abstruse thought, he passed into the land of dreams.

CHAPTER III

THE DISENCHANTED DAY

Mr. Gaffyn's agony in having to make up his mind became evident in his manner. He darted through doors to avoid his son, and when they were inevitably thrown together at mealtimes he plunged into channels of conversation that were entirely outside the boy's comprehension. To the despair of Mrs. Stabbe, he made pencil sketches on the tablecloth of architectural features that were being introduced into the competition drawings for Grimchester Municipal Buildings. He talked about Pugin, and Scott, and Inigo Jones, about the transition period in French Gothic, about the absurd restrictions made by the Grimchester town council. He talked about a fever that Mr. Cottersby's daughter was suffering from, about the futility of the Government, the iniquity of certain measures that affected rural landlords. He talked about the way the Great Western Railway bungled the handling of steel girders, and the genius of Mrs. Stabbe in making a rice pudding without using an egg.

But of Arthur or of himself, not a word!

Arthur would get up late and have breakfast by himself, with his left arm curled lovingly round a book. He would have three or four warm baths during the day, stroll about the streets, look in the shops, buy sundry bottles of ginger-beer, and sometimes go to the Oval to watch a cricket match. The only personal contact he had with his father would be over a small question of finance. When he had no money left, he would hang about the hall at some opportune moment when his father was either going out or coming in. He would then wriggle about at the bottom of the stairs, and say:

"Oh—er—I say, could you possibly spare me a bob or two! I—er —"

And Mr. Gaffyn would answer very quickly:

"Eh! Oh--er—yes. I—er—"

And he would cough and put down a few shillings, and simply race away through the door.

This mode of life went on for exactly three weeks and four days, before any incident came to break the monotony of it. And then one morning, just after one of the little financial incidents mentioned before, Arthur was startled by his father saying jerkily:

"Let's see, school broke up yesterday; We asked Elizabeth to dinner on Thursday," and he vanished.

Arthur pondered over this statement all day. There was nothing surprising in Aunt Elizabeth paying a visit. On the contrary, it was rather remarkable that she had not been before. But why did his father break the formality of their relationship by telling him of the approaching visit! And why, more especially, did he remark, "School broke up yesterday," as though the two statements were to a certain extent connected. He could not come to any satisfactory conclusion in the matter, and he spent the intervening three days in a greater state of contemplative idleness than usual. The dominant fact that impressed itself on his mind was that the visit of Aunt Elizabeth meant also the visit of Eleanor.

He thought of Eleanor lingeringly, and decided that he would take the earliest opportunity of making love to her. Thursday should be an enchanted day. He would start his life afresh, with the eyes of Eleanor helping him, luring him on to greater and greater ambitions.

Thursday was indeed a very glorious day, and he decided that he could pay it no greater tribute than to spend the morning and afternoon at the Oval. Consequently he persuaded Mrs. Stabbe to give him a packet of sandwiches and a piece of cake and an apple, and he started out for Kennington. He sat the whole day on a very hard bench, with his back to the gas-works, under a sweltering sun, and watched five professionals pile up a huge score for Surrey. It was glorious! It was, in fact, the happiest day he had spent since he left Cullington, and he frequently thought of his life there, and compared it unfavorably with the present splendid freedom of his days. When the last ball was bowled and there was the usual scamper across the field, he got up and stretched himself. He felt rather tired and stiff, and he walked along the asphalt walk toward the exit gate. He had not gone twenty yards before a boy came clambering over the benches and almost stepped on his toes. He looked at the boy's face, and the boy looked at him. It was Seedy Simpson! Instinctively he cried out:

"Hullo, Seedy!"

And instantaneously his mind became occupied with several peculiar psychological impressions. In the first place, he was immediately conscious that the relationship between Seedy and himself was not what it was. It was very apparent that Seedy knew all about him, and what he'd done. It was also apparent that he was a little uncertain how to act. Arthur thought he detected an expression on Seedy's face as though he wanted to be friendly, but was frightened. At the same time his father's remark, "School broke up yesterday," flashed through his mind. What a fool he was, himself! He might have known that he would meet some of the Cullington chaps there, especially Seedy, who always rushed over to the Oval directly he got back. And perhaps there were some more of the Cullington boys about, and Seedy was afraid of being seen with him I He believed he would be friendly if it weren't for that. It was very contemptible to be afraid of your own opinions. All these thoughts passed through his mind before he heard Seedy say:

"Hello, Gaffyn!"

That in itself was an acknowledgment of a different state of things, for at school it was always 'Moods.' That's what Seedy and most of the others called him at school. "Moods"—on account of his preposterous remark to the form-master that he did not feel in the mood to play cricket—a remark that seemed so incredible and un-English that it eventually passed away among the limbo of Cullington mythology, and was not believed.

The two boys looked at each other self-consciously, and it was Arthur who came to the rescue and proved himself the man of the world by saying:

"Hayward played a great game."

Seedy looked relieved, and answered:

"Corking! That was a spiffing drive over the dock!"

Arthur struck his shoe with his cane and blew out his cheeks.

"Been beastly hot, "he remarked.

Seedy said "Yes, beastly," and looked in the direction of the pavilion.

Arthur felt that it was necessary to relieve his friend of the suffering he was going through on his account, so he said:

"Well, I must be going; got some friends coming to dinner."

The idea of "friends coming to dinner" was a brilliant inspiration. It showed that he did not wish to intrude himself on Seedy, and also that he was very much a man of the world.

Seedy said, "Oh, so long then; I'm looking for my cousin."

Arthur returned to Eccles Square feeling that an ugly cloud had gathered on the horizon of this enchanted day. He was angry and depressed. Was it to be always like this? Would this wretched business be always cropping up! He felt angry with Seedy—if the positions had been reversed he would not have behaved like that—but more angry with fate which had side-tracked him into this contemptible position. Seedy's attitude stung him into a desire to show these people what he was made of. He would prove that he had the right stuff in him, that he was, moreover, in some ways superior to them,—yes, even to Seedy, and Baynes, and the Rook, and the judges, and the bishops, and all the rest of them. Be damned to them! He paid his twopence on the top of the bus at Waterloo Bridge with cheeks whose scarlet flush was not caused entirely by the heat. He arrived home feeling sullen and pugnacious.

Aunt Elizabeth and Eleanor had already arrived, but he could not face them in his present mood. The inevitable warm bath and a change of clothes wrought a more equable frame of mind, and he went down to the drawing-room with the, incident of the afternoon but a rankling impression.

Aunt Elizabeth was curiously unlike Mr. Gaffyn, except for certain formations about the chin and nose. She was very stout, and had a round, plump face and brown es, and a wonderful flow of conversation, the bulk of which was heralded by the prefix, "they say."

She did not apparently indulge in any opinions of her own; her whole mental outlook was directed by the mysterious consensus of opinion embraced by the word "they." "Perhaps the principle "they" was the newspaper that was delivered every morning at her door. She read it all through religiously, and held a not unpopular superstition that anything which appeared in print was ipso facto true. 'They' also consisted of some half-dozen friends and relations whom she was in the habit of meeting, and who also read and implicitly believed in the same newspaper. It also included Edith.

Edith was a Gaffyn, the most masterful, brilliant, and successful of the Gaffyns. Aunt Elizabeth called her "cousin," but she was indeed but a very distant relation. She came of a different branch of the family altogether, the Shropshire Gaffyns, who counted among their numbers a general, a knight, a member of parliament, and even a bishop. They were presumably the original Gaffyn stock, whereas

Mr. Gaffyn's own family history was very obscure. A student of sociological questions might have imagined that at some time during the last generation some wayward son had broken away from the Shropshire family tradition and wandered to London, and married an actress; or had become an artist, or done something else entirely disreputable.

Edith herself had married Robert Yardley, a very successful consulting engineer. They lived at Bradehurst, in Surrey, and had three young children. Edith was young, barely twenty-six, but she expressed something of the insolent force of her tradition in her manner, in her strong capability, and in the proprietary sway she held over this poor and ineffectual branch of the family.

So great was Aunt Elizabeth's veneration for Edith that she frequently varied her phrase "they say" with "Edith says," and sometimes it would be "Edith says that they say," and occasionally, "They say that Edith says."

On this particular evening when Arthur returned from the Oval, he did indeed interrupt Aunt Elizabeth's dissertation to his father on the wonderful things that "they" said about the remarkable things that Edith said about the amazing things that Edith's children said, but he was too immediately occupied when he entered the room with gazing into the swimming eyes of Eleanor and thinking to himself: "Yes, by Jove, how awfully jolly it will be to be married to you" to follow this discourse very closely. He had a curious feeling that Eleanor knew of what he was thinking, and that she was blushing with pleasure at the thought of it. He looked away and felt a little ashamed of his boldness.

When they were seated at dinner, Aunt Elizabeth turned the fire of her battery upon Arthur. She said:

"Well, Arthur, I hear you've left school."

Almost automatically Arthur replied:

"Yes, school broke up last Monday," and he instinctively glanced at his father, and then looked away. How Very rum I Why bad n't he thought of that before! His father was very busy with his soup. If Aunt Elizabeth had come before the end of the term, she would have wanted to know why it was. Now perhaps she would never know "the reason why." But he dreaded to be cross-examined. Of one thing he felt certain. If it came to the point, he would have to tell. He might prevaricate, but for some reason or other he simply could not tell a deliberate lie in front of his father. Fortunately, the incidents of leaving school did not interest his aunt so much as the more immediate demands of his future. She said:

"And what are you going to do in the world!"

And Arthur made the only appropriate reply:

"Oh, I don't know. Aunt."

Aunt Elizabeth rattled the bangles on her little plump wrist as she negotiated the soup, and said:

"Well, you mustn't become like your father and never know your own mind. Do you want to be an architect! They say architecture's very overcrowded. Or a builder! They say building is a very good trade to be in, if you're clever. They say there's a lot of money to be made at it."

Arthur again said he didn't know and looked at Eleanor. He felt that the conversation was too personal and sordid to be carried on before her. Her eyes were watching him with an intent sympathy. How splendid it would be to have those eyes always watching him, always reflecting his own hopes, and sorrows, and joys!

Aunt Elizabeth was still holding forth to his father about the building trade, and he fancied that once Mr. Gaffyn mumbled:

"Yes, he has a talent, I think, for drawing'

And Aunt Elizabeth replied:

"Well, I shouldn't let him be an artist, whatever you do. They say there's no money at all in it. Look at the pass bys. They say Tom Naseby is one of the cleverest landscape painters in the country, and I know, as an absolute fact, they have the greatest difficulty to pay eighty pounds a year rent for that place of theirs at Hammersmith. Lena has to go out and do fashion-drawing, or typewriting, or something. Charlie goes to a common grammar school. They say it's awful; so rough and all that. No; Edith says she thinks you ought to make him a builder. Why, what with your influence and that, I should think you could put him on to a lot of good paying work, eh?"

Mr. Gaffyn pulled at his little tuft of beard, and Eleanor smiled and said:

"I don't believe Arthur is half practical enough to be a builder."

"Not practical! Fiddlesticks! He's got to be practical. Everyone has to be practical these days. Edith says we've had too many dreamers in our family, as it is. There was your Uncle Brian; he went mooning round the world. They say he died out in some South Sea island among a lot of naked savages. That was a nice thing I and then there was Harvey; he came to no good. He was always trying one thing and another, chopping and changing about. He never left a penny."

"He may have had a very happy life, 'remarked Eleanor. angel! She became to Arthur at that moment more adorable and desirable than ever. He did not hear the biting diatribe that Aunt Elizabeth indulged in in reply to this remark. A sudden dazzling vision filled his mind; it was the vision of a home. He could see the room quite clearly, a sunny white-paneled room that looked out into a garden full of flowers. The bees were droning lazily, and the birds were singing in praise of the glory of the day. He was seated at the end of a polished table, his own dining-table, and opposite to him his wife was smiling into his eyes with that provoking mothering expression. He would be rich, of course, and famous, and surrounded by beauty, and love, and the song of birds. He felt a curious little stab of pride, as though he knew he were predestined for these things. He would be in some way exceptional.

"They say that Robert Yardley is making three thousand a year, if he's making a penny. He's a clever man, if you like. My word! yes, I should say he is. Now, there's a good line to go in for—engineering. Of course, Arthur wouldn't be clever enough for that; besides, they say it costs a lot of money at first, hundreds of pounds for the apprenticeship, and then it 's years before you earn anything. But I don't know; I should think one could pick up building. You know; get someone else to do it for you, and all that sort of thing—sublet it—isn't that the expression? I shall speak to Edith about Arthur and see what she says."

Aunt Elizabeth dabbed her lips with her napkin and prepared to go upstairs.

Mr. Gaffyn said:

"If you care to see them, I could show you some of the drawings for this new competition we're going in for. The Grimchester Municipal Buildings."

"It seems to me" replied Aunt Elizabeth, waddling toward the door, "that you waste a lot of money over these competitions, John. Edith says that they say these competitions cost a lot of money, and you stand a very poor chance of getting them, when all's said and done. I should think it would be much better to get hold of jobs privately, even if they're not such big jobs. You don't stand the risk, and you don't have the expense."

Arthur saw his aunt disappearing into the studio, followed by his father. Eleanor lingered for a moment by the door. It was the golden opportunity. He looked at her wistfully, and could not for the life of him think what to say. The fat-faced maid, Ada, entered the room with a tray. He followed Eleanor to the door, and his voice felt hard and dry as he said:

"Are you keen on drawings!"

And Eleanor was so very composed and at ease. It almost irritated him.

"Why, of course I am. Uncle's drawings are always wonderful." And she laughed kindly.

Arthur stuck his hands into his trousers pockets, and they went into the big studio. Mr. Gaffyn spread the plans and elevations out on the center table, and Aunt Elizabeth looked at them through her spectacles, and kept on making little clicking noises with her mouth and repeating:

"Oh, well, I hope you get it, I'm sure."

Eleanor leaned over the drawings and declared that they were fine, and that she was sure Uncle would get the job; and Arthur leaned on the table as near her as he dared, and watched the little lobe of her ear with the tress of light-brown hair above it. After that they filed upstairs again to the drawing-room, and Aunt Elizabeth talked about rents, the indolence of work-people, the almost uncanny intelligence of Edith's children, the movements of various remote members of the royal household, about cuts of bacon, and the best place to buy cork carpet.

At ten o'clock the ladies prepared to go, and it was only for less than five minutes that evening that Arthur found himself alone with Eleanor. She came downstairs ready to depart, while Aunt Elizabeth was carrying on a whispered conversation with Mr. Gaffyn on the second landing.

Arthur was in the dining-room, and he came out into the hall and grinned at her, and Eleanor smiled at him in her kind way as she buttoned her glove.

"Yourself, then "was the brightest thing it occurred to him to say.

Eleanor replied, "Yes, we're off. You must come over and see us."

"Rather, I'd like to."

There was a pause; then Arthur said:

"How's Angela?"

Angela was a parrot, a bird that Arthur was not the least little bit interested in, but it came to his mind on thinking of Aunt Elizabeth's house.

"Poor Angela! She's not been at all well. "Eleanor talked at considerable length about Angela, and Arthur looked at her with bis burning eyes, and thought; "Oh, dear, I wish to goodness I could say the right thing to you. I'm just desperate about you, can't you see?"

But all the time she talked about the wretched parrot, and he was forced to reply: "Oh, I say!" or "What bad luck!"

It was a subject of conversation that gave absolutely no loophole for endearing advances, and it was eventually interrupted by the sound of the slow and painstaking process of Aunt coming down the stairs. Arthur walked with them to the comer, and saw them on to a bus, and Aunt Elizabeth's last words were:

"Well, Arthur, we must write to Edith about you. I shouldn't hang about, though. I should start doing things. Make up your mind firmly, and then go in and do it. That's what they say."

She panted on to the step of the bus, and so occupied was Eleanor in piloting her mother through the perilous journey over the backboard and into the body of the bus that she did not get an opportunity of turning around and waving to Arthur. He watched it swerving out of sight.

It was an unsatisfactory termination to what he had so hoped would be an enchanting day.

CHAPTER IV

THS JUDGMENT OF EDITH

Five days after the events chronicled in the last chapter, Arthur was seated one morning at half-past ten in the dining-room, reading a book. He was, as a matter of fact, awaiting his breakfast. He yawned rather impatiently, and suddenly his father came bustling into the room from the studio. They exchanged a noise with their mouths that was their usual morning greeting if they should happen to meet. Mr. Gaffyn went to the bureau and fussed about with some papers. He was just about to depart when he suddenly said over his shoulder:

"Oh—er—Edith Yardley has written—asks you down—might perhaps go, eat."

Arthur replied:

"Oh! When!"

"She says—er—tomorrow."

"Oh, all right."

Mr. Gaffyn went back to the studio, and Arthur pondered over this latest development. By saying "might perhaps go, 'he knew that his father meant that he wanted him to go. It was as near a direct order as his father ever gave. He would certainly have to go, and just as certainly he knew it would be an awful bore. He also knew for what purpose he was being sent. He was to be examined, cross-examined, and to have his mind made up for him, for Edith was notoriously the only Gaffyn capable of making up her mind. Every important problem in the family was submitted to her. Personally, he detested her and everything about her, and this was a feeling which he suspected was cordially reciprocated. However, there was no help for it. It would have to be gone through with. He tried to comfort himself with the reflection that in any case it was in the country, which for the moment he would be glad to get back to. And then, travelling was in itself very attractive, and he might see something of old Yardley in the evenings. He was a decent old chap, and could talk quite intelligently about cricket.

He spent the day in the usual manner, and even extended his normal activities to the point of buying three new collars and a shirt, and discussing exhaustively with Mrs. Stabbe the question of whether one pair of socks would last till he returned. On the following day he caught a train early in the afternoon, and arrived at Bradehurst at four o'clock, where he found a trap that had been sent to meet him. The drive took twenty minutes, for "Lorriemuir" the Yardleys' house, stood high on chalk soil, and commanded a fine view across Surrey.

It was a large, new, red-brick and stucco building, standing in its own grounds and surrounded by gravel paths, clumps of mixed shrubs, and occasional oblong beds of standard roses.

When the trap drove up to the door, it was greeted with the loud barking of two small dogs. And as he descended, Edith came across the lawn to meet him. He had not seen her for nearly two years. The Yardleys had been living at Manchester for part of that time, and on the occasions when they came to London, he was at school. They had only taken up residence at Bradehurst during the previous winter.

Edith Yardley was a good-looking woman with brilliant colouring and had masses of gold-brown hair banded tightly under her hat. She was tall and well-proportioned, and she moved briskly but without flurry. There was something about her face a little hard, and about her manner something more than a little imperious. She was one of those people who instinctively take control, and whom others instinctively obey. Men for the most part admired or feared her, and women either adored or hated her.

She was wearing a white print frock that gleamed in the sun, and from her waist was suspended a bunch of keys which jingled as she walked. She looked like a hospital nurse, except for the straw hat with its black velvet band.

She called out across the lawn, in a fresh strong voice:

"Well, Arthur, did you have a good journey?"

"She's bright, and hard, and metallic—" Arthur thought, as he replied:

"Oh, quite decent, thanks."

She called up to someone in a room upstairs, and a maid appeared and took possession of his bag. Edith shook hands and led him indoors.

"Chappie will show you your room and the bathroom," she said. "Then come down to the dining-room. We shall be having tea quite soon."

The dogs continued to bark, but on the first-floor landing this noise was drowned by the sounds of laughter and yelling on the other side of the door, and the disturbing truth dawned upon the visitor that there were children! Of course he knew that Edith had children, but he had overlooked the fact. He had never associated with young children. He did not know how many there were, or what they were like, and how he ought to behave to them, and he was terrified. There appeared to be two bathrooms, one of which was occupied. It may be observed at this point that these bathrooms were the most impressive features to Arthur of his visit. They appeared to be the mecca of all the conscious activity of the place. At an incredibly early hour in the morning taps would start running, and people would commence whistling or singing in them, and this would continue throughout the day. Other rooms in the house were used, but only in a vague, migratory sort of way, and when people appeared in them, they seemed to have just come from the bathroom, or to be just going to the bathroom. Nurses and maids in new print frocks would bustle in and out with brass cans and towels, and would wash, and splash, and scrub either themselves or the children from dawn to midnight. And all these attendant satellites of Edith's appeared unconsciously to imitate her. They walked with the same sure sense of conscious strength and superiority. They were equally cheerful, equable, and consciously moral. During his visit Arthur came to the conclusion that when Edith awakened in the morning at six-thirty, her first thought was, "What uncomfortable thing can I do today."

She had not sufficient imagination to conceive anything dramatically uncomfortable, like wearing a hair-shirt, so she confined herself to doing hundreds of little, fidgeting, uncomfortable things.

To Arthur's mind the house was the acme of discomfort and discord. There was not a comfortable chair in the place, except in Mr. Yardley's smoke-room, which was kept locked. The decoration was like a hospital; sanitary paints, oilcloth and tiles. Whatever the weather was like, every window in the place was kept open night and day. The children slept in the open, on the veranda, and were fed on sterilized milk and various health foods. They were brought up on some new system which Edith one day explained to him. It had an Italian name, and it seemed to consist in letting them do exactly what they liked, and in encouraging them at all times to make as much noise as they were physically capable of. The meals were heralded in by a crescendo of sound, the barking of dogs, the yelling of children, and the breezy clatter of maids, culminating in a vigorous banging on gongs; and when it came to the point, there seemed to be nothing to justify all this noise, there being very little to eat, except clean napkins and mysterious sections of unattractive-looking health foods lurking behind parsley. A paraphrase of the old school tag occurred to Arthur's mind at lunch-time on the second day: "A great mountain is in travail, and a ridiculous nut fritter is produced."

The children, moreover, found in him a splendid objective on which to exercise various principles of their educational training. They were at that age when it is a little difficult for an inexperienced eye to determine sex, but he had a shrewd suspicion that the eldest child was a girl. They were encouraged at all times to be natural and frank, and Arthur reaped the full benefit of this. At the very first tea this eldest child asked him if he ever cleaned his finger-nails, and also asked him why he didn't speak more distinctly. They pulled him about, and shouted in his ear, and asked him endless embarrassing questions. If Edith spoke to him, he was conscious of all their eyes being fixed upon him in critical expectancy.

The eldest child—she was certainly a girl—corrected his pronunciation of words and pulled him up over his facts. It was his first experience with young children, and he had never imagined that the good God could have created anything so heartless and cruel.

He made a desperate attempt to be friendly and playful with them, to enter into their mode of life, but he found it impossible. He simply could not stand their noise, their excessive inane vitality. He hated them more passionately than anything he had so far hated. He would slink out of the house at times, harbouring vindictive ideas toward physical violence.

"I would like to get hold of that eldest girl" he thought once, "and take her down the garden behind the summer-house, and bash her in the eye."

It was with the greatest difficulty that he kept these criminal instincts under control. Neither did Edith in any way tend to ameliorate his outraged feelings. The only remarks she would make to check this infantile hooliganism would be:

"Now, Gladys, my pet!" or "Be careful, darling!"

Breakfast was at half-past seven, and everyone was expected to be down on time. Arthur could not for the life of him see why, as they had nothing to do all day except wash each other, they should start at this unreasonable hour.

In the morning Edith wore a print frock and an apron, and she rattled and glittered about the house, doing all her uncomfortable little things, washing the dogs, counting the linen, checking the housekeeper's books, and weeding in the garden. Everything tended to make Arthur feel a drone and an encumbrance. He tried to keep out of the way, but he was rapidly caught up in the vortex of this bustling life, where everyone except the children was doing their duty so zealously and cheerfully. In fact, the whole household seemed to have the word "duty" stamped upon its brows. Even over the matter of the baths, Arthur was aware of a different point of view from his own. He was in the habit of having a bath because he derived a certain amount of sensuous enjoyment from it, but to the Yardley household the bath was merely the symbol of the clean and godly life. It was, in fact, not right to enjoy a bath; one ought to have a bath, and that was the end of it. And this view held good throughout the whole functioning of the household. One got up early, not because one wanted to, but because one did n't want to. Meals were not pleasant diversions; they were medical functions where the right and proper nourishment was administered to the blood cells. Walks were not a form of natural enjoyment; they were calisthenic exercises for the benefit of the mind and body, and were always taken at regular times and in the direction of the most salubrious spot.

On the very first morning he was darting from one room to another, trying to find some sanctuary from the restless aggression of this house, when he met Edith in the hall, carrying some blinds. She said:

"Arthur, I wonder whether you would mind just putting these blinds into the rollers in the nursery?"

Arthur had no mechanical genius at all. He lugged the blinds upstairs and examined them and the fittings for half-an-hour. He then made an effort to force the blinds in somehow and succeeded in pinching his fingers. After he had managed to get them in the wrong way up, Edith came in. She smiled superciliously, and said:

"You're not very practical, are you?" and with a few deft touches of her competent fingers put the matter right.

She then sent him for a screw-driver and a gimlet and told him exactly how to fix the brackets. But he became so flustered and irritated by the fact of her watching him that he did it all wrong even then. And she said in her quiet voice:

"I expect you had better let me do it."

It is always galling to be made to look ridiculous, but to be made to look ridiculous by a girl is intolerable. He went out for what he called a "mooch." But this did not save him from further ignominy. Edith was always finding him these little uncomfortable jobs, things which she must have known he would not be successful at. And he thought to himself:

"Damn it! she's putting me through a sort of exam; she's going to report on me."

Even over that little question of the 'mooch' there was trouble. For as he came strolling up the path in time for lunch, he noticed Edith watching him from the bathroom. As he was putting up his hat and coat in the hall, she came downstairs, and remarked as she went through to the dining-room with some vases:

"They didn't teach you to walk very well at Cullington. You ought to hold yourself up."

This remark annoyed Arthur very much, and he went upstairs and banged his bedroom door with unnecessary violence.

One source of disappointment at Bradehurst was the fact that Mr. Yardley only put in an appearance twice during the ten days Arthur stayed there. Edith said he was working very hard, and could not often come down. On the first evening when he came home, he was apparently dog-tired. He arrived home at half -past eight, and after supper sat smoking a pipe, and occasionally muttering monosyllables. He was a very big man, older than Edith, with deep gray eyes and a sense of breadth and power about him. He blinked at Arthur sleepily, as though he would be friendly if it weren't so much bother.

Arthur was impressed by the fact that, although Mr. Yardley had come down from town and had been working hard all day, his supper was identical to that which the rest of the family usually had; that is to say, it consisted of cold boiled fish, done up in some yellow sauce, and stewed fruit and custard, and the drink was hot water. It occurred to him as being an incongruous meal for a person of Mr. Yardley's bulk and appearance.

There was something about Mr. Yardley that Arthur liked; and he liked him especially because, when he was there, he was the only comfortable thing in the house. He came down again on the Saturday following, and on Sunday was apparently allowed to have his breakfast in bed. In any case, he did not appear till nearly lunchtime, when he strolled heavily about the garden and examined the standard roses, as though he had seen them for the first time. Arthur observed him from his bedroom window, whither he had gone under the conviction that the propitious moment had arrived to change his one pair of socks. The three children came racing out on the lawn, pushing each other about. Mr. Yardley turned slowly and regarded them with the same expression of wondering awe that he had extended to the roses. They might have been the strange phenomena of some scientific experiment, and he the professor, a little uncertain how to account for them.

Edith came round the comer, carrying a basket and a pair of scissors. Arthur heard her well-modulated voice talking to Mr. Yardley about the flowers, and Mr. Yardley replying in his deep purring tones. They passed under the window.

"That's a rum thing," thought Arthur. He wasn't very clear about what was rum except that—well, when Mr. Yardley and Edith passed under his window, they were quite alone. They would not know that anyone was listening, and yet Edith spoke to him in exactly the same voice that she employed when telling the cook not to put onions in the vegetable pie. Arthur didn't know, but he thought: "If you're very keen on anybody, I believe you have a different voice for them, when you're alone. I believe I wouldn't talk like that to Eleanor, not when—when everything had come off."

It was a glorious morning and he sat musing by the window, keeping just out of sight. He wondered whether they were keen on each other, these two. He tried to think what it would be like to kiss Edith. He decided that it might not be bad. Despite everything, he could understand that someone might find something attractive about Edith. She had a lovely complexion and all that sort of thing, and yet—she ought to be different. Was old Yardley keen on her It was a very funny business, all this business of people being keen on each other.

On Sunday afternoon old Yardley "mooched" with him round the garden and the lanes, and they got on famously. He talked about cricket and boxing, and told him some amusing stories about his grandfather, M. Jules Carbonnet.

On Monday morning Arthur went to the station to see him off, and much to his surprise, just as the train was coming in, Mr. Yardley slipped something into his hand. He had no time to comment, for the broad back of Mr. Yardley was disappearing into a first-class carriage, and the train had left the platform before he realized that he was gripping the milled edge of a sovereign.

That evening Arthur was sitting at a table and trying to read and to make himself comfortable on a highbacked chair at the same time. Edith came into the room; she spent most of her evenings going in and out of doors. She brought a work-box and suddenly sat down at the table deliberately opposite to Arthur, and said:

"Arthur, I want to talk to you about your career. Tour father has asked us for our advice. He 's not very capable of making up his mind, and there is a fact I think I ought to tell you. He is very hard up, and it will be necessary for you to earn your own living at once. Now the point is: what are you going to don't"

She threaded a needle with unerring precision, and continued:

"Robert, as you know, is a very practical person, and we have discussed you. It appears that you have some talent for drawing. Is that so?"

Arthur felt himself going hot and cold, and the irresistible desire to lose his temper expressed itself in his:

"Oh, I don't know."

Edith was consciously tolerant with him. Her voice became more suave and deliberate.

"All the artistic professions are, as you know, very difficult It might be years before you could earn your own living, and your father is not well enough off to keep you till then. We are writing, therefore, to suggest a compromise. Robert thinks it would be a good idea for you to be a designer. It appears that one may quite quickly make money at designing, if one applies oneself. And you would thereby be able to adapt your natural talents to commercial ends. Robert is therefore sending a letter of introduction to Mr. Fred Blinkinshaw, of Blinkinshaw and Bepstow. He knows the firm very well. They were the biggest decorators in England. He is sure they will help you all they can. What do you think about it?"

The principal thing he thought about it was: what on earth has this all got to do with Edith? Why should Edith give him advice? Why should Edith have to break it to him that his father was hard up? Why should Edith have to work the introduction, and do everything else? He doubted very much whether it was Mr. Yardley's advice at all. It was probably all Edith. He looked at her, her proud capable face frowning slightly at some linen material she was sewing, and the lamplight silhouetting in golden streaks the heavy masses of her fine hair. He felt an unpleasant sense of impropriety that this girl, for she wasn't so very much more, should know all about him, and these sordid affairs of his home life. He wriggled in the uncomfortable chair and said:

"Oh, I don't know."

And then his mind became occupied with his father. The poor old guvnor! He visualized that pathetic figure spending the rest of his days leaning over a drawing board, or taking expansively to McIlrane about the details of chimerical jobs that he would always dream of getting and never get. His heart ached, and he was glad he was going home to-morrow. Of course he would work and help his father. He didn't want to be told by Edith what he ought to do.

He sat there ruminating on what it meant to be a designer, when Edith got up and left the room. As a matter of fact, she went to a little room upstairs where there was a writing-desk, and she wrote a letter which ran as follows:

My dear Bess,

We have had Arthur here for ten days and he is returning to-morrow. I am afraid he has all the characteristics of the Gaffyn male! And curiously enough he is in appearance rather like his Uncle Brian, who died in the Cook Islands. I acknowledge that he is rather good-looking in a sensuous kind of way, and he has certain attractive manners, but for the most part he is lazy, too fond of comfort, and hopelessly unpractical. I have talked him over with Robert, and Robert, who always likes everyone, thinks he may be artistic. So now I think I have an idea. I am sending you a letter of introduction, signed by Robert, to Mr. Fred Blinkinshaw. Let us see whether they can make a designer of him. It will be a happy combination of art and commerce. Now it's no good talking it over with John. He will never make up his mind. Tell him we have discussed it, and say that Arthur is quite keen on it, and then post the letter and get an appointment. I'm sure this will be a good solution. We are all, as usual, very fit. Many thanks for the recipe for chocolate shape.

Your affect.

Edith.

On the following day Arthur returned to town. Edith came to the gate to see him off. She said:

"Well, good-by, Arthur. You must come and stay with us again."

And Arthur mumbled:

"Yes, rather."

At the station he purchased three penny cakes of chocolate and two of butter-scotch from an automatic machine and secured a comfortable comer seat in a carriage. On the way up, he gazed out of the window and munched his well-deserved delicacies meditatively. Just as he arrived at the fourth packet, and the train was rumbling through some pleasant meadow-land, he muttered:

"Lord! what a cow!"

But whether this remark was addressed to a genuine species of its kind which was indeed gazing abstractedly at the train, or whether it was a mental reflection upon the character of some person occupying his thoughts, we will not attempt to determine.

CHAPTER V

MESSRS. BLINKINSHAW & BEPSTOW

All the world knows the famous house of Blinkinshaw & Bepstow. With its huge central block of buildings in Soho, and it's equally imposing branches in Manchester, Glasgow, Paris, and Montevideo, the tentacles of its ramifications exert their influence in every part of the civilized globe. It combines the laudable ambition of supplying the public with "the maximum of taste 'in furniture, decoration, and upholstery, with the silent workings of huge financial operations. Everyone knows a Blinkinshaw & Bepstow cretonne or bedroom suite, but no one knows the details of the vast ululations of capital that flow secretly behind the balance-sheets of this very distinguished firm. Huge hotels spring up, are stamped with the hall-mark of Blinkinshaw & Bepstow's crowning reputation, pass into other hands, and either succeed or fail. Great liners ply the waters of the Atlantic and Indian Ocean, and their proprietors are justifiably entitled to charge the maximum rates, because their ships have been "decorated throughout by Blinkinshaw & Bepstow." To say that your house has been done up by Blinkinshaw & Bepstow is to say that you have done the very best and the most expensive thing. You become at once a very desirable member of society.

When you enter the premises of Blinkinshaw & Bepstow in Soho, a tall military-looking man in pale-blue and gold ushers you through a cunning arrangement of double doors, and deposits you in a sort of large marble atrium, where you stand on a thick-pile Turkish carpet, and blink feebly into the mysterious lights and shadows. You are allowed a few moments to accustom yourself to your exalted location, when a very old gentleman with snow-white hair and gold pince-nez comes forward and looks into your eye. He has a melancholy but sympathetic expression. He seems to want to convey the idea that your sorrows are his sorrows, that your hopes are his hopes, that he has no other object in life than to be kind and gentle with you. You mention some vague project, but he does not reply. He leads you reverently into the shadows, and switches on electric lights. You find yourself in gorgeous fitted rooms of carved oak and tapestry; knights in armour scowl down at you from galleries; huge Chinese vases stand dumbly for you to bow your knee before them as you pass. You are impressed. You lose all sense of time or social values. The mission you came on is forgotten; neither does your cicerone remind you of it. He speaks in his soothing, melancholy voice, and extols the fading glories of the crafts. He becomes your brother. You are like pilgrims wandering hand in hand in search of revelation. Your imagination riots with the moving possibilities of it all. That Chinese lacquer bed with the maroon hangings; how gorgeous that would look in the little white room at home! But the dear old gentleman shakes his head. There are tears on the brink of his eyes. He does not seem to want to part with the lacquer bed. He touches the smooth surface lovingly, and tarns away. You feel that he is too overcome to speak. And then your desire increases. You become passionate. You follow him doggedly and other ideas present themselves, but at the back of your mind is the vision of the lacquer bed. Over an inlaid Dutch table he becomes lyrical in his quiet way, but you can tell by his eyes that he knows how you are suffering. He, too, is suffering, and there is a poignant moment as you hover by a Boule cabinet. Suddenly he turns to you, and his eyes are clear, as though the struggle is over, as though some sympathetic chord in yourself has moved him so deeply that he is forced to make a concession to you. You find yourself seated at a desk, writing. The Chinese bed is yours; and everything you have is his. What does it matter! Are you not fellow-sufferers? Is the world so pitiable a place that a few hundred pounds one way or the other will affect it?

You part from him, you don't know how, and find yourself in the street You walk gaily homeward, dreaming and humming snatches of half -forgotten melodies, and it is only when the dim shadows of evening creep over the city, and your wife says, "Did you remember to order that ceiling paper for Lucy's bedroom?" that you realize that there is a genius behind all the works of God and man, the indefinable quality of getting the very uttermost out of life. Wasn't it Carlyle who extolled this quality so profoundly!

On a certain evening in the early autumn, Arthur found himself on the top floor of the premises of Blinkinshaw & Bepstow. He had not passed through any of the experiences enumerated above, for several very good reasons. One was that the firm was officially shut, and great dust-sheets covered the more important objects d'art Another was that he was there in a purely officeseeking capacity.

On the other hand, his experience on the top floor was almost as surprising and unsettling as our own on the ground floor, when we entered to order Lucy's bedroom paper. He described it afterward as being "rampageous." You must picture him at that time, a trimly built young man with rather dark, dreamy eyes, brown hair, and an olive skin. Under his arm he carried a small folio of drawings made by himself at odd times, and he awaited hesitatingly the realization of his first business appointment, to meet a Mr. Prank Leffbury, described as tie head designer of the firm. And suddenly he found himself in an atmosphere that recalled his schooldays gone mad. There were several large studios and smaller studios partitioned off by wood partitions and glass windows, and although it was late in the evening, a lot of young men were in the large studio, some howling comic songs and others fighting with rolls of paper. It is not at all like a business. And then he found himself in another smaller room, with real walls and a trapdoor leading through to the big studio, and he gazed at the back of Mr. Leffbury, who called out in a break voice:

"Hello! Do you want me?"

And he turned around, and Arthur beheld an elderly, thick-set man with a gray beard, who at first glance gave more the impression of being a sailor than a decorative draughtsman. He was in his shirt sleeves and he wore a low collar and a dark blue tie. His eyes were keen and kind behind the thick steel spectacles.

"My name is Gaffyn, sir," Arthur said timidly. "I have an appointment."

And then the seafaring designer cried out:

"Oh, yes, I remember. Someone spoke to me about you. Come in. Pull yourself a cigarette. No, I expect you're too young. Sit down a moment I must get this bloody drawing settled."

And he called through the trap-door. It was all very bewildering. And it did not become less so when a young man named "Henry" entered. He was a gorgeously apparelled young man with jet-black hair brushed right back, and he and Mr. Leffbury carried on the most remarkable conversation Arthur had ever heard in his life. It concerned a red-ink tracing that Mr. Leffbury was working on, and the talk was a mixture of foul language, profanity, ridiculous badinage, and a quite intense seriousness. Arthur was fully convinced that under the extravagant manner of their discourse, they really were discussing the best way to treat a certain section of a building. At one moment Mr. Leffbury would say:

"Oh, no, my darling; where is your intelligence! Where do you get the light for the entre-sol?" And at another point Henry would tell Mr. Leffbury "not to be a bloody old fool, but to use his gump."

So keen did the discussion become that they rushed out of the room to examine some other plan, and Arthur was forgotten. He examined some amazingly clever water-colour drawings hanging on the walls, and peeped furtively at large plans of buildings and architectural "blues. "This was a business not untouched with romance. And then Mr. Leffbury returned, rolling a cigarette, and he said:

"Now then, old chap, show me what you can do."

And to Arthur's surprise the head designer found virtues in his futile drawings. There was "a nice feeling" in this, "an undeniable quality" in an amateurish study of apple-blossoms, "a good instinct for line "in a desperate attempt to design a repeating pattern. Mr. Leffbury licked his cigarette, and his eyes glowed with a quiet excitement. He talked eagerly about the great future of the crafts, the illimitable possibilities of this studio at Blinkinshaw's, the genius of great artists of whom Arthur had not heard, and suddenly he remarked:

"God Lord! I've got to go up to Rugby to-night. What is the time?"

It was, perhaps, this remark which settled the matter in Arthur's mind. Outside was the drone of traffic and the tooting of horns. All around the room were scattered plans and sketches of royal palaces, imperial institutions, colossal liners, and hotels. They lay there in embryonic lines, vast unborn adventures awaiting the magic touch of this little bearded man lighting his cigarette, who remarked casually: "I've got to go up to Rugby" as though it were the most ordinary thing in the world. In a flash Arthur felt himself for the first time in touch with the great moving world. Things were being done here. There was movement.

"I shall like this" he thought.

And then Mr. Leffbury said:

"Well, if you like to come on, Gaffyn, I can find you a little niche. There's plenty of work, but we have a very good time. There are no restrictions. Provided you work like a blasted slave, you can do any old thing you like. Just hark at those devils!"

This latter remark referred to a noise coming from the outer studio. Some of the young gentlemen were apparently giving imitations of the coyote-house at the zoo.

Mr. Leffbury's eye alighted on a large drawing mounted on a light wooden frame, which some one had apparently just started. He fidgeted in front of it, as though annoyed that he could not have a go at it. He puffed excitedly at his cigarette, and then suddenly he turned away, and striking a theatrical attitude exclaimed:

"Gaffyn, in this little room we control the decorative destinies of Europe."

At the same instant young Henry came bursting in again, and Mr. Leffbury called out:

''Henry, isn't it a fact that in this little room we control the decorative destinies of Europe?"

And the brilliant youth answered:

"Oh, to hell with the decorative destinies! What have you done with my clothes-brush, Pat"

The clothes-brush was found, and some tobacco borrowed, and Henry went out. And then Arthur said boldly:

"I think I should like to join, if you can arrange it, sir."

"All right," Mr. Leffbury answered. "Come in on Wednesday, any time you like. I shall be away to-morrow. And then I 'll tell you what to do. And for God's sake don't call me sir. Good-night!"

CHAPTER VI

FRANK LEFFBURY

It is not known, and it probably never will be known, except to a favored few, that at the time when Arthur was starting on his career—that is to say, in the late nineties—a certain man made a great and heroic effort to revolutionize the crafts in London. His ambition was nothing less than to introduce something of the spirit of the medieval gilds into the arena of commercial London; to instil into the minds of an influential crowd of materialists the enthusiasm for an ideal, the complete submergence of the individual in the interests of society, the sense of fellowship and cooperation conspiring toward a common search for beauty; something of the spirit that raised the spires of Westminster and Amiens. And some who knew him very well were amazed not that he failed, but that he came so near succeeding, and that the reason of the failure was not attributable to the outside forces which opposed him, and which, indeed, he almost mastered, but to disloyalty and abuse of privilege from within.

The man who made this heroic effort was a man quite unknown to the general public, the employee of a large firm, and his name was Prank Leffbury.

He was one of a family of seven children of a poor bootmaker in Leicester. The father died when he was nine, and he was the second son. His elder brother who was thirteen, was found work in a printing-house, and at the age of ten Frank was taken from school and employed by the Midland Timber Corporation at their wharf on the canal. He, and his brother, and his mother, who took in the neighbors' washing, managed to support themselves and the younger children for two years. At the Midland Timber Corporation's wharf Frank's work was purely mechanical, assisting the men in loading and unloading, running across the yards with messages, and holding the planks for the great saws. But, as he afterward confessed, it was here that he fell under the spell of his first love—wood! He got to like the smell of it, the sight of it, the possibilities of it. He spent long hours in the firm's sample room, and in a short time found no difficulty in differentiating between East India satin-wood and West India satin-wood, and the various kinds of bird's-eye maple. He learned the capacities of wood, and their whims and eccentricities. There was, moreover, a world of romance in the cases that showed the veneers from strange trees in different parts of the world.

"It was wood "he said to Arthur one day, "that first gave me the lust to know other things. And as a matter of fact, you cannot have a much better subject to start on than wood, which has been one of the best friends to man. I remember that it was one day during the lunch-hour on the wharf, after I had been examining the grain of a fine specimen of sycamore that had just come in, that the great idea came to me. It had been raining, and suddenly the sun came out. I was looking at the canal and thinking of the wonderful journey of the sycamore, and its history and romance, when I became imbued with the great desire not only to know all about wood, but to know all about everything else. I made up my mind that I would acquire all knowledge, everything I Everything there is to learn I would set out to learn. I would read all the books that had ever been written. I would find out just exactly why everything is and what it is, and wherefore. I was ten years old then." He sighed, and added, "I am now an old man and I have n't learned very much, but I thank God I can still go on learning."

During the short time he had spent at the national school he had not been taught to read, except the very simplest words, so he devoted his spare moments to drawing. He used to draw the barges on the canal, and the timber yards and the mills. At the age of twelve he had an accident, losing two fingers of his left hand in the machinery. He spent three months in the Leicester Infirmary, and a man in the bed next to him taught him a little about reading. His mother used to call and complain about the difficulties of supporting the family without his help. Before he left the infirmary a plague of typhoid broke out in the town, and two of his younger sisters died. When he returned home he found the family in dire straits. He went back to the timber yard for a few months, and then his mother decided to take the family up to London. A cousin at Walthamstow had offers his eldest brother a situation in his shop, which was a stationer's and small printer's, and it was thought that the third brother, who was now eleven, might make himself useful there. Mrs. Leffbury could get employment in a laundry, and there would probably be no difficulty about finding work for Prank.

The family arrived at Walthamstow on a bleak day in November, and occupied two rooms and a lavatory, which the cousin had been kind enough to secure for them. On the following morning his mother told Frank he had better go out and find work. He thought the matter over, and decided that he would most likely find employment in some trade where his knowledge of timber might be of use. He wandered about till he came to a builder's and timber merchant's, but they did not require assistance. He tried one or two other places without success. On the way back he observed a small cabinetmaker's shop. He went in, and a gaunt old man in an apron and steel-framed spectacles came forward.

"Do you want an assistant, sir?" Frank asked.

The old man shook his head and started to move away, and Frank turned to the door. By the side of the door was a plank of polished birch. As the old man was only two or three yards away, Frank remarked:

"That's a nice piece of birch."

The old man looked at him with his melancholy eyes and said:

"Why"

"I say that's a nice piece of birch."

"What do you know about birch, my boy?"

"I know something about birch, and also teak, and hazel, and oak, and mahogany; in fact, most of them."

The old man gazed at the small boy, rubbed his brow and said:

"Hm."

Then he looked round his shop with a bewildered expression, and asked:

"Do you know anything about joinery!"

And Frank said:

"Yes, a bit."

The old man beckoned to him to come into a room at the back. Fixed on a winch was the framework of the lower structure of a Boule cabinet He was evidently in difficulties. He was restoring the cabinet, but getting into trouble with the veneers.

"You've got an interesting job there," said the small boy.

The old man explained the difficulties of the problem in a doubtful voice, as though he thought it was a waste of time. But at the end of his discourse Frank said:

"I can tell you where I think you're wrong, Mr. Brackett."

And he explained at length what he would do under the circumstances.

The old man muttered "Hm" at intervals, and took off his spectacles, and wiped them, and put them back again. When the discussion was finished he sat wearily on a chair, and looked at Frank.

"What is your name," he said.

"Frank Leffbury."

"H'm." He thought for a long time, but eventually rose and leaning against a small, black, iron, fireplace, expectorated gloomily into the meager grate.

"I might try you for a bit," he said at last.

They went back again into the shop, and after very careful deliberation Mr. Brackett agreed that Frank should come for a week on trial. Then, if satisfactory, he should receive eight shillings a week "to make himself generally useful."

Frank went, proved generally useful, and stayed with old Brackett for nine years.

It was in some respects a very satisfactory period. Old Brackett employed no one else, except occasionally when there was a great rush of work, as, for instance, the demand for a coffin. He himself had a fair, but rather limited knowledge of his profession. He taught Frank a certain amount, but for the most part he had to find things out for himself. He worked at Mr. Brackett's from eight in the morning till six in the evening, and every evening he went to the Polytechnic, attending the antique, life, and design classes, and occasionally going to lectures.

Mr. Brackett was a Baptist, a very religious man, and extremely conscientious about all his business dealings. He raised Prank's salary at regular intervals, and at the age of twenty-one he was receiving twenty-three shillings a week. It was as well that he had attained this princely income, for the maintenance of his family fell more and more upon him. His elder brother married a girl from a tobacconist's shop and went to live in Streatham, and his mother developed such attacks of rheumatism that she became almost a cripple. The third brother had made no startling success after his entry into the stationery world, and the youngest was still too young to earn money. Of the two girls, now aged twelve and fourteen, the eldest had also been drafted into the stationery business, but the younger stayed at home to wait on her mother.

At the age of twenty-one, restless desires and ambitions took possession of Frank, and he had almost decided to make a plunge into some more adventurous mode of life and to leave Mr. Brackett, when that gentleman solved the difficulty for him by dying, being buried in one of his own coffins. It was a misfit, a coffin he had made for a local tripe-dresser, but unfortunately, he had taken the wrong dimensions. Frank Leffbury did not find any great difficulty in securing employment, for he had by that time developed into a really brilliant draughtsman, and he had all the mechanical knowledge of the cabinet-making trade at his back, also. He eventually took a situation at Prothero's, a small decorator in Bayswater. He received a salary of thirty shillings a week, but out of this he had to pay his fare to and from Walthamstow; also to wear a clean shirt at least once a week, and a dean collar at least twice a week. He stayed there a year, and then quarrelled with Mr. Prothero about the design of a panelled room. He left one evening in a rage and never returned.

For twelve years after that he lived the life of a journeyman draughtsman, moving about from one firm to another. He acquired the reputation of being a very good designer, but a very difficult man to deal with. He was, indeed, restless and dissatisfied. And his dissatisfaction was not confined entirely to material things. The material did certainly weigh heavily upon him. He was always vaguely desiring happier conditions of life, a better home and furniture, the chance to travel, freedom for himself; but always these longings were suppressed or crushed by the insistent demands for the immediate material support of his family.

But this was not all. He came at that time under the influence of William Morris and other pioneers struggling for the spiritual freedom of the masses. He visited the Fabian Society, and talked with people whose ambitions were evolutionary. He was appalled by the realization of the social conditions from which he had sprung, and among which he earned his daily bread. He was torn between the overpowering claims of the artist and the reformer. He wanted to do something really big, not just to earn money. He went on working, and studying, and hoping. At the age of thirty-three his ambition "to acquire all knowledge" had, in any case, reached the point where he was acknowledged to have one of the most retentive memories in London for architectural detail. He was a complete authority on decorative style; he was a very clever mathematician and took a delight in conic sections and algebraic speculations; he had studied physics and the theory of light; he knew something of Egyptology and, for some reason or other, had studied subaqueous plant life; and he could tell you how the Chaldeans built their temples of reeds. He could, moreover, speak French and German, and had read Don Quixote in Spanish. As a friend of Mr. Blinkinshaw's remarked one day, "If that man Leffbury had ever had any education, he might have been quite a clever man."

He was, in fact, not only a clever man, but a very remarkable one, and, like a great many other remarkable men, the texture of his life was curiously uneven. He had great ideals and ambitions, and at the same time yielded to ridiculous vices and weaknesses. Normally of a temperate disposition, he would occasionally get riotously drunk. As far as everyone knew, he led a clean life—in fact, there could be no doubt of it; one had only to look at his sane, healthy face—and yet he had an uncontrollable liking for filthy and improper stories, of which he possessed an unlimited repertoire.

His language was at all times coloured by extravagant and indecent terms, and he had a nice turn for profanity.

As he grew older this side of his character became emphasized, and he also developed moods when it was impossible to know how far he was acting, and how far he was being sincere. At the age of thirty-four he was head of a studio in Manchester, where he lived for ten years. It was at that time that he came into touch with Mr. Fred Blinkinshaw.

The Blinkinshaws had started a small cabinet-making and upholstery business in the suburbs of Manchester, when an uncle of Fred and James Blinkinshaw died and left the two brothers fifteen hundred pounds each. They immediately moved their business to a more central position, and at the end of three years were one of the flourishing houses of Manchester. James was frankly a materialist, what Mr. Leffbury called "one of the claws and talons crowd" but Fred, was a man with imagination. He met Frank Leffbury, and marked him down as a man to be secured by his firm. James did not see the necessity,—it was an unnecessary expense,—but Fred, despite his more imaginative disposition, had the greater force of character, and he won the day. They approached Leffbury, and he was engaged as their head designer at a salary of three hundred and fifty pounds a year, a considerable sum at that time.

The result was almost immediately successful, and the Blinkinshaws secured some good contracts in competition. At the end of six years Blinkinshaw & Co. was one of the biggest concerns in the north of England, and Mr. Fred cast his eye longingly on London. There was considerable misgiving about this, James being terrified at the risk, but eventually Fred got in touch with a Mr. Septimus Bepstow, who ran a large wholesale house for the manufacture and sale of brass beds and bedroom furniture, in the East End. He was also an ambitious man, and he had considerable capital. There were many board meetings and discussions, but eventually Blinkinshaw & Bepstow took an old Georgian house in Soho and started business. Prank Leffbury was again appointed chief designer. The concern wobbled for several years, till the imaginative Fred came to the conclusion that the thing was not being done on a big enough scale. By some means unknown to anyone but himself, he persuaded a well-known nobleman, who was a notorious speculator, to invest a huge sum of money in the business, and it became a limited liability company. Large factories were erected in the suburbs, and vast sums were spent on advertising. In a few years the Blinkinshaw & Bepstow "note" in decoration became a byword throughout the land. All the biggest contracts came into their hands, and the Georgian house in Soho was extended till it occupied the whole of two blocks.

At the age of fifty-three Prank Leffbury found himself the chief of a staff of twenty-five designers working for one of the biggest limited liability companies in Europe. But in the meantime he had passed through many mental vicissitudes. All his sympathies were with the theory of cooperative workmanship. He detested these big commercial enterprises like poison. He had assisted at the launching of the arts and crafts movement, and was a member of the Art Workers' Guild. He found himself, almost reluctantly, in a position of power, and the receiver of the colossal salary of five hundred pounds a year. It was a larger sum of money than had ever been paid to a designer before, but his conscience told him it was something in the nature of a bribe. He would have liked to have broken away and to have been a free-lance again, but he seemed to be held as in a vice by the conditions which surrounded him. His mother had become bedridden, his two sisters were still dependent on him, and he had to move the family to a house in St. John's wood. He had to work like a slave, and he knew not the meaning of the word "liberty."

One night in the summer he was working alone in his room at the top of the building in Soho, when a feeling of depression came over him. He had been to an exhibition of the arts and crafts during his lunch-hour. There were, perhaps, twenty people in the building, examining the somewhat futile exhibits. He was thinking about this, and of the hopelessness of the movement. The window was open and outside he could hear the dull roar of London, like the growl of a beast of prey. The contact of these two impressions operated on him in a queer way. The growl of the beast was like the mighty, irresistible roar of commercialism, and the memory of the Arts and Crafts Exhibition like the pale ghost of some hapless idea. He stood up, leaned out of the window and lighted a cigarette.

Suddenly a phrase came to his lips in the way that a phrase will sometimes come to a person of a certain type of creative genius, before the thought which created the phrase has had time to very clearly formulate itself. The phrase which occurred to Prank Leffbury was:

"Why not start from the other end!"

It was odd, but this very simple and laconic query ease to him in the light of a revelation. He peered eagerly into the street, and watched the lights flitting hither and thither.

'Why not start from the other end'

It was so absurdly simple! He was fifty-three years old, and it had not occurred to him before. Trying to put it concisely to himself, it amounted to this:

'Instead of trying to oppose commercialism, why not use commercialism? Commercialism is a fact, deep-rooted in the lives of the people, ineradicable. The arts and crafts movement is an excrescence on society. It has nothing to do with the fundamental purposes of being.'

He puffed fiercely at his cigarette, and the simplicity of the idea dazzled him. The hour and the man was peculiarly opportune. Blinkinshaw & Bepstow was not only a big firm, but they promised to monopolize the entire decorative industry of the country. They had already bought out two very old and well-established firms in the city, and it was rumored that the Blinkinshaws privately held large quantities of shares in firms who were their reputed rivals. It was on the road to becoming a comer in the trade. The strength of his own position was undeniable. He knew that the Blinkinshaws knew that no one could take his place. He commenced to dream and to formulate his scheme. His scheme, roughly speaking, amounted to this: He would form a spiritual commonwealth within a material oligarchy.

He would gradually build up around him a coterie of men imbued with his own altruistic views. There would be no violent and dramatic denouements. The thing would work itself. The whole system would find itself permeated with the doctrine of the fellowship of man, and they would go forward in a reverent search for beauty. So strong would the position of this coterie become that they would gradually be able to force into working order some of the rules of the ancient gilds. There would be a revival of the apprenticeship system. There would be mutual cooperation. Men would be taught their trade thoroughly and efficiently. There would be sick benefits and pensions, and the opportunity for study and travel, and eventually there would be co-partnership. The Blinkinshaws would be swamped, and a gild in its truest sense would be formed.

However fantastic these ideas may appear to an outsider, Mr. Leffbury must be given the credit of believing them practicable, and he must also be given the credit of having no personal ambition in the matter at all. On that night when he listened to "the growl of the beast," he visualized the day when the beast should growl to a more melodic phrase, and he pictured himself, when the reeds were piping to the happier England, creeping away among the shadows, unknown but desperately happy.

He turned to the pencil elevation on his bench and muttered:

"I shall never get this bloody drawing done to-night; that's certain!"

Such was the man under whose aegis Arthur commenced his professional career.

The syllabus of study which Mr. Leffbury drew up for Arthur consisted of the following: Two days a week he was to spend in the studio at Blinkinshaw & Bepstow's, making tracings and doing any work he was capable of, and observing closely the work which was going on. On the other four working days he was to go to South Kensington Museum and make sketches in pencil and colour, and also drawings to scale of such objects as Mr. Leffbury suggested. On two evenings a week he was to attend an architectural class at the Regent Street Polytechnic, and on two evenings a life-class. On Thursday evening he was to attend some lectures on historic ornament, and on Saturday a cabinet-making class. On Sundays he was advised to go out into the country and sketch, and in his spare moments he was to read everything he could get hold of—scientific books, essays, lives of the painters, history, biology, fiction, the newspapers, and reviews. He was, moreover, to keep his mind alert for impressions, and to train his memory, and above all things, to keep cheerful.

He found the last instruction the easiest to follow, for he started out on this professional pilgrimage with buoy ant spirits. He certainly felt rather bewildered by the variety of the manifold activities he was to pursue, and he would at moments wonder, when he was doing a certain thing, whether he ought not to be doing something else. But it was all amazingly exciting. He was to be a citizen in the best sense of the term. He would eventually be independent and would be able to help his father, be as insulting as he liked to Edith, and marry Eleanor. The affair of the penknife would be forgotten, and he would become great and successful, and people would look up to him. He found the atmosphere of Blinkinshaw's extremely entertaining, and the studio reminded him of a glorified school. They were nearly all very young men, with the exception of Mr. Leffbury, and there was the same schoolboy spirit of ragging, and fooling, and noise going on all day. But there was the added glory of independence. Many of the young men were getting quite large salaries, and they dressed like Piccadilly dub-men. They took cabs, lunched at expensive restaurants, and took girls to the music-hall in the evening. They would turn up for work in the morning, and boast of the previous evening's adventures, being rather proud of looking washed-out and exhausted. He soon found among them a remarkable variety of character.

There was the brilliant youth, 'Henry,' whose other name was Waldren. He had tremendous animal spirits, and drew divinely, but he gave Arthur the impression of being shallow and insincere. There was George Arthur, a Scotsman, with rather a cruel, sensual face, who made most astoundingly clever water-colour drawings. There was a young man with a smooth child-like face, named Bertram White. He was reputed to be the cleverest designer in the firm, next to Mr. Leffbury, and was in charge of one section of the studio. Despite the innocence of his appearance, he was notoriously the heaviest drinker in the place. There was a very tall boy, named Hazell, who was also clever and who also drank. There was a Yorkshireman, named Levistock, with dark hair and olive skin, who nurtured a sullen resentment against the whole social system. He would sit on his high stool, and fidget with his pencil, and growl about the tyranny of capital all day. There was Jimmy Long, a round-faced, gladsome creature, always pursuing the chimera of what he called "life." There were two

Frenchmen, named Tonquet and Luneville. They were employed principally on French interiors, or what the rest of the studio called "the lousy Louis'." They seemed rather bewildered by the boisterous atmosphere of the place, but Tonquet made himself popular with his imitations, which were very good. He could imitate birds and animals, and water running down a sink, and wood being sawed. Luneville was of a more melancholy disposition, but he was greatly admired not only on account of his work which was excellent, but on account of his exhaustive knowledge of obstetrics and other unmentionable subjects. There was a Swede named Larsen, who spoke very little English, but who gave amazing exhibitions of feats of strength. And there were many others that it took Arthur a long time to individualize.

The life and liberty in that studio seemed an incredible thing for a business house to tolerate. There was apparently no rule beyond the fact that the work was done. And the work was indeed very well done, and always on time. The whole studio would occasionally work all night, if a big contract were being competed for. But apart from that, the young men were at liberty to keep their own hours. They could smoke, sing, swear, wear ridiculous clothes, go out for drinks or meals as often and as long as they liked, fight with rolls of paper, give imitations of leading actors, have moods, telephone to chorus girls; everything was tolerated as long as the work was done. This was all part of the system instituted by Mr. Leffbury.

The heads of the firm knew, of course, the kind of life that was led upstairs, and it is known that many stormy board meetings took place with regard to it. Mr. James Blinkinshaw and the other directors wanted to have the same rules of punctuality and behavior apply to the studio as to the rest of the establishment, but Mr. Fred supported Mr. Leffbury.

"You have to remember, gentlemen, 'he once remarked at a board meeting, "the success of this firm is primarily due to the studio, to the craftsman. I acknowledge that this man Leffbury is a madman, but the point is: he gets the work done. The number of skilled draftsmen is limited, and we have the pick of the bunch. If we lose Leffbury, one of our rivals will get him, and probably some of the other designers will follow him. And then you have to remember, 'he added, smiling indulgently, "these men are—er—artists in a sort of way. This—er—lack of discipline—shall we call it?—is perhaps one of the peculiarities of the artistic temperament."

The board laughed at this extravagent statement, and Mr. James Blinkinshaw exclaimed:

"Artistic fiddlesticks! This is a business, not a bear-garden."

Nevertheless Mr. Fred carried the day, and Leffbury was allowed to conduct the "bear-garden" on his own lines.

Arthur found the contrast between the noisy vitality of the Blinkinshaw studio and the austere seclusion of South Kensington very striking. This was in the days before the new and somewhat commonplace building, which at present houses the finest collection of works of art in the world, had been erected. It is true that in those days the corridors were badly lighted, and the central courts were dim, but there was a peculiar mystery and fascination about the place, which has since been spirited away. Arthur soon learned to love the museum. He loved the silence of it, and the heavy chiaroscuro of corridors filled with furniture and plaster casts; the sense of beauty brooding across the centuries and transfixed in little passages of wood, and stone, and ivory, and damask. These objects, imprisoned in their cases or resting dumbly against the walls, seemed eloquent of a common purpose. And on certain days in the autumn when a heaviness was in the air, he would wander forth and meet the ghosts who fashioned them. They would come whispering through the galleries in the polyglot garments of past centuries, with all their loves, and hatreds, and passions that moved them in their day forgotten, and only their lips moving in a kind of worship.

He remembered once coming across a woman's workbox made in the seventeenth century. It was exquisitely embroidered in coloured silk needlework, and partially padded. There were some quaint formal figures representing the story of Hagar and Ishmael, and the colour had faded to an almost uniform tone. Arthur could not account for it, but the box produced in him a peculiar feeling of tenderness, and every time he passed it he was conscious of little thrills of vibrating emotion. Who was the dear ghost who haunted the work-box? And what was she to him, or he to her?

The museum was filled with these ghosts; and more especially did he like the little fragments of things, for they were the most ghost-ridden. Tom pieces of tapestry, broken sections of architraves, an incomplete caryatid, a Roman base without the column; in these things there was little left but the indestructible spirit. It was as though the great heart of the world reached out to them across the centuries, and would not let them go.

He loved the colour of things, colour that had been burnished by the sun of Italy and Arabia, colour evolved from the molten furnaces at Limoges, the colour of Chinese porcelain, the colour of Persian rugs. What was it about colour that stirred the emotions! Why did the vision of a combination of colours in a certain rug or on a painted plaque set his pulses throbbing, while another combination left him cold and indifferent.

It was very exciting, the threshold of this new life! He was no longer a schoolboy; he was a man. He would develop and express himself for what he was worth. At Blinkinshaw's there was the great lure of the living world, the promise of wealth, cleverness, dazzling but obscure possibilities, the commanding figure of Mr. Leffbury, and the varied attractive qualities of the other men. At the museum there was the great lure of the dead world with its undying whispers.

Between these two centers four years of his life passed rapidly. By a sort of algebraic progression he was gradually drawn away from the dead world to the living world; that is to say, by Mr. Leffbury's system of instruction he gradually ceded days from museum study to the practical work of the Blinkinshaw studio, till at the end of that period his whole time was at the disposal of the firm. But it must be acknowledged that as this progression worked toward its inevitable conclusion, his own state of mental happiness did not develop in a parallel degree. Notwithstanding the stimulus of vitality at Blinkinshaw's, he began at the end of that time to develop moods of dissatisfaction there which he did not experience in the museum. He made progress as a designer, but showed more promise as a colourist than as a practical draftsman. He divided his companionship between Levistock, who talked of "the tyranny of capital" and Jimmy Long, who quoted Omar Khayyam.

He learned to smoke cigarettes, and to swear, and to talk about politics and women. He shaved, wore high collars, and fell in love promiscuously, and once desperately with a girl called Myra Henness, a student from South Kensington School. She was a small, pert, little thing, with very bright colouring, and she wore short hair and a jubhah. He spent many restless days and nights on her accounts, and they ambled round the museum together, and giggled and pushed each other surreptitiously. Once he told her about the work-box and how it affected him, and she laughed and said:

"You're so funny."

And curiously enough, he thought at the time that it was rather attractive, the way she said this. It was not till he visited her home at Netting Hill one Sunday afternoon that the disillusionment came.

Alas! for the cruelty of youth! He met her three sisters and her mother. The sisters were like Myra, only their legs were too short for their bodies, or their bodies were too long for their legs, whichever way you like to conceive this unfortunate physical defect. In any case, the appearance of these sisters reacted on him disastrously. Myra appeared to him after that less like a girl than like a species, and a species of an almost repelling kind. The mother, also, was unpleasantly suggestive of what Myra would be like in thirty-five years time. He avoided her, and spent his Sundays sketching barges up the river.

He continued to live with his father, who took an absorbing but uncritical interest in his work. He talked at great length about his drawings, and the objects he had drawn and studied, but he gave no opinion upon their merits, or made any reference to his career and future. He never asked questions about his comings and goings, or proffered advice upon any subject at all. He was even apparently unaware whether Arthur received a salary or not. In any case, at the end of that time Arthur was receiving a pound a week from Blinkinshaw, and he had nothing to spend it on except himself, although it was very evident that the Eccles Square establishment was being run on most parsimonious lines. Scores of times it occurred to Arthur that he ought to suggest that he contribute to the household expenses, but when it came to the point, he simply could not bring himself to speak of such a matter to his father. The very mention of such a thing would be too embarrassing and painful It would be cruelty to his parent. And so they continued their daily companionship without any show of affection, and with all the finer impulses of mental communion suppressed.

It was not till nearly the end of this fourth year that a series of little disillusionments combined to weld him into a normal state of restlessness and discontent. It expressed itself succinctly in a remark he suddenly made one day to Levistock:

"I don't see what all this bally business of bedroom suites and machine-made papers has got to do with art."

The profession he had slipped into appeared to him as a naked means to an end, a way of making money in one of the least objectionable ways, but nothing more. And something told him that this was not, and never would be, satisfying.

Sometimes at odd moments in the museum, inspired by the contemplation of the work of medieval craftsmen, of French weavers, and Italian silversmiths, and the spirit of the painter-priests who depicted the Passion of Christ on a little gilt diptych in the thirteenth century, he felt thrilled with the desire to "go and do likewise." But when he was brought up against the actual conditions which prevailed in a studio turning out drawings for a modem limited liability company, the whole thing wait to pieces. The buoyant optimism of his early days was strangled by the realization of the cynical attitude of his fellow-workers.

Gradually he discovered that the dignified exterior of Blinkinshaw's was only a veneer. It covered the old wormwood of commercialism with a cynical impressiveness. The swarms of well-dressed salesmen who had the management of the work in their hands, were utterly ignorant and unscrupulous. They had no other ideas than that of making the work pay the uttermost farthing, of putting in "shoddy" wherever it could be managed without showing, of introducing faked material where real material had been paid for, of beating down the subcontractors and the workmen so that in the end they could show a good profit on the job in their statement to Mr. James and Mr. Fred Blinkinshaw. These gentlemen would be in and out of the gorgeous bar of the "Queen of Rumania" all day long, drinking and standing each other whiskies and sodas, arranging secret "deals" and "dos." On the occasions when Arthur visited this alluring establishment he would observe them leaning heavily against the bar or whispering together in the comers, and the remarks which reached him were always of this nature: "I got him by the short hairs, dear boy"; "I can put you on to a very cheap line in hardware. A friend of mine—"; "If you could introduce Mr. So-and-so to me, I'd make it all right for you over that—"; "Well, I'll tell you what I'll do; I'll share the commission with you if you'll persuade—to place that order for lino with—."

"These are the men "thought Arthur, "who really have 'the decorative destinies of Europe "in their hands."

And then he learned that the rare antique furniture was mostly made at Walthamstow. It was one of the jokes of the firm, and the dear old gentleman who sold it with tears in his voice had the reputation of being the cutest salesman in London. The disillusionment in regard to the studio took longer to detect, but in its effect was even more disturbing than the other. He soon found that in spite of all the cleverness and plausibility of these young men, there was no loyalty to Mr. Leffbury, and no loyalty to an idea. Every man was for himself, and there was the rumour of a plot by Bertram White and Waldren to usurp Mr. Leffbury and to get the control of the studio in their own hands. He could not analyse his own feelings in the matter. He wanted to get on himself and to be successful, but something told him that that was not and never would be everything. He could not define the quality of his discontent, but he knew that it was there, like a stranded thing.

But still he went on, for the reason that there was no alternative, and indeed this spirit of discontent did not permeate all his days. He had the divine recompense of youth and an uncrushable faith in Mr. Leffbury.

In company with Jimmy Long he discovered the delights of the little French and Italian restaurants in Soho. It was Jimmy who suggested the inspiring institution of sharing a bottle of Beaune between them for their lunch, and they would return to the studio in a roaring state of optimism. Sometimes they would go to Pollini's to dinner in the evening, and afterwards visit a music-hall, or sit over their coffee and talk. They would talk about art, and socialism, and the chaps at Blinkinshaws and Mr. Leffbury and his ideas, and foreign countries, and free trade, and musical comedies, and eventually and always about women, Jimmy was a companionable little beast, an averred sensualist, but by no means a fool. He was older than Arthur, and these four years gave him a patriarchal right to lay bare his impressions, and to impart his records of successful enterprises in the dubious pursuit of the erotic passion.

That phase of life was very exciting. Somewhere in the world there was at that moment, walking quietly and unknowingly, that woman, that divine and wonderful person who was going to dovetail with all the vague desires of his heart. His eyes were always searching for her in the crowd.

Often after lunch these young men would stroll down Regent Street arm in arm, with their hats at jaunty angles. And there they would see the most adorable women of every description, walking briskly or looking into shop-windows, their little chins and noses peeping from under most alluring head-gear. Some of these would be alone, but they were invariably the sort who just glanced at our cavaliers and then hurried by. And those that did look, and even grinned at them—well, both these young men held very decided views about women of that sort.

"Besides," as Jimmy remarked one day, "they're usually so damned unattractive."

Occasionally at a music-hall they would look down from some dizzy elevation upon visions of inaccessible loveliness. To the strains of disturbing music, beauty would hold out her arms in her great central appeal. The young men would hold their breath and gaze mesmerized across the unbridgeable spaces. The world seemed controlled by some ironic Tantalus creating unnecessary allurements, and chaining the feet of heroes out of their reach.

And as Arthur found the conditions of his professional life more and more disillusioning, the closer did he hug his ideal of womanhood. He would wander down the Brompton Road at times and look in the antique shops. And he would think to himself:

"One day I shall buy that old shawl for her, and that little oval mirror to place upon her dressing-table. Perhaps she will come along here with me, and we will choose some of that violet glass to place upon our sideboard."

Sometimes perverse moods would come to him, sullen desires for expression. If she should prove inaccessible! Society had such cunning arrangements. However dearly one loved a woman, when it came to the point one practically had to buy her. One had to have money, to be a social entity. And all this was very difficult and ill-regulated. It was the James Blinkinshaws who could afford to buy.

One day in spring he walked across the park. The rhododendrons were out, and there was a feeling of movement in the air. A carriage swung round the corner by the Achilles statue. In it sat a finely dressed woman. Her face was proud and insolent, and provokingly beautiful. She gave the boy a half-glance of disdain and looked away. The thought flashed through his mind:

"I'd like to have you, and break you."

He had the momentary prescience of some hour when he would face a woman like that, as proud, and disdainful, and beautiful as she. And he would be proud, too. It would be a competition of pride and strength, and he would triumph.

He spent his summer holidays with Aunt Elizabeth and Eleanor. His father was always to come, but failed to turn up at the last moment, owing to "some urgent Work he could not leave."

As time went on he discovered grave deficiencies in Eleanor. She was kind and lovable, but he probed her and found a point where things became vacant and unsatisfying. She was not the lady of the work-box, who haunted his dreams.

CHAPTER VIII

SELF-EXPRESSION

During those years which preceded the South African War there was a great wave of industrial prosperity in London, and the house of Blinkinshaw & Bepstow rode flamboyantly on the crest of that wave. Nothing seemed to go wrong. Nearly every big competition they entered was secured. The contracts that the firm had in hand must have amounted to several millions of pounds. Salaries were increased, the studio was enlarged, and extravagance was the order of the day. And yet it cannot be said that as the line of fortune took this upward curve the spirits of our hero made a corresponding sweep. In fact, they seemed to take a diametrically opposite course.

School-life had inured him to a certain amount of immoral talk and profanity, but what depressed him was the underlying keynote of cynical indifference. Nobody cared. Every man was for himself. Not only was there a lack of loyalty to "Pa" Leffbury, but he and his ideas were the secret butt of endless obscene mirth. Moreover, the fashion of excessive drinking increased as the prosperity of the firm became more assured. It was a known fact that many of the salesmen would drink anywhere from fifteen to twenty whiskies and sodas during the day, and the drinking was not confined to the salesmen. The young gentlemen of the brush and pencil held their own. It became the fashion to boast of one's physical capacity for consuming alcohol. The laurels of prowess in this direction passed from one brow to another; from the ingenuous-looking Bertram White to Henry Waldren, from Henry Waldren to Hazell, from Hazell to a very charming young gentleman from Budapest, named Kaponyi, who invariably arrived in the morning holding his head and saying:

"Gott! vot a night it vas!"

The tilting of glasses, and the whispering and scheming would commence in the bar of "The Queen of Rumania" at eleven o'clock in the morning, and would continue until this delectable place of refreshment closed its doors reluctantly at half past twelve o'clock at night.

The only satisfaction Arthur derived from having to earn his living in this atmosphere was the sardonic reflection that Edith was responsible for his introduction into it.

And the only note of relief amid these disintegrating forces was the figure of Frank Leffbury. He appeared strangely impervious to the shallowness and insincerity of his associates, as though by the force of his personality he could move mountains. He stood there like a good mariner in a treacherous sea, with his eye upon the compass and his trust in the crew. It seemed to matter to him less whether a contract was secured, or whether people were scheming to overthrow him, than whether the section of a certain cornice were a thing of beauty. He insisted on believing in everyone, and in the validity of his ideals.

Arthur asked Levistock one day his opinion of him, and the reformer said:

"Leffbury's all right, only he 's a sanguinary fool. He's trying to run with the commercial hounds and hunt with the idealistic hares. He 's trying to graft the ideals of St. Francis on the fangs of a man-eating tiger. He doesn't stand a dog's chance of succeeding."

"Why shouldn't he succeed?" said Arthur.

''For a hundred and one reasons. And the principal one is, you can't have a revolution in the crafts without having a corresponding revolution in society. He's starting at the wrong end. The first thing we've got to have is what Shaw asks for—equal distribution of wealth, every man, woman, or child, irrespective of age, sex, or character, to have an equal wage, and the abolition of private property. Then you can begin to talk about ideals."

They were in the museum at the time, and Levistock peered at some old Spanish ironwork and sighed.

"Does it ever strike you how ridiculous it is that we should have a museum at all? All these things ought to be in the homes of the people, but instead of that, it's considered so remarkable to see a beautiful thing, a decent piece of wrought-iron, for instance, that one has to put it in a museum, and people come and stare at it open-mouthed. They starve and underpay the people, and then they erect a place like this, and stuff it full with decent things, and then they say: "Look what we are doing for you, you dirty dogs! We're helping you and educating you. We're showing you what you ought to have in your own homes. Whereas the swine know all the time that the very commercial conditions which they impose make it impossible for the people to produce these things in their homes. It's like leading a muzzled dog up to a juicy bone."

The reformer blew his nose, and Arthur took this opportunity of interjecting:

"But the museum belongs to the people."

Levistock grinned superciliously and stuffing his rather grubby handkerchief into his sleeve, replied:

"Yes, and so does the army, and the navy, and the general post-office, and Hampstead Heath and the crown jewels! How does it help them? What's the good of owning India and Australia, if the baby at home is starving?"

This struck Arthur at the moment as being such a dazzling argument, he could think of nothing to reply.

The pendulum of their discussion swung backward and forward. Arthur was by no means convinced by the arguments of his colleague, but he was undoubtedly impressed, and his impressions were further accentuated by certain visits which they paid together to the more squalid regions of Walham Green and Hammersmith. Levistock, moreover, provided him with printed matter giving figures of the appalling pauperism in the East End of London, particulars of the sweating, and low wages, and the spread of vice and disease. On the other hand, he was furnished with the details of the rent-roll of certain dukes and landowners who held the very districts where these appalling conditions prevailed. And the knowledge of these things depressed him intensely.

One afternoon Mr. Leffbury accompanied Arthur to the museum. They went for the purpose of taking notes of Italian doorways for the design of a courtyard that was to be added to the house of a wealthy manufacturer in Yorkshire. The said gentleman seeing nothing incongruous in introducing to the bleak moors architecture designed for a sunny clime, and having the money to pay for it, the work was to be done "as per instructions."

It was a humid day in April, and Mr. Leffbury was in one of his perverse moods. He spoke very little to Arthur as they went along on the top of a bus, except to use language with regard to the Yorkshire manufacturer that was almost as humid as the day.

In the museum he gradually calmed down, and they strolled about among the carved doorways, and wellheads, and fonts, and examined the "Gates of Paradise" of Lorenzo Ghiberti. Then suddenly his mood changed, and he talked about Italy, where he had never been, excitedly. And he said to Arthur:

"Go to Italy while you're young, Arthur. None of these things are any good to you when you're old."

He looked at a low relief by Donatello, and exclaimed:

"My God! what pigmies we are! Just look at this! Doesn't it make you despair? See how the forms emphasize the lines of the architectural setting. Do you note how the old devil gets his deepest shadows just where the light is strongest? Look at these dancing girls! Are n't they darlings! And yet you don't want to love one individually. They take their place too well. It's the whole thing you love. How the word nature has become abused. Imagine this treated by Jacques, the R.A. You would find five, pretty, realistic, chorus girls. You would immediately debate within yourself which one you would like to take out to supper. You wouldn't see it as a whole. It would just express the academic nimbleness of the lecherous, well-fed Jacques. When you go to Italy, Arthur, keep this in mind, think of yourself. Express yourself. Don't be mesmerized by reputation, or by what people call 'nature.' Did you tell me you were going to Italy?"

Arthur said "No" rather breathlessly.

"Strange! Perhaps I dreamt it, or there was something about you associable with the Donatello relief."

He talked about Italy very vividly, just as though he had been there. He talked about the bambini on the foundling hospital in Florence, and about other Delia Robbias, and about the Church of San Miniato, and Fiesole, and the pavements in Sienna, and Venice at night-time, and Naples in the spring. And Arthur became very excited, and kept on thinking to himself:

"I should go to Italy while I'm young."

So intimate and confidential did Mr. Leffbury become that Arthur became bold enough to lead him to the workbox, and to tell him about the peculiar way it affected him. Mr. Leffbury looked at him quickly, and after a pause said:

"Arthur, you have one of those faces that the world will love to torture."

He became silent after that, and then sighed and suggested that they should go and have some tea. They went out into the Exhibition Road and walked down toward South Kensington station, where there was a teashop. It was getting dark, and as they walked along Mr. Leffbury said ruminatively:

"Everybody has a work-box handed them when they enter this silly business we call 'life'. Everything else is puzzling, incomprehensible. But about the work-box there can be no mistake. It's put in our hands. And when we die, we leave it behind. And others follow on, and take up the work-box. The things we make are scattered, but the work-box remains. And so those others who come after us know us less by what we made than by the love that we imparted to the making."

He again paused, and then added: "I can well believe in your lady of the work-box. The ghosts that hang around work are the most insistent of all."

As they crossed the road Arthur looked at his chief's face. It was pinched and worn by a life of struggle with uncongenial surroundings. He was getting old. In another environment and with better opportunities he might have been one of the world's recognized successes. He had more brains, character, and imagination than the majority of men, and yet the verdict of Levistock was the general verdict: "Old Lufbery's a sanguinary fool." They all thought that. They laughed at him behind his back.

And as Arthur glanced at him, his heart was touched with pity and pride. Pity for the pathetic figure of the man, and pride that suddenly, with one little sentence, he should have lifted the veil and given a glimpse of bis soul to Arthur.

"The love that we impart to the making."

A wonderful secret to carry through one's life! And what did the James Blinkinshaws care; or the shallow draftsmen; or the salesmen with their unquenchable thirst? "I can put you on to a good thing, dear boy, if you'll introduce me to So-and-so."

At the door of Blinkinshaw's they parted, and Arthur ran into Jimmy Long.

"Hello" cried Jimmy. "Where have you been? I 've got a hell of a hump. Come and have a drink."

"I 've been to the museum with Pa," Arthur replied.

"Oh. Was the old man amusing? Tell me something amusing, for God's sake!"

"Yes. He was in quite good form."

Arthur found himself let into the bar of "The Queen of Rumania"; and Jimmy calling for "two gins and bitters. Miss Parkisson."

He sipped the gin and glanced round the bar, where the usual crowd had congregated. Some men were having oysters and stout, and others drinking port wine and sherry. Arthur involuntarily wondered how much a week these men spent on these comforts, and how much they allowed their wives for housekeeping. The cold greenish light, and the glittering mirrors and blood-red mahogany, and the two great pale blue Doulton-ware vases of hideous design suddenly brought home to him the sordid ugliness of this atmosphere. He touched Jimmy's arm, and said:

"Let's go somewhere else. I can't stand this place."

"All right, my lad."

They strolled out and went into Oxford Street Arthur was still quivering with a strange sense of excitement. He wanted to talk. He said:

"Right-o. You haven't told me what the old man said"

"Why he talked about all sorts of things. He said he thought I was going to Italy."

"You're not are you"

"Oh, I don't know. I may go one day soon."

This seemed so interesting a proposition that Jimmy insisted on having another gin and bitters in the bar of Pollini's, and they eventually entered that gay establishment with a walk not devoid of swagger. They sat near the band and ordered chops and a bottle of Beaune. Under the influence of these good things and the moving strains of waltz music, the multiple activities of Arthur's sentient being rioted exceedingly. He became extremely garrulous. He looked into the eye of his friend and realized for the first time that he was the dearest chap in the world. The room was an enchanted place. They toasted each other and swore undying friendship. They glanced at the other tables, where incredibly beautiful women dreamed into the eyes of their lovers or sparkled with a genial appreciation of the splendid glamor of this life. The remarks that Mr. Leffbury had made to him became diffused by the riotous interplay of the senses. Much that he had said became transcendent, and the rest was gloriously obscure. But he kept on thinking to himself:

"I'm not going to tell Jimmy everything he said. It was, in a sort of way, sacred."

But he talked of Italy. Before the Beaune was finished he had definitely invited Jimmy to accompany him the following year to Italy. They would go to Paris, and Monaco, Bordighera, Genoa, and so on down to the south. Then to Sicily "to see the Byzantine stuff" and perhaps go across to Egypt and up the Nile, and return through Algeria, Morocco, and Spain. There would be art, music, adventures, red wine, and romance.

They moved to a recess and had coffee and a liqueur, and pursued luxuriously the wild helter-skelter of their thoughts. They lost the sense of time and place, and became intently conscious of the consuming fires of an idolatrous present. It was absorbing, tremendous. Jimmy suddenly got up and said he had just caught sight of a friend he wanted to speak to. Arthur beheld him talking to a lady with dark hair, near the door. He laughed.

"What a devil Jimmy is" he thought indulgently. He seemed to be rather a long time, so he gave him up at last and went out into the street.

He spoke genially to several people in the street about anything that came into his head and was told by a lady in Oxford Street to "go and fry his silly, shiny face." He took this speech in very good part and laughed uproariously, and eventually managed to find his right bus. As he sped along in the night air, he recollected that his father was away. He and McIlrane had gone off in pursuit of some elusive job in the north of England.

"What an old rascal Jimmy is!" he thought again.

Nearly all those chaps did that sort of thing. Well, well, what did the old man say? Express yourself. Yes, he would do that. He felt peculiarly virile and unselfconscious to-night. Thank God for youth! He would not grow up and become like Pa Leffbury. He would not reach the other's age without going to Italy and experiencing all those things which are the prerogative of youth. As he descended from the bus, the various thoughts that had raced through his mind on the journey began to crystallize into one concrete idea.

"That rascal Jimmy! Go while you're young! Express yourself!" And then came the reflection that his father was away. The concrete idea concerned the Welsh maid, Ada. She slept in a room on the top floor, and Mrs. Stabbe slept in a room on the floor below.

When he let himself in his heart was beating rapidly. The house was all in darkness. There was no sound but the rhythmic tick of the hall clock. He hung up his hat and coat, took off his boots, and crept upstairs.

"I 've seen her looking at me slyly, in such-and-such a manner" he thought to himself. Images raced through his brain. Little expressions and postures that he had hardly noticed at the time. They became pregnant with meaning. He stole into his bedroom, leaving the door ajar. He laughed softly to himself, and put on a dressing-gown. He was very much himself to-night, a dynamic force demanding expression. He went out again on to the landing. The clock still ticked and in the distance traffic rumbled; someone was whistling for a cab. On the opposite side of the landing was his father's bedroom door, a ponderous dark tiling that might have been open or shut. He went by it without looking, but half-way up the next flight of stairs, he had to turn and peer back at it. And then he crept back and passed his hand over the face of it. Yes, it was shut. He started off again, but with less confidence. On the floor above he listened outside Mrs. Stabbe's room. He fancied he detected the faint sound of heavy breathing. He passed on, but his eye could not help straining over the bannisters to see the angle of that door below.

''Curse the ghosts that haunt these inanimate things!" 'he thought testily.

He reached the top landing. Opposite to him was the door of Ada's bedroom. He was shivering with a nervous agitation. He looked down the staircase once more. He almost expected to hear the door creak, and his father come out. He could almost hear the tones of his gentle voice:

"Er—who is that?"

But he knew that his father was not there. And then he began to see that it would really be easier if his father were there. That shut and silent door! It was so like his father, who had never said, "Arthur, do this or do that"; who had only been like a sentinel on the outskirts of his life, silently watching, expressing nothing, but exerting a deathless influence.

"These others who come after know us by the love that we impart."

He gave a little cry and crept downstairs again. As he did so, he thought he heard a door on the top landing open stealthily and then close. When he reached his own landing the house was again silent, except for the grandfather clock below, solemnly ticking, like some insatiable monster devouring the fateful seconds that would never return.

CHAPTER IX

"RACING AWAY INMTO THE UNKNOWN"

One day in the early summer a disturbing disruption took place in the house in Eccles Square. Since Mr. Gaffyn's return from the north of England it was apparent that something had gone wrong. He had seemed more abstracted and restless than ever. Edith turned up in one of her most masterful moods. She took temporary possession of the household. The maid, Ada, was dismissed, and the upper part of the house was let to an auctioneer and his wife. Mrs. Stabbe, Mr. Gaffyn, and Arthur were confined to the ground floor and the basement, and the expenses of the establishment were reduced to a minimum. Edith spent rather less than a week effecting this reorganization, and before she left she took Arthur aside and said that, as she believed he was now receiving twenty-five shillings a week, his father thought that he might contribute ten shillings a week to the household expenses, and perhaps he would hand this over to Mrs. Stabbe every Saturday.

The suggestion made Arthur furious, for the reason that he was certain that his father had never thought anything of the kind, and also because it was what he had wanted to suggest himself for a long time, but had never been able to bring himself to the point; and lastly, because it was just like Edith's "managingness" to come butting in and telling him what he ought to do. As though the family couldn't arrange a little thing like that without her interference!

He said, "Oh, all right," in a voice that must have conveyed the idea that he very much resented parting with ten shillings a week, whereas he had already made a mental resolution that he would make it fifteen.

It was a curious feature about the relationship of this family that Mr. Gaffyn never appealed directly to Edith about anything. If there was some matter which disturbed him and about which he could not make up his mind, he always asked Aunt Elizabeth to call. And then he would hint at it in a vague, sketchy manner, beginning his sentences in the middle. Aunt Elizabeth would talk the matter over and sleep on it, and then get Eleanor to write a letter to Edith, And Edith would act instantly and deliberately, without consulting anyone, although she had a way of talking to the others as though it was all their idea.

When the family gathered together Mr. Gaffyn still had the habit of addressing Elizabeth, who would repeat exactly what he had said, only with more completed sentences. Edith would say nothing until he interjected:

"Better, perhaps,—er"

And then Edith would say:

"Why, of course that would be an excellent idea." And then she would set forth what the idea was, and Mr. Gaffyn would believe implicitly that it was his idea, and so in a way it would be, for Edith had the genius to know what it was that Mr. Gaffyn would probably want to do, if he could but formulate the resolution in his mind.

The domestic upheaval affected Mr. Gaffyn considerably. He seemed worried and distraught. Arthur did not know whether his father was aware that he contributed his fifteen shillings a week to the house, but he noticed that at times Mr. Oaf regarded him with a kind of nervous anxiety. He would occasionally fidget about the dining-room after meals, as though he were going to speak to Arthur about something personal. He would even get as far as:

"You—er—I want—er—"

And then he would fly off at a tangent, and make some safe remark about general matters.

After a little while, however, the household in this more restricted manner settled down to a normal state of affairs.

It was, indeed, almost exactly a year later that the sudden and tragic event occurred which severed forever all chance of a more tangible understanding between these two.

Arthur had been attending some lectures on the Italian Renaissance, and he returned home one evening about half-past ten from one of these. As he let himself in, he noticed that the light was on in the dining-room. This was rather unusual, for his father invariably dined at half-past seven and then spent the rest of the evening in the studio. "Perhaps he has a visitor" he thought.

He did not hurry. He hung up his hat and coat, and then went and washed. After that, as he did not hear a sounds he opened the dining-room door quickly and peeped in. A strange sight met his gaze. The dinner had been cleared away, and the table was littered with papers. His father was sitting huddled up on a chair by the fireplace and apparently doing nothing. The boy had an immediate presentiment of some calamity. He ran forward and touched his father's shoulder, but the elder man did not speak. He gave an almost inaudible moan and continued to gaze on the floor.

Arthur rushed to the staircase and called down to Mrs. Stabbe in the basement.

That lady came bustling up, the contagion of alarm depicted on her white face.

Between them they helped Mr. Gaffyn across the passage to his bedroom. He hardly appeared to know them, but he murmured once very softly:

"No, no, please don't trouble! No, no, it's—quite all right."

Arthur rushed across the square and had the good fortune to catch a doctor who had just returned from a visit He was a young Jewish doctor, named Schultz. He came at once. When he had examined the patient it was only necessary to glance at the doctor's face to see that the affair was critical.

Mrs. Stabbe was crying. She said:

"O Lord, sir, I was afraid of something. The master seemed so queer. He called me after dinner and got me and Mr. Alcott from upstairs to witness his signature to some papers. One paper was his will, sir," she added in a whisper.

During the rest of that night and the five days which followed, the mind of Arthur became focussed on the central terrifying fact—his father was dying. He became dimly conscious of other people and incidents happening around him, but they were only shadows emphasizing the main issue. He was aware of Aunt Elizabeth and Eleanor being constantly present with their help and sympathy. He was aware of the young Jewish doctor, with his pale face and dark hair, who struck him as being too temperamental for a doctor. He gave more evidence of emotion than anyone. He was aware of Edith arriving on the following afternoon, and by some means or other converting the house into a professional hospital in the course of a few hours. He was aware of the arrival of a competent-looking hospital nurse, and of the enormously helpful genius of Mrs. Stabbe, who rose to the occasion in an incredible manner.

Other people were there vaguely. McIlrane darting furtively in and out of the studio and looking scared; several old friends. But all these people had little reality. The central fact itself had little reality until that ominous evening of the fifth day. He was in his father's bedroom, and the nurse was standing by the bed. His father was breathing in a peculiar way, and the young Jewish doctor arrived. He stooped down by the bed and made some observations. Then he came over to the gas fire, next to Arthur. They stood there silently a long time, watching the figure on the bed. Then suddenly the doctor said in a dreamy voice:

"Racing away into the unknown."

It was not till that moment that the truth stood out naked and relentless. He tried to steady himself, and said:

"I suppose it is so."

The young doctor patted his shoulder and turned away.

After a pause, Arthur followed him and whispered:

"Will he ever be conscious again?"

And the doctor replied:

"I'm afraid not in this world."

He looked at Arthur sympathetically, and then turned and spoke to the nurse.

He went into the next room and found Aunt Elizabeth crying. Eleanor came up to him and kissed him. He kissed her in return, and was conscious of a little thrill of comfort Edith was writing letters at a desk, and there was no sound but the scratching of her pen and the gentle sobbing of Aunt Elizabeth. After a time the young doctor came in. He went straight up to Edith and said:

''I think I will call Dr. Pellescourt. It will be more satisfactory for everyone."'

Edith nodded her head and said:

''Yes. Very well. Do so, then.''

She licked the edge of an envelope, and the doctor fidgeted nervously with his watch-chain, and went out. Arthur went across the landing again and looked at his father. There was no apparent change. He felt that he could not stand the strain of that peculiar breathing. He returned once more to his relatives. Four times during the ensuing half -hour he wandered to the bedroom and back. Then the bell rang. There was a sound of some one speaking in the hall. The young doctor came nervously across the passage, followed by an elderly man with a pointed beard and a heavy tread. They went straight into the bedroom. Arthur did not move.

They seemed to be there an interminable time. At last they both returned and came into the sitting-room. The younger doctor introduced the elder man to Edith. He said:

''This is Dr. Pellescourt.''

The elder man nodded casually, but not unkindly, at the rest of the room. He looked tired and rather bored. One gathered that it was not an interesting case. Eleanor darted across to him and said:

"Do you think there is any hope, doctor?"

The elder man looked at her rather peevishly and answered:

"Everything possible is being done."

He went out into the hall, and the younger man whispered something to Edith. Edith immediately sat down, wrote a check and gave it to him. The younger man went into the hall, and the door slammed. There was another long silence. The auctioneer who occupied the upper part of the house came home. Arthur heard McIlrane creeping across the hall and whispering to him, and then the auctioneer saying:

"Dear! dear!"

He went upstairs on tiptoe. In a few moments there was the smell of food being cooked. The auctioneer and his wife were preparing their supper. At half-past ten Edith said:

"I don't think there is any need for you and Eleanor to stop, Bess. There is nothing you can do. I will stay here to-night. I will sleep on this sofa."

Aunt Elizabeth cried once more and was persuaded to have a little brandy and water. She and Eleanor took their departure.

When they had gone, Edith said:

"You might as well lie down, Arthur. I will call you if it is necessary."

Arthur did not answer. He stood staring at the fire. He went in once more to see his father. It was very painful. He did not feel like crying. He felt horrified. After a time he returned to the sitting-room and drank some brandy. He heard McIlrane go out of the front door, and Mrs. Stabbe bolting the shutters in the basement. It became much stiller after that. He could hear his father from the sitting-room. There was no one now but the nurse, and Edith, and himself. Edith produced some knitting. She again said:

"Hadn't you better go to bed, Arthur? There's no point in sitting up. I will call you if it is necessary."

He looked at Edith. "She is doing her duty," he thought. He watched her fingers, almost fascinated by their dexterous movements. Without saying anything, he eventually went into his bedroom, and lay on the bed. He was trembling. He felt that there was no question of sleep.

"Racing out into the unknown! "The phrase recurred to him again and again. What did it meant Was there really anything after. The episodes of the week rushed through his mind. The night when he had come home and found his father in the peculiar position by the fireplace, with all the papers scattered on the table. And Mrs. Stabbe's prescience of fatality, because she had been called in to witness the signature to a will. And then the arrival of the doctor, and the desperate effort it required to make up one's mind what to do next. He remembered that he almost automatically sent a telegram to Edith, even before despatching one to Aunt Elizabeth. Very vividly he remembered the arrival of McIlrane at nine o'clock in the morning, and the peculiar way he seemed quite unable to realize what it meant. He remembered McIlrane saying, after he had explained the position to him as well as possible:

"I'm awfully sorry. H'm! well, well. I suppose I'd better not consult him about that templet that Higgs & Hanwell have sent us, instead of sending it straight to the surveyor at Brinton Marsh."

McIlrane had never been able to realize the seriousness of the whole thing. He seemed to look upon it as some ridiculous interruption to the fine artistic intimacy he shared with Mr. Gaffyn. He looked at the others rather suspiciously. He kept on going in and out of the studio and standing in the hall, as though he expected someone to come out and say:

"It's all right. You can go in now."

And during those days and nights Arthur had stood mostly in his father's bedroom, listening to the terrible sound of his breathing. Mr. Gaffyn had been conscious at times, and Arthur had waited patiently, ready to snatch at any comfort, or at any sign of a disposal to speak. On the afternoon of the third day he had been leaning over a chair by the gas-fire, when he happened to look up. And suddenly he realized that his father was looking at him intently. His clear gray eyes were wistful and childish, and strangely enough he did not look away.

Instinctively Arthur walked across to the bed, and touched his father's hand.

His father continued to gaze at him, and perhaps for the first time in their lives these two continued to look at each other without self -consciousness.

Arthur lowered his head and said:

"Father!"

Mr. Gaffyn had seemed to try and speak, but the boy could not catch what he said. Then suddenly he had shut his eyes and gripped Arthur's wrist. His hands seemed abnormally bony and cold. He pinched the boy's flesh with the flat part of his hand, but the fingers had no grip. Then he had seemed to shiver and become comatose. The nurse had come into the room and busied herself with some preparation. The patient had not opened his eyes again that day in Arthur's presence. On the fourth and fifth days he had opened his eyes, but to Arthur's grief he obviously did not see him. He just stared upward and occasionally muttered to himself incoherently. He was already in some world of his own. He was occupied with images the vision of which no living thing could share. And then to-night had come that sudden portent:

"Racing away into the unknown."

The boy was utterly exhausted. It had all come so suddenly and terribly that he could not grasp the significance of it. He was simply aware of a nameless horror which he was too worn-out to face. Within a few minutes of resting his head on the pillow he fell into a restless slumber. This slumber seemed to last a very short time, when something chilling brought him back with a start. His eyes became aware that it was already daylight, and, moreover, that a cold hand was pressed against his brow. He started up.

"What is it?"

In the dim room he realized that Edith was leaning over his bed, and that he was wrapped in an eider-down coverlet. Her clear voice was saying:

"Arthur, we did not wake you. He never regained consciousness. It was quite peaceful."

He jumped from the bed, and gasped:

"What do you mean"

He pushed by her and out into the passage, and entered his father's room. The light, filtering through the blind, revealed that grim and definite acknowledgment of the Central Fact. The gas-stove was out. All the medicine bottles had already been cleared from the small table by the side of the bed. They would not be required again. The nurse was asleep in the next room. His father was lying with his eyes closed, and his face looking incredibly young and beautiful. But perhaps the fact that struck the boy more than anything was that all the clothes had been removed, except one sheet. The window was open and it seemed intensely cold. He felt inclined to cry out:

"But he'll be cold! How frightfully cold it is. Are you quite sure it Isn't it somehow unnecessary to do all this so quickly!"

He felt curiously angry with Edith. It was so characteristic of her. Why did she always come interfering and doing things in this way. The cold-blooded thoroughness jarred his nerves. He wanted to give way to the floods of passionate grief that were pouring through his heart, but he stood there atrophied, shivering. He became aware of a heavy coat being put over his shoulders, and Edith's voice saying:

"Arthur, you must be very brave. It is all for the best."

His teeth chattered, and yet he could not cry. Suddenly he felt an arm round his shoulders, and Edith's cool firm lips pressed against his cheek.

"You mustn't stand here, Arthur dear. You will catch a cold. Come into the other room, and I will make you some tea."

He continued shivering, and allowed himself to be led into the sitting-room. The fire was burning brightly, and the nurse was sleeping on the sofa. He sat in the easy-chair by the fire. Almost against his will his eyes followed Edith about the room. What an extraordinary woman she was! She had been up all night. She had not changed her frock, and yet she looked perfectly fresh and calm. She moved with brisk, deliberate movements to the tray on the side-table, and then took the tea-caddy from the cupboard. The kettle was already simmering on the fire, and in a few minutes a cup of tea was thrust into his hands. The nurse continued sleeping, and Edith went to the desk, and began writing letters. It was very silent, and he became aware of the clock ticking in the hall. It reminded him of a certain night, the night when he nearly took advantage of his father's absence. He wondered whether his father was listening to that tick, and whether he knew now what had passed in Arthur's heart.

Soon began the manifold signs of the day's normal activities. The clatter of milk-carts, the whistling of errand-boys, the buzz of traffic, some letters falling into the box. Everything would go on just the same. Presently there was the faint sound of sizzling, and the smell of bacon being fried. The Aleotts upstairs were preparing their breakfast. Edith went below and awakened Mrs. Stabbe, who had been away too, during the night while Arthur slept. At nine o'clock McIlrane came, and Edith led him through the studio and shut the door. In a little while he came out on tiptoe and left the house, and as he passed through the hall Arthur heard him sobbing like a child.

All day long Arthur sat by the fire, or moved restlessly from one room to another. And all day long Edith untiringly coped with the various problems and situations which arose. Aunt Elizabeth and Eleanor arrived at ten o'clock, and shed tears on Arthur's face, but he did not respond. He stood there, dazed and curiously dependent on Edith. She made him eat, go out and send some telegrams, and buy some stamps. At odd moments he found her looking at him in a queer, wistful way. She did not give him anything difficult to do, but she encouraged him to be occupied, and would not leave him alone for long. Numerous people called during the day, including another cousin whom Arthur had forgotten, named Walter Gaffyn. He was a chartered accountant, a small man with a dark mustache, and as he entered the hall Arthur heard him say to Edith:

"I say, this is a bad business! Dear, dear! I am sorry!"

He demanded full medical details, seemed rather disagreeable and was plainly irritated by the whole thing. He was very anxious to know when the funeral would be, as he had arranged to take his wife to Bognor for the week-end. He was boisterously friendly to Arthur, and cried out:

"Why, it's years since I saw you, Arthur! How you 've grown! Getting on all right in business? You're in the furnishing line, aren't you? You must come over and see us. We're always in on Sunday evenings."

He slapped Arthur's back, and took his departure.

Mr. Edwin Beck called. He was apparently Mr. Gaffyn's solicitor. He spent some time in the bedroom talking to Edith. Then he entered the sitting-room and made a remark to Aunt Elizabeth that amounted to the original reflection that "in the midst of Life we are with Death." He shook Arthur's hand and said:

"Please accept my deepest condolences. I shall hope to see you on Saturday."

He then took some papers out of the desk, and also his departure.

This strange dream went on for days till the funeral was over. All sorts of people came and went. People whom he did not know came and pressed his hand, and proved to him by a glance of the eye that they understood. Others whom he did know proved by a glance of the eye that they felt that the whole thing was a personal inconvenience, and an affair to be got through with—with the least possible discomfort. Amid it all, the one person who gripped his imagination was Edith. What did Edith really think and feel. His dislike of her passed into a sort of amazement, and from amazement into a curious reliance.

On that last dreadful day when he stood in the churchyard, like one in some fantastic dream, and the Krugman was droning forth the wisdom of St. Paul, and the small groups of silent figures in their somber clothes were gazing with awestruck self-consciousness at that ghastly oblong hole in the earth, as if aware that for each one of them that would be the inevitable goal, for some reason or other he glanced at Edith.

She was looking down, her strong face rather paler than usual, and her beautiful hair visible under her black hat. She stood very erect, and on her low, white brow there seemed the same inexplicable calm that always characterized her. In that setting she appeared somehow distinguished. There was the calm pride of conscious moral strength. It was as though she had arranged the whole thing as an expression of herself. It was a duty that his father should die. It was a duty that she should come and help him die. It was a duty that she should show sympathy, kindness, and firmness to her less competent relations. It was a duty to use her ability, her power of organization, her pride, to help these weaker vessels.

When it was over and they moved back to the carriages, he almost unconsciously drew near her! as one might in a world of abstract fancies cling to the presence of a concrete fact.

He rode back in the carriage with her, and Aunt Elizabeth, and Eleanor, and Aunt Elizabeth spoke in a subdued but relieved voice of the way the Reverend Leggatt had read the service. She gave a brief list of the people who had been at the funeral, and also a list of some who had not put in an appearance. Edith replied in quiet monosyllables, and Arthur and Eleanor did not speak.

"We think, Arthur, it would be nice if you would go home and stop with Bess for a little while. She will be very pleased to have you, and then we can discuss the best thing to do later on. Mrs. Stabbe will look after the place. Mr. Beck is coming at six o'clock, and he wants to speak to you about the will, you know. "

This was all said kindly, but with an air of finality. It was curious that the implied arbitrariness of this arrangement did not annoy him. He was, in any case, in no mood for opposition, and he derived at that instant a queer sense of satisfaction at being ordered about by Edith. He surprised himself by saying:

"What are you going to do?"

"We are staying to-night at the Grosvenor. We shall be returning to Bradehurst to-morrow."

"Oh, I see. Are you coming up again soon?"

Edith gave him an odd little glance, and answered:

"Yes. On Friday. I have to bring Mildred up to see the dentist."

CHAPTER X

THE BUNGALOW AT BODIESHAM

There was surely never a drier or more illuminating script than the will of Mr. Gaffyn. Certain pictures and furniture were left to Aunt Elizabeth, a tall-boy to Edith Yardley, some architectural books and £50 to McIlrane, and £50 to Mrs. Stabbe. To his son, Arthur, he left the remainder of his property, amounting to shares and capital producing approximately one hundred and ten pounds a year, the freehold of the bungalow at Bodiesham, and the remaining furniture at 14 Eccles Square. There were no other provisos or instructions.

When Mr. Beck solemnly read the document through to Arthur across a leather-top table, the legatee was at a complete loss as to what it all represented. The one thing that stuck in his mind was "the bungalow at Bodiesham." What on earth was the bungalow at Bodiesham? He had never heard of such a place. When Mr. Beck, who spoke very slowly, clearly, and precisely, eventually had to relinquish what to him was obviously the unqualified joy of reading a legal document out loud, and when he had put it down, and taken off and wiped his spectacles, and cleared his throat, Arthur ventured to ask him what the bungalow at Bodiesham was.

Mr. Beck smacked his lips in the pleasurable anticipation of further declamation, and said: "The bungalow at Bodiesham is a property three miles from the Sussex coast. It is a two-story building that your father built himself about twelve years ago. It was not quite completed at the time of your mother's death, and as far as I know has never been occupied. The reason for this, I do not know. I have no evidence that the bungalow was ever even put in a house-agent's hands, though I believe it is quite a desirable property and on a very salubrious part of the coast. It cost something between fifteen hundred and two thousand pounds to build, and has three acres of land attached. It is near some sand-dunes. It is possible that your father had the idea of opening a golf-course there, and making the pavilion into a club-house; though perhaps from lack of capital, or some other reason, the scheme never materialized."

Mr. Beck stabbed with a pen into a sheet of blotting-paper, and looked at Arthur as though he expected some comment. Being disappointed in this respect, he continued:

"Well, now, Mr. Arthur, this matter is for you to decide. You are quite at liberty to sell the bungalow, or to let it. There is no proviso in the will with regard to it. It is simply left to you. Personally, I should advise you to let us place it in an agent's hands for letting. I think we ought to get at least sixty-five or seventy pounds a year for it, and it will mean that addition to your income. Would you like me to send my clerk, who is an experienced man, to look it over and report? Or would you care to go and have a look at it yourself? Or what?"

Arthur said very deliberately:

''I should like to go and look at it myself."

Mr. Beck entered something in a note-book with a fountain pen, and said:

"Very good."

Arthur surprised himself by further supplementing his sudden resolution with:

"I will go on Saturday."

Mr. Beck again wrote something, and again said:

"Very good."

He then rose and held out his hand, and added:

"If you will report to me on your return, I will endeavour to get these little matters settled as expeditiously as possible. "

On the following Saturday Arthur caught an early train that landed him at the market town of Lanby-Wodehurst. From there it was a seven-miles' drive across low-lying country to Bodiesham. He hired a trap from the inn, and decided that as it was a glorious day and he did not know how long his "inspection" would take, he would engage the man for the single journey only. The village of Bodiesham consisted of an inn, about five cottages, and a smithy. After dismissing the driver, he learned from the very ancient smith that the bungalow was about half a mile further on, along a track through what he called "the leas." The leas was a gently undulating country of grass slopes, sand, and patches of gorse.

In this invigorating air in which there was a strong smack of the sea, he walked briskly along. The depression which had followed on his father's death became mellowed by the gaiety of the day, and almost succumbed to the virile impulses of youth. Suddenly, as the track led eastward over a rather higher elevation of ground than usual, he beheld a narrow belt of dark pine-trees, and silhouetted against it, with its front facing south, was the bungalow.

He walked more quickly, and was aware of being strangely agitated. His eyes devoured the white lines of the bungalow, and he tried to take in every detail at a glance. A hundred yards from the face of the building was a grass bank. Between the two were evidences of the beginning of a formal garden, and on the top of the bank was a young elder-tree. Instead of going straight to the central door of the bungalow, Arthur made for this bank, which commanded an uninterrupted view of it, and sat down beneath the elder-tree. As he gazed at the lines and proportions of this white building, he felt his heart swelling within him, and suddenly he broke down and cried for the first time since his father's death. He was troubled for the moment to account for this excessive feeling, but gradually the whole truth of the thing came to him.

He knew his father's work so well, and this was so—him. It was so characteristic and—of this he was quite sure—it was the finest thing his father had ever designed. It was a labour of love. He felt the love of his father in every line of it. It was very, very simple, and he knew the infinite trouble his father would take to get a thing simple. He could tell the love the other had expended over getting the proportions of the graceful columns just right, and the beautiful cornice that bound it all together. Over the central hall was a dome, and on either wing was a broad veranda. It was rather on the lines of an eighteenth-century colonial house, but with all sorts of characteristics of his father.

The windows and the doors were peculiarly his father's, and no one else could have designed that fanlight above the central porch.

A labour of love! The whole tragic import of that phrase came home to the youth as he leaned forward on the bank.

The bungalow had been "not quite finished at the time of his mother's death." His father had been secretly building this for her. He was going to give it to her as a surprise. He had lavished his whole soul upon it. His labour of love! And then, "it had not been occupied. I have no evidence that the bungalow was ever even put in a house-agent's hands." O fools and blind! As though his father could do that! He had probably visited it sometimes in secret, and sat beneath the elder-tree and dreamed about it on this very spot. And then this strange characteristic of the man; he passes it on to Arthur without a word I He does not say: "Arthur, this is a sacred place to me and to you. I want you to keep it sacred. "He does not admonish him any more than he had admonished him when he sent him to school. He does not give a hint. He does not even say "to my dear son, the bungalow at Bodiesham which I designed and built for my beloved wife." This would have been the most ordinary, generally accepted wording, even for an old dry-as-dust like Beck, but his father, who he knew was overcharged with emotional impulses, merely said, "to my son, Arthur, the bungalow at Bodiesham."

The boy sat there gazing at this strange legacy, and dreading to enter it. It was as though his father, by his very silence, had bound him irrevocably to the tragic heritage of his unexpressed emotions. Already among the weeds which clustered on the formal garden, he was beginning to visualize the pictures which this setting was intended to disclose. The boy forced back the tears, and taking the key which Mr. Beck had given him, walked across the lawn. He had great difficulty in getting the lock to accept the unaccustomed attentions of the key, but at length he stood in his father's hall. The plaster had cracked in places, but there was no evidence of dampness. The foundations must have been sound. The walls were quite bare, and there was no furniture of any sort in the bungalow. In some of the rooms he discovered an odd plank or two, and a trestle, and on the upper landing some rolls of ceiling paper that had never been used. Two of the bedrooms were without fireplaces, but all the main constructional part of the building was sound and finished. On the ground floor was a beautiful L-shaped room with delicate plaster paneling. It would have made a splendid room for music.

"O God!" the boy groaned to himself. "What am I to do with this!"

What did his father mean him to do with it, this deserted legacy? He must have thought of it. He must have had Arthur in his mind's eye when he said "to my son, the bungalow at Bodiesham." Was it to be a sanctuary, or merely a means of increasing his income? He somehow could not believe that. Whenever his father wished him to do a thing, he expressed that wish by some vague implication. With his uncritical mind which touched nothing but his work, with his peculiar faculty of seeing both sides of a question at the same time, in the affairs of the world he was a negative quantity. And yet, as Arthur wandered about that house, he felt that he knew his father for the first time, that he was more intimate with him than he had ever been.

He entered the principal bedroom and looked out of the window. Across the dunes a narrow strip of sea lay quivering like a white ribbon. He opened the lattice and sighed, and as he did so a little incident impressed him. Some martins had made their nests under the eaves of the roof, and as he sighed two of them fluttered away with a cry. Eavesdroppers! That was quaint; he hadn't thought of it before, the meaning of the word. They listened at the bedroom windows of the happy and the wretched. They heard people sob in the night, and they heard the laughter of children in the early morning. On this day they had heard him sigh as he entered the heritage of his father. They would flutter away and tell the other birds. There would be a bond of understanding. Somehow he felt glad that the martins had made their nests under the eaves of his father's house.

He stood at the window a long time, watching the sand glittering in the sunlight. What was he to do? Did his father mean him to come and live here? It would surely be possible to live on a hundred pounds a year, given a house. He could live simply, and work, and study. It would be a glorious place to study, silent and beautiful; rather lonely, perhaps, but he would get used to that. And he could wander about, and paint the sand-dunes and the sea. The martins went swirling by beneath the window, and overhead a lark was praising the beauty of this peerless day. What a contrast to the fetid atmosphere of Blinkinshaw's! Indeed, a glorious legacy! His decision was made. He would come and live here.

Immediately he desired to return, to make all arrangements so that he could come at once. He went quickly all over the bungalow once more, determining which rooms he would make use of. He would use three; the kitchen for his meals, the largest bedroom to sleep in, and the bedroom facing north as a studio.

Ruminating on the fair prospect of these resolutions, he walked at a good pace back to Lanby-Wodehurst, and had the good fortune to have only forty minutes to wait for one of the trains which occasionally connected this sleepy town with more active centers of civilization.

When he broached the subject of his resolve in the evening, Aunt Elizabeth exclaimed:

"Goodness gracious! you can't do that! You can't go and live alone. They say man wasn't made to live alone. You'll go mad. Besides, how are you going to manage? You can't cook and all that"

And Eleanor said:

"I'm afraid you'll be very lonely, Arthur. Are there any cottages near? Perhaps you could get a woman to come in and do for you."

"I'm certain Edith will think it's preposterous" continued Aunt Elizabeth.

"It's nothing to do with Edith" answered Arthur, the gall of anger rising, "and you needn't write and let her know until I've gone. I shall just arrange it with Beck."

When Mr. Beck was informed, he went through all sorts of tricks with his nose and throat to get his voice to the right timbre of chilling dissuasion.

"The place requires three or four hundred pounds at least to make it habitable. You will have to pay twenty pounds a year ground-rent, and if you live there, there will be rates and taxes. Oh, no, my boy, you want at least three hundred a year to keep that place up."

"I can manage to live there on eighty pounds a year," answered Arthur.

"But you won't even have eighty pounds a year. By the time you have paid the rates and taxes, the cost of removal, the—er—incidental expenses in connection with the winding up of your father's estate, you will have nearer sixty pounds a year."

"Well, I can live on sixty pounds a year" replied the boy doggedly.

Mr. Beck shook his head and shrugged his shoulders.

"There is no electric light or gas."

"I can burn candles."

"Did you test the drains!"

"No."

Another shrug of the shoulders.

"Well, I can only advise you as an old friend of your father's. I have no power to force you to act contrary to your wishes. I will simply point out that if you will allow us to let the bungalow, your income will be about two hundred a year, which, with what you earn in your profession, will soon place you in a position of—er—comfort and security. You will soon, perhaps, be considering the question of marriage, eh? And then there is your career to be considered. What can you do at Bodiesham to develop your career? You will have barely sixty pounds a year, and no opportunity that I can see of augmenting it. You will not be able to entertain; you will be cut off from all society; and you will not even be able to keep up the estate. Why, the place requires two gardeners for a start,"

And then Arthur surprised himself by saying:

"I shall be going down to Bodiesham this day week."

Mr. Beck looked distinctly irritated at this, and he again shrugged his shoulders and said:

"Very well."

He then rang the bell for his clerk, and Arthur shook his hand and departed.

He next visited Mr. Leffbury and explained the matter to him. Mr. Leffbury sighed and said:

"O Lord! you are a lucky devil! I wish I could go and live in the country. Sixty pounds I Why, you can live like a bloody king on sixty pounds a year in the country. Take your water-colours, and come and show me what you're doing now and then."

He avoided the big studio. He was afraid of what might be said about his father. There was no limit to the cynical flippancy of the young designers. But on the stairs he met Jimmy Long. Jimmy said:

"Hello, Gaffyn. I'm awfully sorry to hear about your guv'nor."

And Arthur pressed his hand and did n't reply. They looked at each other for a few moments, and then Arthur said:

"I'm leaving. I'm going to live in the country."

"Are you really? When are you going?"

"On Saturday."

"Jeminy! Well, look here, won't you come and feed with me one night before you go?"

Arthur hesitated, and then said:

"Yes, all right. What about Friday?"

"Friday's good. I'll meet you at Pollini's at seven."

'All right."

The following days were devoted to collecting painting material and books, and in arranging the details of having certain pieces of furniture sent by rail to arrive at the time he did.

On Friday Edith came up to town to take Mildred to the dentist. He suspected that Edith would have been informed by Aunt Elizabeth by letter. For some reason or other he felt uncomfortable about this, but fortified his resolution by constantly repeating to himself:

"I won't stand any nonsense from Edith about this."

He made a point of being out when she came but arrived home at half-past five and discovered that she and Mildred were still there.

To his surprise she made no comment about his scheme until just before she left, when she said:

"How are you having your things sent, Arthur?"

''By rail."

''When did they go?"

"Yesterday."

"Do you expect to find them there to-morrow?"

"Yes."

Edith looked thoughtful. Then she said:

"What train are you going by?"

"The 10:37 in the morning."

This was all that was said, and Arthur felt somewhat relieved.

After she had gone he went downtown and dined with Jimmy Long at Pollini's. They had a farewell feast and drank a great deal of Beaune. Arthur felt the need of this humanizing society. Over the red wine he unburdened himself to Jimmy. He told him every little thing about his thoughts, and feelings, and resolutions. He talked about his father, and the mystery of death, his shame at the affair with Ada, his ambitions. The conversation rioted among the problems of life and love. They discussed Mr. Leffbury again, and the future of Blinkinshaw's, and again and again returned to women and beauty, and the mystery of life. Arthur forgot his previous promise to take Jimmy to Italy, but instead invited him to come and spend the summer holiday at the bungalow,—an invitation that was accepted with warmth. But they did not get drunk; although when Arthur parted from his friend, the latter stood a certain risk of missing his last bus owing to his insistence on quoting Omar Khayyam to a policeman in Charing Cross Board.

Saturday was a gray day with low banks of clouds blowing up from the west, but Arthur set forth on his new life in a cheerier frame of mind than he had been in since the beginning of his father's illness.

He arrived at Lanby-Wodehurst at half-past twelve. To his disappointment, his furniture and effects had not arrived, but he arranged with a local carrier to send them on immediately when they did. There was a train due at 2:05. They would probably be on that.

He took his bag, which contained a few clothes, sketching materials, and a quantity of food which Aunt Elizabeth had insisted on his taking, and started out to walk.

He covered the first two miles briskly, the breath of the sea in his face, and then the bag began to feel very heavy. He changed hands frequently and had a long rest. At the end of the third mile he regretted not having indulged in the desperate extravagance of taking the trap. He had no idea that a bag, which seemed so unnoticeable to carry from a bus to a train, could become such a dead weight. But he trudged on, consumed with a desire to reach his new home. At the end of the fourth mile he again rested and debated whether he wouldn't open the bag and have some lunch, but his anxiety to become installed in his father's bungalow overrode this wayward temptation.

It was nearly three o'clock by the time he reached the bungalow, and both his hands were blistered and his shoulders ached. He was trembling with exhaustion when he finally deposited his burden in the kitchen.

Despite his weariness and the inner craving, he felt it necessary to go all over the building again carefully. Yes, it was very exciting. He eventually returned to the kitchen and opened the bag. He took out a loaf, and a packet of tea, and some butter, and a tin of corned beef. And then an unfortunate fact presented itself. He had several tins of things, but no tin-opener. Moreover, he knew he would be able to collect some wood for a fire, but he had forgotten to bring a match.

This was very annoying, but he cut himself a large hunk of bread and buttered it, and leaned against the window-sill and dreamed of the glorious life of freedom before him. He also had an apple which Eleanor had thrust into his overcoat pocket, and which he found very acceptable.

After this repast he once more wandered over the bungalow and visualized his things in the places he had planned for them. It was half-past three, quite time they arrived. He went out into the garden and sat for a time on the bank. Then he went up into the pinewood and collected some twigs.

"I'll borrow some matches from the old chap who comes in the cart" he reflected.

Then another disquieting thought occurred to him. He had forgotten to order any candles. He had no means of lighting after dark. However, it was summer-time; it didn't get dark till nearly nine o'clock. He would manage. Besides, after the things had come, he would go into the village and see what he could get.

He wandered round the pine-trees and up on the dunes, keeping the bungalow and the road always in sight; but no cart came. At five o'clock he began to think it would be jolly to have some tea, but he had no means of lighting a fire. He did not like to leave the bungalow in case the things came, and he could not remember noticing any building nearer than the village half a mile away. He went inside and ate some more bread and butter. At half-past six a fine rain began to fall, and he went upstairs and sat on a trestle by the bedroom window. The trestle was a great comfort. It was his only piece of furniture. It was not till nearly seven that the alarming idea came to him that the things might not come at all This was Saturday. If they didn't come to-day, they certainly wouldn't come to-morrow. There was absolutely nowhere to lie down (he couldn't balance himself on the trestle), and he hadn't a rug, and no light or fire. It was certainly rather disgusting. He would probably be able to get something to-morrow in the village, but he daren't leave the bungalow to-night; and he had no other comforts than bread and butter, and a suit of pajamas and a tooth-brush.

He stood patiently by the window, and the room began to get very chilly; it was certainly going to get dark to-night earlier. The wind was moaning gently through the chimneys, and outside the pewits went swirling by with their plaintive cry.

"I mustn't get depressed by this" he thought, and he walked briskly about the rooms, his footsteps on the bare boards echoing all over the bungalow.

Every five minutes or so he would go to the window and peer out. Once he heard a cart rumbling on the road and ran to the door, but it was only a farm cart laden with Swedes lumbering through the rain. After it had gone he thought:

"What a fool I am! I might have borrowed some matches from that man."

The rain increased in violence, and he gave up all hope of his things arriving that night. He cursed his luck and tried to determine how he would spend the night He tested the effect of lying on the floor, but wherever he indulged in this recumbent luxury, it seemed incredibly drafty. He eventually decided to try lying in the comer of the L-shaped room in a recess, with his head on his bag.

Suddenly—it must have been after nine—he heard the crunching of wheels on the road. He ran to the door again. Hooray! There, indeed, was a small cart, with a lantern on its left side, pulling up at the gate.

As he ran down the path toward it, he had time to reflect that it was a very small cart to bring all his effects. When he reached the gate, a man got down from the seat and said:

"Yes, that's right," Arthur answered.

The man grumbled and went to the back of the cart, and Arthur joined him.

He pulled out what was apparently a camp-bed covered with a canvas, and a mattress similarly treated. Arthur peered at them

"These aren't my things, are they?" he asked.

"Eh?"' exclaimed the man. "Garffyn, ain't it,—the bungalow!"

"Yes, that's right."

He looked at the label. It was certainly addressed to him, and there was a large box also covered with canvas. He helped the man bring in these mysterious things. When they were deposited in the hall, he ventured to remark:

"But these are not the things I was expecting. I am expecting some furniture."

"Furniture!" exclaimed the carrier.

"Yes, I had it sent off on Thursday by freight-train from London."

"Freight-train? From Lunnon! Lord, whoy, you woan't get they for a week."

"But what are these, then!"

"I don't know nothing about it. I bring these from Wodehurst. They come from Lunnon by passenger-train. I believe Mr. Cheneyad a telegram from Lunnon to bring un on at once."

"Oh, I see" said Arthur, and he gave the driver a goodly proportion of his week's income.

"Well, this is an extraordinarily rum thing" he thought after the man had gone.

The bed was a very neat little camp-bed, and the mattress was quite dry under its canvas cover. The top of the box was somewhat flimsy and he was able to open it with his hands. He pulled it near the kitchen window, but he could not see its contents, so he groped among them. Almost the first thing he felt was a packet of candles. Then he again cursed, because in the excitement he had forgotten to borrow a match from the carrier.

However, he groped further, and lo and behold; there was a packet of safety-matches. He was able to light a candle, which he propped up in the fireplace. He then rapidly examined the rest of the contents of the box. There was a tin of mixed biscuits, a piece of cooked bacon, some cheese and some condensed milk, a rug, a sweater, a small spirit-stove and a tin of spirit, some apples and bananas, a screw-driver and a hammer, a corkscrew and a tin-opener.

There was no card or evidence as to where this amazing package had come from. It is quite possible that Arthur would never have been able to satisfactorily determine this point had it not been for the fact that the sweater was wrapped in a piece of brown paper, and inside was an old torn label of Messrs. Marshall & Snelgrove. The relict of the address on the label amounted to:

Mrs. Yardl
Brad
S

CHAPTER XI

ARTHUR HAS TWO VISITORS

It is always tiresome to the free spirit, or to a gentle egoist like Arthur, to have to acknowledge that something which "they" say is, in effect, the truth. It was particularly galling to Arthur to be forced to swallow the incontrovertible platitude of Aunt Elizabeth, "They say that man was not meant to live alone." But as the days, and weeks, and months went by, this statement leered at him, showing its white fangs of naked veracity. It was, indeed, an appalling wretched time.

It is true that on certain days when the sun shone, and he got into a snug position on the dunes, or down by the harbor of Fareshaven, with his water-colours and "Whatman paper in full working order, life was a very complete and satisfying business. He became conscious of nothing but the virile thing growing under his hands. He wanted nothing else.

But when he returned to the bungalow, and more especially when the evening came on, he could not disguise from himself his unutterable loneliness. With his own furniture, which arrived five days after it was due, he fitted up the three rooms as he had planned. He did not put up his own bed, as he found Edith's camp-bed quite comfortable, and it did not seem worth the bother to change. He had a good supply of books, and he read Marcus Aurelius; and Walt Whitman, and Emerson, and Vasari's lives of the Italian painters, and the Decameron of Boccaccio, and the Life of Benvenuto Cellini, and the novels of Tolstoi, and Turgeniev, and Anatole France, and Joseph Conrad. But the written words of these fine teachers could not compensate for the lack of contact with his fellow-man. He visited the village as often as he could and talked to the smith and the farm-hands, but he did not make much progress with them. Occasionally he would visit the village inn, drink ale in the bar, and try to strike up a friendship with the village people, but he was always aware of them looking at him rather suspiciously, and his voice seemed strained and self-conscious in contrast to their rich homely burr.

If he had followed his inclinations, he would have packed up and returned to town within the week, but greater than these fears of darkness and loneliness was the fear of being thought afraid, and the dread of being despised by Edith and his other relatives. He had set out to live alone in the bungalow, and here he would stay until a reasonable excuse should present an opportunity of release.

Every week or so he wrote to Aunt Elizabeth or Eleanor, and occasionally sent post-cards to Jimmy Long or Levistock. He could not bring himself to write to Edith. In the first place, there was no message with the things she had sent. He had no official intimation that they came from her. He felt that she ought to have written. And in the second place, the gift had somehow annoyed him, made him feel ignominious. He would have been in a desperate state if they had not arrived, and this very fact made the gift the more objectionable.

The days seemed incredibly long, and the nights infinitely longer. The hours when he became immersed in bis work, or inspired by some illuminating thought transmitted from the pages of a book, were merely gleams in an infinity of wretchedness. The memory of his father was always with him, and the tragic atmosphere of the bungalow, with its eternal suggestion of still-born happiness. Whether he lay on the bank in the sun, in the shadow of the veranda, or in his silent bed at night, he was always aware of the sterile purposes of this unhappy building. The unexpressed love of his father and the inexpressible love of his mother were they gone! Dead to him forever? He thought, and thought, and thought, and drew comfort from Emerson and despair from his own perverse moods. He wrestled with a thousand desires and inclinations and touched the lowest rung of human experience—self-pity.

One night the wind rose and howled in the chimneys and rattled the windows. Arthur suffered paroxysms of physical fear. He thought he heard some one walking in the rooms below, and the bannisters creaking. He had no keys to the rooms, and he expected every moment to hear the handle of the door turn stealthily; his heart almost stopped with fear.

He lay there a long-time trembling; then he thought to himself:

"After all, what does it matter! Suppose someone comes in and kills me, will it be worse than this living wretchedness! Who would care if I were alive or dead!"

He saw himself in a detached way, a lonely boy without love or friendship. Did he want to live? He struggled hard to keep back the tears. What did life hold out for him that he should be afraid of death? And yet something was telling him he must not think like that. But he was lonely, lonely, lonely. He reached the rock-bottom of this dark well of silent self-pity. He seemed to see his soul stark and desperate, suspended in space, out of touch with any living contact. The very desperateness of this despair suddenly fired a spark that lit the dark places of his yearning heart. He jumped from his bed and walked firmly to the door, and opened it. He shouted in a loud voice into the empty spaces of the house:

"Hello, Hello!"

There was no answer but the wind wailing relentlessly, and yet he felt somehow comforted. He walked up and down the room, his physical fears assuaged, but moral fears, like pale ghosts, hovered at the back of his mind.

"I can understand," he thought; "one has to fight, and fight, and fight. I can understand, if one lives too long alone, one goes mad. It is because one is not complete. No living thing is complete; it is all connected with the rest of life. Physical things are connected by the law of gravitation, spiritual things by the law of love. Man is spiritual; he belongs to the rest."

He spent what the French call a "white night" trying to adjust the impulses of his egotistical desires to the iron bars of philosophic reflection which were being smelted in the white-hot furnace of his suffering. When the dawn came he felt that something had been destroyed in him, and something had been born.

There were many more nights such as this, nights spent in striving to solve imponderable problems, to grapple with unspeakable fears, to find within himself some satisfying faith. But the dominant force which kept him faithful to his father's bungalow was the force of personal pride, a curious, elusive, egotistical force which seemed more powerful than reason or philosophy.

In August Jimmy Long kept his promise and paid a visit, staying for a week. To his surprise the loneliness seemed to impress Jimmy less than it did himself. The weather was fine, and his former colleague seemed conceit to spend the day in semi-nudity, bathing, lying in the sun, and smoking. Inside the bungalow he howled popular melodies that made the windows rattle and found infinite delight in grilling steaks and experimenting in strange dishes that had an unfortunate habit of sticking to the pan. He pronounced "it's great life."

After he had departed on Saturday the place seemed lonelier than ever. For the first few days it was unbearable, and he said to himself:

"I shan't be able to stand this much longer."

Many times he was on the point of packing up and going off to London, but from day to day he put it off. It was late August. Aunt Elizabeth and Eleanor were in Wales. Edith he had not heard from since he left home. There was no one he could go to.

He went out for long rambles, and once stayed a night in lodgings in Littlehampton. And every time he returned, the bungalow seemed lonelier.

He had made over a hundred water-colour drawings in the open, and he did some still life, some real "hard" drawing. He made a careful study of an old rusty anchor he found on the beach, and sketches of teazels and sea-holly and poppies, and on wet dais he made drawings of the interior of the bungalow. He also wrote verses, and one he dedicated to "The Lady of the Work-box."

In September he caught a chill and was feverish for two days and nights. He stayed in bed and lived on milk which was delivered by a woman from a farm a mile away. When he recovered from this he was excessively weak. He lost interest in his work and sat about the garden or the bungalow, occasionally reading, but for the most part doing nothing. He felt himself getting into a low, maudlin state, and that some great effort was required of him. He started writing down his experiences in the manner of a person who is expecting to die, but the result did n't please him, and he tore up the manuscript. As he got a little stronger, he went in for reading aloud, and learned passages from Shakespeare and Milton, which he declaimed in his most theatrical manner to the bare walls. The old physical fears by this time had vanished. He had no terrors of the darkness, but a peculiar numbed indifference was getting possession of him. His letters to Aunt Elizabeth and Eleanor had gradually become rarer, and he had refused again and again their offer to come and stay with him for awhile.

It was on the second day of October that the thing happened which was destined to be the indirect cause of a change in the whole tenor of his life.

It had been a dull day without rain, but with a great deal of humidity in the air. It was about half-past six, and was already getting dark. He was carrying some faggots into the kitchen from the yard when he heard the noise of an automobile coming slowly along the lane. To his surprise, it came to a stop at the gate of the bungalow, and lay there panting and gasping, like a thing that has had an exhausting journey. A man in motor-goggles and oilskins leaped down from the car and approached the house. As he came to within about a dozen yards, he cried out:

"Arthur!"

Arthur came round from the side of the bungalow, and approached the visitor. He recognized him as his cousin, Walter Gaffyn. On catching sight of Arthur, he shouted:

"Hello! Arthur, old man! I have had a job to find you. I 've come over from Bognor. We're living there now. I heard you were here; thought I'd give you a look up. How are you?"

Arthur replied:

"I'm all right, thanks. Will you come inside!"

They went through the front door, and Walter continued shouting:

"Well, you are a rum chap to live here like this! How on earth do you manage! Get a woman in to cook and so on, I suppose f Why, it's quite a nice property. Bit lonely, I should think. Tell me all about it."

Arthur said there was really very little to tell, and he lighted a paraffin lamp, and led the way into the room in which he had his meals. He made a hasty mental calculation of the food there was in the house, and said:

"Will you stop to supper! I have some er stew and stuff, nothing very special, but if you 'll stop—"

"No thanks. I'm afraid I must get back to dinner.

We dine at eight. You haven't a drop of Scotch, I supposed

Arthur said he regretted he hadn't, and Walter roared out:

"Oh, that's all right. You've heard the news, of course?"

"What news!"

"Why, about the Yardleys."

"What about the Yardleys!"

"What! Do you mean to say you haven't heard? It's been in all the papers."

"I'm afraid I hardly ever see the papers. What is it?"

"Lord! what a rum chap you are! Not see the papers! Living the simple life, eh?"

And Walter Gaffyn laughed with boisterous incredulity.

"What is it about the Yardleys?" Arthur repeated.

Walter swelled with the importance of a person with news. He twirled his dark brown mustache, and said:

"Robert Yardley was found dead in bed last Monday night."

"Dead!" exclaimed Arthur. "Good Lord!"

Walter seemed satisfied with the success of his first pronouncement. But his sense of dramatic effect forbade him to rush all the details into the one statement. He looked at Arthur, and then added:

"But that's not all. The point is,—and this is why there's been a good deal of talk in the papers,—he did n't die in his own bed!"

Arthur looked at his cousin questioningly, somewhat impatient of the studied delays.

"What?—what bed?" he stammered.

And then Walter, with his nice sense of climax, delivered the culminating bombshell in a stentorian voice:

''He died suddenly in the night in the flat of Miss Renee O'Brien, a lady described as an actress.''

Arthur's mind rioted with a hundred visions. He gasped:

"But what—why was this—And why was it in the papers!"

Walter thoroughly enjoyed the effect of this astounding news. He started out to elaborate his important information. He replied:

"Why was it in the papers! My dear boy, there was a post-mortem. You can't suppress a post-mortem. The papers were all over it, like flies on a tart. 'Sensational death of a famous engineer!' 'Regrettable story,' and so on. Everything came out. The woman, of course, was a prostitute."

The mind of Arthur became keenly occupied with the vision of Edith. Good God! It was incredible! Edith! He tried to think of her as they broke the story to her, as she gave evidence, as she stood by the body that once ... as the people looked at her in the court. Would she be proud again? Could she ever look proud again? Could she ever look as he was visualizing her at that moment, as she looked at his father's funeral, standing strangely erect and her eyes cast down, insolently proud of her calm strength.

"Good God! it will break her! She is finished" he thought.

Walter was grinning at him with smug satisfaction. He was saying in a more confidential manner.

"Of course, I never could stand Edith, Arthur. And I gathered from what I saw at your place that you couldn't either. Of course I'm sorry for her; it'll break her up, I should think. The disgrace of it! Talk about a clean cop! No hushing up anything like that. But Lord! she never knew how to manage Robert. He was a nice chap. I used to like Robert—a man of the world and all that sort of thing. Beastly bad luck for him, eh? The disgrace, you know! Won't matter to him much now, anyway! Ha, ha! But, Great Scott! I went there once or twice. Robert would come home to dinner about half -past eight. Give him cold fish for his dinner! Did you ever hear anything like it Cold fish! Cold fish!"

Walter broke out into paroxysms of incredulous interjections. It appeared to be all most amusing and preposterous to him. Arthur felt a wave of anger at his cousin. What a disgusting cad the man was! Fancy being able to laugh at such a tragedy!

And then, after all, it was true; he had not liked Edith, but she was extraordinarily good. She had come out very well at the time of his father's death. She was very kind in her peculiar way. She had done a lot for him. He had never been grateful to her, not a word. Underneath all her apparent hardness there was some mystifying quality. And now in this dark hour there was that—pride, was n't it. He felt a desire to see her, to see how she would take it all, to see her proud face humbled, perhaps softened. She was an abnormal woman in her way. Certainly, this little cad had no right to laugh at her.

"I knew this would interest you if you hadn't heard"

Walter was running on. "That was partly why I came over; and just to see the country and so on. You must come over and see us. Lucy will be delighted. Do you get any shootin' here to Snipe or wild duck, why?"

Arthur said "No" and thought of Mr. Yardley walking among the standard rose-trees at Bradehurst and smoking his pipe, while Edith, with her basket and scissors, clipped the dead shoots and spoke in her calm, detached voice about the artificial manure that Scatter & Company were advertising in their trade catalogue.

"A good lay-out here for a golf-course, what! Was that your governor's idea, do you think? This pavilion, why the club-house, m—yes. Too far, of course, from town. Poor old Robert! He was a good player. He had one of the longest drives I've ever seen; usually came a cropper on the green; a bit inclined to pull. I wonder they hadn't let you know. Well, you are a rum 'un, living here alone. I should get one of these country girls to keep house, I think. Ha! ha! ha! The simple life. Oh, my word!"

"I must go to her" Arthur thought suddenly. He hadn't any idea what he would do or say when he went. He could not analyse his motives for wanting to go. But he knew very definitely that he would have to go.

'Come back with me to dinner, and stop the night. Lucy 'll be delighted."

"No, I can't do that, thanks."

"Not? Well, you are a rum chap! I must be off, then. Give me a hand with the screen, will you."

CHAPTER XII

PARIS AND BACK

It was a quarter of eight in the evening when Arthur arrived at Bradehurst station. As he was not expected, and a trap was an expensive luxury, he walked the two miles to the Yardley house. It was quite dark, and on two occasions he took the wrong turning, so that he did not eventually arrive till past nine o'clock. He felt peculiarly nervous and agitated. He did not know why he had come, or what he was going to say when he saw Edith. He half-hoped she would n't be at home. He walked up the gravel path and rang the bell. A maid whose face was unfamiliar to him opened the door. He asked for Mrs. Yardley, and the girl showed him into the drawing-room.

When the maid retired he balanced himself on the edge of the settee, and his heart was beating at an unreasonably rapid rate. He sat there for less than three minutes, when Edith entered the room. Any ideas he had entertained that he would see a crushed and broken woman were instantly dissipated by his first glance at her. She said quietly:

"Arthur! How kind of you to come. You'll stop the night. I'll have your bag taken upstairs."

He could not but be struck by the curious change in her. Her face was flushed, and her eyes were rather bright. She gave him the impression of some primitive creature that, driven into a desperate position, was straining every nerve and sinew to fight for its life. She looked, if anything, prouder, more alert, more commanding. She had herself tremendously in hand.

"She's a remarkable woman" Arthur thought, and he stood by the fireplace, not knowing what to say.

He was conscious, moreover, that in her attitude to him there was some fundamental change. She was glad to see him. She motioned him to be seated, and she herself sat down. Her head was silhouetted against the dark comer of the room, and in her poise, there was something indicative, almost majestic.

He felt ashamed of the silence that he did not know how to break, and he said haphazardly:

"I'm leaving Bodiesham. I find it too lonely."

'Ah! I expect it is. It's good for a time, though, to live alone."

He answered:

"Yes, of course; I liked it in a way. It did me good, I think. I see things differently. I did a lot of work, and read a great deal. I was very wretched at times. I went through all sorts of things."

He was surprised to find himself exchanging these confidences with Edith. They were, in a way, a sort of defense. He couldn't say, "I'm awfully sorry to hear about your trouble" or make some trite remark to this effect. He tried to show by his change of manner that he understood, that he was sympathetic.

She did not answer for a while. Then, still gazing at the fire, she said:

"I am leaving here, too. I am going to London. All my maids left suddenly on Wednesday. I only have the woman who opened the door to you. "What are you going to do?"

"I haven't made up my mind."

She smiled sadly and answered:

"That's always been a trouble, hasn't it? Come! I 'll get you some supper."

"Can I help? I've become fairly domesticated."

"No, don't you bother. It'll be a change for you to be waited on."

In ten minutes she returned and said:

"Come! It's all ready."

As they walked across the hall, some sardonic voice—in fact, his cousin Walter's—whispered:

"Goldfish. Cold fish!"

But on arriving in the dining-room, the anticipations of this mocking spirit were confounded. For lo and behold! there was an omelette, and some sort of bird in a casserole.

They sat down, and Edith served.

The supper was surprisingly good, and afterward Edith asked him if he cared to smoke. They talked scrappily about commonplace matters. Nothing was said about the tragic thing which lay so heavily at the back of both their minds.

He stayed three days, and then returned to London. Aunt Elizabeth and Eleanor welcomed him with open arms and copious weeping. How dreadful it all was! And how was dear Edith taking it? Who could have suspected that that amiable man, Robert Yardley, could have been such a villain 1 There was enormous discussion, and many and various disclosures of unpleasant details.

He looked at Eleanor. Her eyes were just as kind and mothering as ever but there was about her something small and insignificant compared to Edith.

It is to be feared that he used Aunt Elizabeth's house rather like a hotel during his week's stay. He went to see Mr. Leffbury and showed him a few of his best water-colours. He went to picture-galleries and museums and wandered about London. He went out to dinner with Jimmy Long, and Levistock, and others, and visited theatres and music-halls.

He found London at that time a very disturbing place. The South African War was on, and the streets were full of cheering people, and there was considerable drunkenness. The music-halls were patriotic in the worst sense of the word. Swearing, blustering jingo songs, flag-waving, and drunken cheering, seemed to be the order of the day and night. The excitement of this life after the austere existence at Bodiesham at times elated him, but for the most part it nauseated him. He found the atmosphere of Blinkinshaw's more feverish and unsettling than ever.

"Thank God!" he thought," or rather, thank my father I have n't got to come back to this!"

It was Mr. Leffbury who gave him the idea which he next acted upon. He visited him very late one evening in his room at Blinkinshaw's. He was in a particularly despondent and bitter mood, but Mr. Leffbury seemed unusually cheerful. He was, as a matter of fact, working- on a drawing which rather pleased him. His little window was open, and he rolled and licked innumerable cigarettes. A wagonette passed below, crowded with medical students blowing penny horns and yelling at the top of their voices. Arthur relieved himself of some of his pent-up misgivings. He told Mr. Leffbury his impressions of London in its present phase, and the head designer suddenly exclaimed:

"My dear Gaffyn, you mustn't go fishing in the deep waters of philosophic reflection with the bent pin of cynicism. You'll catch nothing."

And then he laughed and said:

"By God! that's rather good. I 'll make a note of it, if you don't mind. But honestly, the trouble with you is, you haven't enough to do. The only way to be happy is to be overworked."

He took a clean sponge and washed down part of the drawing he was working on, and continued:

"If one has no imagination, one can be happy on nothing, but you can't. I don't think you've found your right means of expression. Get on with your job. Don't bother about all these other people."

And he waved his hand toward the window.

"Everybody's first job is to save his own soul. Let all these others go to hell in their own way. They 'll find out. You won't do any good interfering with them. If this age teaches us anything, it teaches us the value of selfishness. I'm selfish; that's why I'm happy, and why I sit here half the night working on these bloody drawings."

He peered along the surface of his drawing to see whether it had dried, and then suddenly looked up and said:

"Why don't you go to Paris and study painting!"

"Paris I couldn't afford it."

"Yes, you could. You could go to old Berthelot's. It's one of these municipally endowed places. You pay about two francs fifty a week. And for the rest, you can easily live on twenty francs a week in Paris. He's an excellent teacher. I feel you 've got something in you. You might do something big. Go out after the big thing. Hunt round till you find your right medium. Don't be discouraged if you don't do a Rembrandt during your first term."

At half-past ten the next morning Arthur was in Mr. Beck's office. He explained that he wanted to raise some money to go to Paris and study. Mr. Beck pointed out that, owing to his extravagances in living at the house at Bodiesham and letting himself in for rates and taxes and other expenses, he was already living beyond his income. The legatee was obdurate, and the upshot was that some shares invested in a gas company were sold at a great loss, and Arthur found himself in possession of one hundred and twelve pounds in cash. "I shall be able to live in Paris for two years on this "he thought.

He brought his painting materials from Bodies ham, bade farewell to Aunt Elizabeth and Eleanor, had a great night out with Jimmy Long and Karolyi, and then took his departure from London.

He secured a room in an obscure comer of Montmartre and attended M. Jules Berthelot's academy. He found the life there different from the Quartier Latin life which he had read of. The students at M. Berthelot's were nearly all English and American, earnest young men anxious to "make good." He met them in class, but saw very little of their private lives. His stay in Paris was principally noteworthy for the friendship which he established with a young Californian named Leslie Hales.

He was a large-framed, slow-moving young man with a peculiar intentness of expression. Arthur had never met anyone quite so interested in life. He had a clear gray eye, and a habit of thrusting his head forward and listening, as though everything he heard was of tremendous importance and value. Arthur found unending de light in going around with Hales. It was like taking a very intelligent child about. He liked to watch his face and see the effect of every new experience reflected on it. Extremely kind-hearted, rather sentimental, not very deep, but tremendously anxious to be deep, Leslie Hales regarded all the passing phenomena of daily life as symbols of revelation to stir the depths of his soul. He was amazed, entranced, bewildered; at times even the wonderful fecundity of his expressions dried up at the endless manifestations of beauty and interest being eternally unfolded before him. To anyone with the cynic tendencies of Arthur, he was an excellent antidote.

M. Berthelot was an elderly man with a black beard and a very guttural voice for a Frenchman. Arthur found him difficult to understand at first, but the students had a code of interpretation which they passed from one to the other. He would stand in front of a drawing and make peculiar noises in his throat; then he would close his hand and wave his thumb backward and forward. This would mean that the drawing required more movement. At other times he would look at it, first below, and then above his spectacles, and stick his hands into the flaps of his trousers, which came in front, and say:

"Egh! Egh!"

This meant that the drawing was going on all right.

He was never very polite to anyone, and never encouraging, but he had a faculty of inspiring confidence and even affection.

After the first disastrous attempts, Arthur found painting in oils more satisfying than water-colours. Occasionally, he and Hales would go out to Compiegne and paint twilight in the Barbizon manner. It was enormously fascinating.

At the end of November, Edith wrote. She said she had taken a house in St. John's Wood, near Regent's Park. There was a studio attached to it which she never used. If at any time he wanted to come back to London, he could always make use of it, and as there were two little rooms off it, he could even live there, if he liked.

He wrote and thanked her and said he might one day be very glad to avail himself of her kind offer. He added that he hoped the children were well.

Arthur's attempts at economy were not very successful; neither could he account for the way in which the money went. He seemed to live very cheaply, but there was always the ubiquitous claim of "extras." There were artist's materials to buy, and a few clothes; and then, of course, he had to go about a bit and visit the various theaters, and cabarets, and cafes. Hales was much better off than he was, and he did not like to appear stingy in his society. Besides, in the company of his newly-found friend he was very apt to forget, and to lose his sense of proportion.

So interested were they both in the abstract joys of living that the mere fact of whether they paid one franc or five francs for a seat at a cafe chantant seemed trivial and hardly worth considering.

An incident occurred one night that brought home to Arthur the fact that certain phases of Parisian life were not entirely fictional. He and Hales were returning from the Cafe Rouge, where they had been listening to a black-haired Bohemian gentleman play Liszt with impassioned fervor. They were walking down a quiet street and discussing ethnological characteristics. Arthur casually observed two men ambling in their direction. Just as they reached them he saw Hales fall forward, as though pushed, and at the same moment felt himself gripped from behind. One of the men snatched his watch, his pocket-book, and other available property on the front of his person. It was then that something seemed to stir in the slow-moving Californian. He went off like a firework. It was amazing. All his limbs seemed to be driving right and left, like pistons. Arthur found himself on the ground, grabbing a man's legs, while two bodies fell limply near, one in the gutter, and the other against the wall. Hales was apparently engaged in breaking up a third. A fifth man, who had Arthur's watch and pocket-book, had bolted, and in a few minutes the street seemed to be in a perfect state of revolution. Swarms of people collected, and the noise was deafening. They took different sides; a woman scratched Arthur's face, and another woman tore the first woman's hair. No police appeared on the scene of this pandemonium for fully ten minutes, and when they did arrive they did not tend to soothe the atmosphere. Some people struck at the police, and the chief gendarme shrieked like a madman and was quite incomprehensible. When it was observed that Arthur was English, and Hales presumably of the same nationality, there was more strife and division of opinion. The English were not popular in Paris at the time of the Boer War, and after the police had taken their names and addresses, and the apaches were revived with buckets of cold water and nips of brandy, the two young men were escorted out of the neighbourhood with boos and jeers, and an occasional missile of a more substantial character.

When they arrived at their rooms they counted the cost. Arthur had lost one hundred and sixty francs and his watch, and was badly cut and bruised, and Hales had a lump the size of an egg on the back of his head. Nevertheless, the Californian's eyes were glowing like live coals, and he kept muttering:

"Lordy! Lordy!"

When he looked at himself in the glass he said:

"My! Gaffyn, that was some considerable mix-up. We 'll hear no more of it, you bet. Phew! I've heard say they spring these surprise-packets sometimes, but I never reckoned to get to grips with a real apache."

The horizon of Hales's genial experiences was being enlarged entrancingly. He walked about the room like a cat. Life had never entertained him so lavishly.

"Jeminy!" he exclaimed after a time, "I'm real sorry about your pocket-book and timepiece. You 'll never get them back. Call on me if there's anything you want Paris, why the hub of civilization. Jeminy!" They continued their ethnological discussion till a late hour, with the practical illustration of their evening's experience as a basis.

When Christmas arrived Arthur discovered that the one hundred and twelve pounds, which was to last him two years, was now reduced to rather less than twenty.

On the twenty-ninth of December he told Hales that he was going back to London on business for a few days. It was very apparent that somehow or other he must raise more money. Hales said:

"I wish I could do the round trip with you. I 'll be going over in the spring, anyway. My folks are coming from California. They're going to make London their headquarters and buzz round for awhile."

Arthur did not suspect that this casual remark was to have a very important bearing on his life.

On the very first evening he had spent with Hales, the latter had told him all about his "folks" and given him the full story and details about each one of them. He had, on the same occasion, told him his views on religion, art, and philosophy. He had invited him to come out with him to California when he returned, and to stay with him as long as he liked, as his guest. He had asked Arthur a hundred and one questions about himself, and had deplored the lack of religious feeling in modem France, and also the dearth of good breakfast cereals. He invited him to use his well-appointed apartment as often and in any old way he liked, and to come and take his books or anything else he fancied, without asking.

Arthur was a little aware that if Hales had not seen him again after that evening, he would probably have forgotten him forthwith. Nevertheless, at the moment he was entirely sincere. He had a way of coming up close and saying:

"Now, just tell me exactly what you feel about so-and-so."

He would listen interestedly for some minutes, occasionally interjecting:

"You don't say!"

He did not seem to care to pursue a subject to any degree of profundity. Life was too full of these surprising and entertaining things to waste a great deal of time on any one particular phase of it. His attitude toward life was precisely that of a child with a new toy. His large, kind, sympathetic face was as open as a book, and his eyes reflected the quick sensibility of his mind. Without being excessively clever, he had great breadth of outlook and a certain broad tolerance. Arthur found it was just as difficult to hurt him mentally as the apache found it hard to hurt him physically. He was invulnerable. If in one of his perverse moods Arthur would say something rather cutting, or something which reflected on the character of the Californian, he would observe him turning it over in his mind as he muttered:

"Is that so? Well! well!"

And he would be perfectly certain that the inner reflection would be:

"Well, now, that's mighty interesting."

A fault was merely a reflection of another aspect of the splendid toy.

So prodigiously did Hales talk, and such a wide field of acquaintances did he describe in detail that the casual reference to "my folks" did not stir in Arthur any particular recollection.

He bade his friend au revoir, and returned to London and Mr. Beck.

CHAPTER XIII

ALICE FLIES A KITE

Some there may be whose lives, regulated by the moral bias of their training and tradition, lead through what appear to us the normal processes of predestination. In their youth you may observe them gazing into the rigid perspective of their future. It is true the ebb and flow of material fortune may be an uncertain factor in their development, but so ingrained within them are certain moral precepts, so sure is their fundamental conception of their life purpose, that one has only to glance at some child to say:

"If God spares little Charlie, he will one day become a bishop" or "If Edna makes eyes like that, she is destined to become the mistress of a soap king."

One feels that after childhood everything important is finished. The rest is merely the répétition générale of the drama conceived in the dim ages of primordial lust, and tediously rehearsed during the centuries of physical and moral struggle. The performance itself is an affair of puppets so well manipulated by the Great Producer that we believe they are real actors and actresses. We say: "How magnificent George looks in his sailor suit! And wasn't it fine the way he killed the pirate chief!"

Or we say:

"How exquisitely the duchess handed Mrs. Bung a cup of tea!"

And we applaud these actions as being real and splendid episodes. And when a poet says, "The child is father to the man," we accept it as a whimsical and poetic license, and not as a hard, concrete, scientific fact.

Others there are of whom we cannot take stock. They are the wayward children whose impulses make the history-books uncertain records. Sometimes they lead great lives obscurely; at other times they lead mean lives, although they figure on a great canvas. It has yet to be completely understood that there never was a hero, except a stage hero. Some children have had the heroic impulse more strongly developed than other children, and with the help of grease-paint, and limelight, and the prompter, they have forced their men-or-women children down to the footlights, and made them strut as heroes, and people in the pit have cried: "Hurrah! hurrah!"

But for the most part, we in the pit are clever enough to know that we shout this more for our own satisfaction than because we believe it. We are really applauding the amiable virtues which the actor symbolizes, and which we would so much like to emulate ourselves. We shout because we in the pit are very good critics, and we want to impress the producers with the sense of our approval of that always commendable tag, "virtue rewarded, vice vanquished."

And the difference we note in the eyes of these wayward children is that they already perceive that life is a fluid, and not a rigid business. They gaze into their perspective until they behold some point which becomes the center of a new sphere of experience. At any moment the whole system of life may revolve round that.

Heredity, environment, moods, digestion, nerves, impulses, prejudice, and passion—all these old actors in the dead drama have passed away, but you read the influence of their work on the faces of the wayward children.

It was not without reason that the boys of Cullington School called Arthur, "Moods." And the illustrations he gave of this unreliable quality during the following year were more varied and illuminating than perhaps at any other period of his life. He worried the life out of Mr. Beck. He would turn up and demand that certain interests and shares be sold, so that he might prosecute his studies in Paris. In a few weeks' time he would return and ask him to reinvest this money as he had decided that he would never be a painter; he was coming back to live in London and going into some commercial business. Then he would appear again, probably the next morning, and explain that after all he thought he would complete his studies in Paris. One day he wrote that he had decided to sell the bungalow at Bodiesham, but a telegram arrived before the letter, saying, "Don't sell. Cancel instructions. Calling." But of course he did n't call, or in any case, not for two months, and then it was with the object of raising more money in order to go to Italy. But he never went to Italy. He stayed on in Paris and took to writing essays and verse.

At the end of that year he had expended nearly one half of the capital that his father had left him, and he was as unsettled and undetermined about his future as ever. He became more and more convinced that painting was not his right means of expression, but he hung on in Paris because he liked being there with Hales, and he thought he might as well do there whatever he was going to do, as in London.

Other things also contributed to the general unsettling of his outlook, and one of them was the visit of Hales's "folks" to Paris in the spring.

Hales's "folks" proved to be a mother and a sister. The mother was a diminutive little woman who barely came up to her son's elbow. She had bright eyes and a vivacious manner, and the same friendly, confiding way of talking. She gave everyone the impression of having taken a sudden personal liking to them, and so, indeed, she usually had. The sister was fifteen, and Arthur fell in love with her at once. Alice was a composite of her mother and brother. She had tremendous animation. "She's a streak of life" Arthur thought when he first observed her. She exuded life. Her eyes danced with the eternal fun of the thing. The sun was in her hair, her eyes, her skin, and the joyous movements of her trim little school-girl body. She was very straight and compact, and always gave Arthur the impression that she had just washed her hair. He loved her hair. It was very light brown, and thick and wavy. In some ways she was surprisingly old and self-possessed, and in other ways an incorrigible baby. Her brother called her "Pipsie" for some reason or other, and she called him "Boodles."

They were charming folk, and they all behaved to each other like lovers. Arthur was fascinated watching them. He had never before met people like them. They were so intensely interested in every little thing concerning each other. It was on the second night of their arrival that Arthur was invited to meet Hales's folks at his rooms. And although Arthur knew that the mother and sister had been there nearly two days, they behaved as though they had only just begun to talk about things. They wanted to know exactly about everything in the flat, what everything was and why it was, how he managed about this, that, and the other; what he did if the concierge failed to turn up, how he managed to entertain visitors, how he got to M. Berthelot's studio, where he kept his linen, and, a very important point, what he did about breakfast cereals.

Mrs. Hales's greeting to Arthur was:

"Mr. Gaffyn, I'm very, very pleased to meet you. My son is quite crazy about you and your work. Now just tell me all about yourself. What you think of the life here, and what you think of Leslie."

During dinner they both expressed a wish to visit Arthur's room. Arthur said of course he'd be delighted, only his place was a mere pigsty.

And Mrs. Hales said:

"Why, we'll just love to come."

And Alice added:

"Why, Mrs. Gaffyn, we 'll be just tickled to death."

So they came, and saw, and were tickled to death.

And after they had gone Arthur sighed and thought:

"I wish that girl were ten years older."

And he dreamed of her soft brown hair, and the quick way she had of suddenly looking straight at him.

They stayed in Paris a month, and Arthur saw a good deal of them. He occasionally managed to have a walk alone with Alice, and he found her a fascinating child. She talked to him as though they were old friends.

"I often tried to figure out what you were like," she said one day. "You know, when Boodles gets a pen in his hand, there's no stopping him. He covered reams with a description of you, but I don't think you're a bit like he said. I shouldn't have thought you were English. You haven't any of the 'don't-you-know' sort of thing."

"My mother was French. Perhaps that accounts for it" said Arthur, smiling.

"French, was she? I should have liked to have known your mother. Tell me about her. Tell me all about your folks."

And Arthur told her a good deal, and she kept looking at him with her quick glance of interest and sympathy. Then she said:

"What are your ambitions, Mr. Gaffyn?"

Arthur pondered this comprehensive question for a moment, and answered:

"Oh, I don't know that I'm very ambitious."

And then the child said a surprising thing. As she spoke, he watched her square chin, and her eyes bent on the ground as she swung along with big strides.

"I want you to be ambitious. Everybody ought to be ambitious. I don't mean ambitious to make money or become famous. I mean ambitious to help in the big thing. I'm going to do what I can. I'm going up to Smith College next fall. If I do well there, I'm going to take up medicine. And then I'm going to help people—you know, help in all sorts of ways. There's such a lot to be done. I'm afraid people are very silly and bad, and they want helping. Don't you think so?"

Arthur said he thought they did, but he could not help laughing. She laughed, too, and said:

"It's too bad to laugh at me. I know you think I'm a high-brow."

Arthur said he didn't quite know what a "high-brow" was, but if it was a person who said very wise things at a very early age, he agreed with her.

"But this isn't very wise" she said.

"'People are silly and bad, and they want helping!'" he quoted. "I think that's the wisest thing I've ever heard. I shall always remember that. "

They entered the Luxembourg gardens which were, as usual, full of the kind-faced bonnies with their charges. Some small boys were flying kites. The eyes of Alice danced with delight and she suddenly seized Arthur's arm and said:

'"Will you come here and fly a kite with me one day?"

"Of course I will."

"When! To-morrow?"

"Yes. To-morrow."

Arthur agreed to get the kite, and he did so that very afternoon. He gave an inordinate number of francs for it, for he wanted a fine kite with a long tail, a kite worthy of Alice.

The following morning he called for her at Hales's rooms, and the other two were just as eager about the kite, and wanted to come, too, but Alice said:

"No! you've got to stay home, or go and look at stuffy old pictures. I'm going alone to fly the kite with Mr. Gaffyn. We're going to play around together."

And Mrs. Hales said:

"Mr. Gaffyn, be careful! This young lady has evidently set her cap at you, and when she does that, she's inclined to be dangerous."

And Leslie took Arthur solemnly by the coat-sleeve and said:

"Arthur, I'm sorry to have to tell you that my sister is notoriously the worst flirt in the whole of Los Angeles, and that's a mighty speedy spot."

And then Alice assaulted him with such violence that he was obliged to go down on his hands and knees and sue for pardon. And so they set off alone.

It was an ideal day for flying a kite. There was a gentle breeze, and the blue sky was fleeced with tiny white clouds. They had some difficulty in getting the kite to rise, and Alice seemed to know more about it than he did. She made him run with it about fifty yards, while she held the other end of the cord. It swerved and took eccentric angles above the earth, and then suddenly swung upward. Alice let out yards and yards of slack, and followed it up, and Arthur joined her and they ran across the grass together. They ran and ran, backwards and forwards, till the kite seemed almost a speck in the air.

"Look! look!" Alice cried ecstatically. "Isn't it splendid!"

He looked at her face. She was gazing up at the sky with her lips parted, and her clear shining eyes reflected the blue light of the sky. Arthur was conscious of a complete and satisfying moment. There came to him a tense appreciation of the beauty of that stuff we call "young life." He felt for this small girl a love that was in some way connected with the vibrant splendours of that radiant day. He realized in that moment that the child had suddenly introduced into his life some force that could not be destroyed, epitomizing as she did not merely the vision of a new race and a new friendship, but the vision of youth itself, the most indestructible thing in nature. He thought to himself: "How I would love to have a little girl like you. Some one to worship and lavish all that I have upon, and who would believe in me despite all the world."

He would want nothing more than the touch of her hair, and the right of kindred worship. To stand by her side and gaze up at the sky, and to feel the full force of all living things crying out:

"Aye, it's splendid! splendid! splendid!"

And, indeed, the cup of Alice's happiness was very full on that morning. She made him carry home the kite. And they took a cab, and on the way called at a confectioner's and bought candies, and arrived home very late for lunch, neither feeling at all hungry.

Leslie's greeting was:

"Well, Gaff, did she make love to you?"

And Arthur replied:

"No; but we had a splendid morning."

CHAPTER XIV

A NEW CENTURY DAWNS

To what extent the moody and vacillating behaviour of Arthur throughout the rest of that year was due to the little episode of flying a kite with a school-girl, it would be difficult to determine. It is certain that after the departure of Alice and her mother, he settled down to work in a preoccupied manner. The moods, in fact, did not begin to have any operative effect until the late summer, when, according to the testimony of Hales, the boy began "to prance" in a most disturbing manner. Four times that autumn he went across to London on some wild project, and then returned.

At Christmas time he bade a definite farewell to his friend, announcing that he had decided to return to London for good, and to take up literary work.

The American, who had had definite farewells made to him before, took it with all due solemnity, but in his inmost heart fully expected to see his friend return within the ensuing week.

And so indeed he did, but in this case it was to report on the effect of certain external events upon his mind, events which had the effect of bringing to a head the half-formed slumbering resolutions of the year.

When he returned to London he pitched his camp once more at Aunt Elizabeth's, but he cast his eye longingly on the studio flat that Edith had offered him. He would have liked to have taken it, but he resented this eleemosynary aspect of his friendship with Edith. When he had refused the offer of it and gone back to Paris, she had said:

"Well, I expect it will be here when you come back."

There was an uncomfortable sense of fatality about the way Edith said these things. "It means," Arthur thought, "that I am eventually destined to occupy it."

And for that very reason he fought against it. Every free spirit hates having a destiny. So he stayed at Aunt Elizabeth's, and "mooched" about London in a still unsettled frame of mind.

He visited his friends at Blinkinshaw's and surveyed once more this restless arena of discontent. The Boer War had affected the decorative trade rather adversely. There was an air of uncertainty and suspicion about the place. Several of the designers had been dismissed, and there were rumours and rumours. Arthur had harbored the idea that if things went badly, he could always return there, but now it seemed rather questionable. What was going to happen to him? He felt himself drifting helplessly. He was spending the small capital his father had left him, and he was not sure even now that he had chosen his right profession. He was twenty-five, and was wandering through life without any direct motive or ambition. What was it "they" had said about his family! That they couldn't make up their minds? His father, his Uncle Harvey, who was no good, his Uncle Brian, "who died among naked savages. "After all" he thought, "it doesn't much matter where you die. But one ought to live, somehow."

The last day of that year was the last day of the old century, and Jimmy Long and several others arranged to see the new century in. They decided to dine at Pollini's, then have one or two drinks, and ultimately make their way to St. Paul's Cathedral at twelve o'clock. Arthur was invited to join them.

The arrangement did not work out according to schedule, owing to a sudden demand from Mr. Fred Blinkinshaw for some drawings that had to go off by a train that night to Leeds. Jimmy Long and Learoyd were engaged on them, but not Levistock or Karolyi. Consequently, when Arthur turned up he was taken by a section of the party to the bar of "The Queen of Rumania" to await the others. "The Queen of Rumania" was in quite her best New Year's Eve mood. The saloon was crowded with salesmen and others from the firm, and a good sprinkling of designers. There was considerable toasting and standing treat. By eight o'clock a goodly proportion of these gentlemen were, in Levistock's words, "well oiled." They stood leaning against the bar, with their glasses at incredibly dangerous angles, and glowing at each other with friendly nods and winks.

"Well, good luck, old boy!"

"I deserve it. Go' bless yer. What 'll you have!"

"Good luck, Henry! Good luck, Mr. Smith!"

"Mine's a Scotch and small 'polly.'"

"Well, cheer-o, old pal, and a very happy New Year and many of 'em."

"New century, you mean. Here you are, many new centuries, Mr. Bert! Good luck to you! Ha! ha! ha!"

"Well, I don't mind telling you, dear boy, if my turnover is as good this year as last, I've nothing to grumble about."

"I've done pretty well. I 'll have the same again, please, Miss Purvis; not too much soda".

"Good luck, Charlie! Good luck, Fred! A 'appy New Year!"

It was nine o'clock before Jimmy Long and the others joined them, and as Pollini's was rather full, they all adjourned upstairs to the dining-room of the "Queen of Rumania."

They had chops and steaks and tankards of ale, and became extremely noisy. After that, as there were still more than two hours to put in before the midnight service at St. Paul's, they decided to go to the Oxford Music-Hall. It was several hundred yards to this place of entertainment; consequently, it appeared necessary on the way to call at one or two houses for refreshment. The streets were very crowded, and they went along arm-in-arm, singing and shouting; nor were they by any means conspicuous in doing so. When they arrived in the music-hall, it was so crowded there was only just room to stand up at the back of the lounge. They could not see the stage, but they could hear the cheers when portraits of famous generals were thrown on the screen, and they all joined lustily in the chorus of:

''Sons of the Empire inarching out to war,
With our brave colonials from the distant shore."

They soon tired of this, however, and went to the bar at the back, where were crowds of other young men like themselves, and older men, and coloured men, and dark-featured foreigners, and prostitutes. Some of the party was mislaid here, and they never came across them again. At about eleven o'clock Arthur, and Levistock, and a young man named Kettle left the music-hall and started out for St. Paul's. It took them nearly an hour to reach there. The streets were full of drunken people, and hawkers and impromptu orchestras. Kettle insisted on visiting more public-houses, and became very drunk and quarrelsome. In the Strand they left him in the center of a crowd of people. He was endeavouring to convince a big Canadian soldier that Canada was geographically a smaller country than Spain. He seemed to stand a level chance of being murdered, and the other two were not anxious to share the same fate.

When they came to the upper end of Cheapside it was nearly twelve o'clock. The crowd was enormous, and quite out of hand. They were pressed back against a shop-window. They could see nothing but the people near them, and the great dome of the cathedral looming solemnly against the night sky. The noise was deafening. Groups of people were singing different songs,—patriotic airs, and jingles, and hymns. A line of drunken Scottish soldiers nearby were trying to join hands and sing "Auld Lang Syne," but the song was lost in. the general din. A sailor and a civilian were fighting at the comer of the street near where they stood, and a prostitute was shrieking because some one had torn her hat off. A few individuals were gazing dumbly heavenward, as though prepared to be impressed by the solemnity of the hour, but for the most part it was a composite dirge of drink and disunion. And as they looked round at this heaving mass of fuddled humanity, with its drunken soldiers and sailors, and white-faced civilians, and pickpockets, and charlatans, and loose women and adventurers, the great clock struck twelve. Levistock touched Arthur's arm, and nodded in the direction of the cathedral:

"Hark at it! Two thousand years of the teaching of Jesus Christ!"

And then it was that the naked ugliness of the whole thing came home to the boy. He was not in the mood to reason that, after all, these people were only a small minority, the dregs of a very large and cumbrous civilization, that they did not represent the cathedral round which they held their orgie. He accepted them as in every way symbolical of the age, the product of Christian teaching, and commercial enterprise, and "progress." He would not grant that at that moment there were millions of people sleeping in their beds, or even singing in their drawing-rooms, who were leading decent and courageous lives. He saw only the grim sordidness of it all, the significance of this epic confusion.

Struggle, struggle, struggle—there was nothing else. Through all these two thousand years they had done nothing but fight for the mean and wretched wherewithal to exist. And now, like a great sea, they came surging round the walls of this church which had professed to mother them. Work without love, life without beauty, struggle without hope, disunited, quarrelsome, lascivious, pitiable. He thought of the salesmen in the "Queen of Rumania."

"Good luck, old boy. If my turnover is as good this year as last—"

That was all. The sole epitome of luck, the good turnover! More money, more comfort, more security, more drink. And so they would go on. Another two thousand years, and other men would come. Some would have been "lucky" and some would not, and the prostitute with her towzled hair would still shriek because some one had torn her hat and the crowd was jeering at her.

What did this raging sea care for the gentle eyes of his father, for what was valuable in himself, for the "hare-brained ideas" of Mr. Leffbury? Dash all this high-falutin' sensibility to pieces! Eat, drink, and persuade yourself you're gay; for to-morrow another will take your place!

He hated Levistock for using that phrase, "Two thousand years of the teaching of Jesus Christ."

All the church-bells were ringing, and the sirens from factories and steamers down in the river were hurling their strident challenge to the stars. It sounded like the prolonged shriek of some wild beast that has attained the culmination of its feral passion. He felt faint and exhausted, and he evaded Levistock and darted down a side street. His one thought was, "I must get away from this. "

What was he to do? Were other cities any better than this! Certainly not Paris. Berlin? St. Petersburg! New York? Were they not all on that night giving expression to the triumphant realization of their two thousand years of abortive culture? Could it go on? Was there not already behind it all some dark menace of destruction? He hurried down a side street where great newspapers were going to press. He heard the dull throb of the machines, and in the rooms above the click of typewriters and telephones.

The work-box!

Dot-dot' dash' dash' dash-click' Click secret codes and messages. Intrigues, whispers, rumors, jealousies, personal feuds, secret diplomacy. Already in locked chambers old men were at work, peevish old men who held the happiness of the world in their hands, and they were working without love in their hearts.

In the neighbourhood of Oxford Street he visited a coffee-stall, for he was cold and hungry.

There was a small group of men gathered round the stall, and a thin white-faced young man was arguing testily with the coffee-stall keeper. Arthur could not catch the drift of the disputation, but he could see the profile of the young man, with his collar turned up and his hat right over his eyes, and he heard his cockney voice rise to a whining crescendo:

"Ugh! a lot yew do for people, I must say! A lot yew do!"

And then the gruff voice of the coffee-stall keeper, as he vigorously buttered a piece of toast: I'll do what I can."

'There was something in that. If only everybody would do what they could.

He hurried on in the direction of Bayswater, and let himself into Aunt Elizabeth's house. It was very dark and cold, and he went straight to bed. He fell into a heavy sleep, but awakened a few hours later. He was rather feverish. The woman with the towzled hair, shrieking near the cathedral because the people jeered at her, kept haunting his memory. He felt in some dim way that he was responsible, that he ought to have helped her and defended her. It was very terrible. And then the other voice, strangely comforting:

"I do what I can."

He slept at last, hugging the vision of a fat-faced man vigorously buttering a piece of toast.

THE REFORMER

On the following evening Edith Yardley had a surprising experience. She arrived home about eight o'clock, having attended a committee-meeting of a society that had for its object the better welfare of young and indigent mothers. When the maid opened the door she said:

"Mister Arthur is here in the drawing-room. He has been waiting for you nearly two hours."

Edith said:

"Oh. Thank you."

And she put her muff and chatelaine down on the hall-table, and hurried into the room and shut the door. When she looked at Arthur standing by the fireplace, she was aware that he was laboring under the stress of some great emotion. She did not immediately ask him what the trouble was; she spoke soothingly, apologized for keeping him waiting, and asked him to stay to dinner. But the boy seemed at a loss, and almost incoherent. He said he was not hungry; that he had "just called in." And then Edith showed a touch of that quality which was part and parcel of her genius for management. She went down on her knees and poked the fire until it blazed; and then she rose and switched off the electric light, so that the room was only illumined by firelight. After that she took him by the arm and made him sit in a comer of the Chesterfield. She herself sat in the opposite comer, and shaded her eyes with her hands so that he could not see them. They sat there silently for some minutes, listening to the crackling of the flames. Then she said in a very low voice:

"Tell me what it is."

He started by saying he didn't know; it was really nothing. He just felt rather down about things; that was all. Then he paused, and with some hesitation started telling her about his previous evening's experience and how it had affected him. He gradually became more animated, and leaned forward and conjured visions out of the flames.

"Honestly, I'm frightened. I can't think what's going to happen. Of course I know there are decent people and all that, but God, it's this dead weight in the foreground. It isn't their viciousness so much; there's a lot of rough good-humor and kindness among them. It's their frightful ignorance, commonness, not in the coarse sense, but in the ignorant sense, poverty of idea, poverty of ambition, poverty of taste. Look at their homes, the things they buy if they have money, their ideas of pleasure, of amusement! I've been thinking of it all night. Besides, it isn't a minority; it's the bulk of people. They're no better in Paris. And the tragedy is, so many are contented; they think it's all right. I don't think I'm a socialist. I don't know. I detest politics. Politics are all about economics. I can't see that a man who lives in a palace in Kensington is essentially luckier or happier than a man in one room in Stepney. What I see is the vast untapped spiritual wealth. It's all going to decay."

The boy stopped and glanced at the woman, but as he could not see her eyes, he looked back at the fire.

"I want to do something about this, Edith. I have been thinking, and thinking, and thinking. I want to change my profession again. I want to do what I can. I'm not clever enough to frame policies, or reconstruct the social fabric or whatever they call it, but I could do something, a sort of mission of discontent. Don't you see! I want to keep hammering at the idea that no one must be contented. One must always be restlessly striving for finer things, for higher things. I want to write; not direct propaganda, but stuff that reflects realities, and has point and significance—splays, I think. They have a more direct appeal. Everybody goes to the theater; hardly anybody reads. It isn't only the poor who are 'common.' I thought of a play last night. I worked it all out; at least, a lot of it is vague, but I've got the main idea. Shall I tell you what it is?"

He saw the outline of her face, and her hand shading the fire from her eyes, as she whispered:

"Tell me."

"It is very simple. It is the drama of the conflict of opposing forces struggling for an illusion. In the straggle the people don't destroy each other; they destroy the illusion. It sounds trite, and so are many big things. As I see the world at the present day, we are like the Gaddarene swine rushing down the steep place."

He moved nearer to the woman on the Chesterfield and altered the tone of his voice:

"In this race for material prosperity, suppose one day something should happen. Suppose the big thing we're struggling for should prove an illusion. Let us imagine for instance, all these eat powers and cunning chancelleries who have erected this colossal system of material values so artfully interdependent; imagine one day that the greed and lust for the control of them became so great that they flew at each other's throats, like wild beasts—a colossal war, so great that everybody was in it, every ounce of material value was poured into the thing. And in the struggle the thing itself should be destroyed. That is to say, that all commercial values should be destroyed, and then when they counted the cost, they found that these values were only an illusion, that commercial values were of no value. Then, perhaps, they would return to the work-box with love in their hearts."

He looked up, and seemed to expect her to speak, but she remained in the shadow.

"I have something within me, some sort of gift; I don't know what it is. I want to express myself. I am an artist, I suppose; a person whose mission is to shape things, to influence, to discover beauty which has been there all the time, dormant, perhaps, to some others. But God! how many of these others there are I How dead they are! Buried under the crumbling masonry of this social muddle. And what I feel is, it isn't all economics, it is n't necessary to be rich to see beauty, to find beauty in one's work, to be courageous and to have fine thoughts and feelings. But as it is, this canker of material progression is growing, and growing, and growing, and unless we all do what we can, there 'll be nothing left but the surgeon's knife. Do you know what I mean by the surgeon's knife? The sudden dull rumble of distant guns, and then the end! The blasting of all material values into nothingness, the maiming and slaughtering of young men like cattle. Who was it said 'The central fact of war is the blood and brains of man scattered over a field of mud'! I forget. Nothing like that will count. The surgeon's knife will be very effective. There will be no quarter, no mercy, no abiding by rules, no concession to humanity until the whole of these material values have been exorcized. Then the thing will stop of itself, exhausted. But hearts will break for all time from the sheer pity of it. There will be the desperate reconstruction. Some genius will discover the new point round which the rejuvenated system will revolve. That, perhaps, will be the surprise—the realization that the rigid conceptions of old are dead. Then the world will be ruled from within, and not from without. Why should we wait for this! Why should there not spring up now among the peoples a class something on the lines of the intelligentsia in Russia, people who love the arts and sciences, and the love of work, forming a dead weight to sit on the chests of these old men who rule the world,—an impossible people, you can do nothing with, who refuse to hate anyone, who insist on being intelligent despite their training?"

He leaned forward and held out his hands toward the fire. Then he added:

"Don't imagine I think this could be brought about suddenly. But it's the thing to work for. Imagine it! A sort of freemasonry of love, with its ramifications in every civilized country. It would be tremendous. The women are already restless. They are banding together, and quite rightly. There may come a struggle of the sexes, and it may be followed by the struggle of youth against age. For too long has the world been ruled by the old; the time of the young is coming. Edith, will you help me in this! I don't know how it is, but last night everyone appeared unstable, vacillating. I don't mean the people who had been drinking. They were rolling about like tubs. I mean all the people I could think of, and the people who rule and order and write; and as I surveyed them mentally, you seemed to be the one reliable figure in this shifting kaleidoscope. I had to come and tell you. "

He gazed at her, and she seemed curiously silent and watchful; not a bit like the old Edith who used to come butting in, and arranging, and managing things for people. He liked this new aspect of her. He felt convinced that she would help him, but that she would help him in his way and not in her way; that she understood. Her voice came out of the darkness:

"I'm so glad this has happened, Arthur. It was nice of you to come to me. It makes me proud. Yes, yes, yes, I know exactly how you feel. I have felt these things, too, bitterly. I am older, more experienced; it is all very difficult and—"She seemed about to give expression to some opinion, and then changed her mind. She came nearer to him, and took his hands, and placed them on her knees. In the dim light her face looked pinched and strained.

"Of course! I 'll help you. It will be splendid. You shall come here and work in the studio. You shall live there just as you like. It shall be quite independent of the house. You can come in and have your meals with me, or you can have them sent in to you. You must always confide in me, tell me what you're doing. I'm not clever, Arthur. You give me much greater credit for ability than I really have. But I will help you. I will see that everything is done for you. I will make you a great man."

"I don't know that I want to be a great man" the boy answered.

"But I want you to be a great man. It is the only stipulation I make. The greater you are, the more good you can do. Isn't that so? Oh, it'll be fine! I shall watch you growing and growing, and being talked about, and I shall be very proud."

The fire was dying down, and he could only observe the intermittent glimpses of her chin and brow. He could not see her eyes. A gong rang in the hall, and she said in a changed voice:

"When did you last eat, Arthur!"

He replied:

"Oh, I had some tea and things about midday. I haven't felt like eating. I drank some whisky last night. It always makes me feel rotten."

"You must come and have some soup."

"I don't think I will."

She took his arm and led him into the hall. He again protested, and she smiled and said:

"If you don't come and have some soup, I sha'n't help you to reform the world."

A sudden resentful feeling came to him that she was mocking him, treating him like a baby.

"I'm not going to be bossed entirely by this woman" he thought, and he walked deliberately to the hat-stand. He already had his coat on, when he found her at his elbow. For the first time that evening he looked into her eyes. There was a strange pleading look he had never seen before.

"Arthur, don't you see! I'm sometimes very lonely. You might stay a little while."

Never before could he recollect Edith appealing to him. It flattered his sense of dynamic power. He was no longer the school-boy to be told to wash his hands, or "not to slouch." He had asserted himself, and the act produced a pleasurable sensation. He removed his coat and answered:

"I'm sorry. Of course I wasn't thinking."

He stayed till half -past ten and elaborated his schemes for future work, and Edith discussed the practical details of his home affairs. It would be necessary for him to return to Paris to collect various belongings and settle a few minor matters. In a week's time he hoped to start on his mission to write plays, "stuff that reflects realities, and has point and significance."

He surprised Mr. Beck the following morning by calling on him and returning eighty-five pounds, which he asked him to "put back in the gas-works. "Mr. Beck gave him up as a bad case, and put the money in the bank.

"He will come back to-morrow and want it again" he thought, not unreasonably.

His one regret in cutting short his student career in Paris so precipitately was the severance of the companionship of Hales. He thought the whole matter over and decided that the best plan was to tell the big Californian precisely all about it. So he invited him to dinner at the Caf6 du Bourse, which was a favorite haunt of theirs. The cooking was excellent, and the management supplied a red wine in old bottles covered with cobwebs. Some evilly-disposed people used to aver that Monsieur Badet had a special breeding-place for cobwebs, which he applied to comparatively new bottles, but these people were generally indigent students who resented the fact that they were not at the moment in a position to purchase the good fare at Monsieur Badet's table.

In any case, the cobwebs always gave an added piquancy to the occasional imbibings of Arthur and Hales, neither of whom knew anything about wine. When the cork was drawn. Hales would put his nose to the top of the bottle and say: "My that's a mighty fine bouquet, Gaffyn." And when Arthur had sipped it, he would say: "By Jove; this wine's jolly good to-night." Consequently, why should anyone begrudge Monsieur Badet his innocuous assiduity!

Certainly on this occasion the cobwebs were prolific. They covered the label and hung in cloudy mists round the neck of the bottle. The waiter apologized for disturbing them when he removed the cork.

"Well, I'm very, very sorry you're going," Hales remarked, as an oval dish of whitebait was set before them. "Now just tell me exactly how it all came about."

Arthur started diffidently and apologetically, and then described the scene on New Year's Eve. He became eloquent, and Hales was kept busy interjecting: "You don't say!" or "Is that so!"

When the picture was completed he remarked inevitably:

"Well, now, that's mighty interesting!"

"Tell me," Arthur said. "What is New York like! Or the other American cities?"

"Well" replied his friend, "on the stunt you're going on, it's much of a muchness. Of course, there are some striking dissimilarities. There's less drink, ever so much less drink. We're a comparatively temperate folk, and our domestic lives are, for the most part, pure and sweet. But when it comes to what you call 'materialism.' My! we have Europe guessing."

Hales swirled some claret round in the bottom of his glass; then he said:

"I get the drift of what you're after, Gaff; and I admire your attitude. Where I think you're a bit wrong is in judging a people by some external S3nnbols. That bunch of hooligans who loafed round St. Paul's on New Year's Eve don't represent England, any more than those apaches who tried to do us up in the Rue Quatre Septembre represent Paris. Society is a big thing. It's come down through a lot of very dark work. We're only a small fraction of a big tradition. The majority of people are dead, and we're just clearing up the mess a bit."

"On the contrary" Arthur said, "it seems to me that the majority of people are unborn. And the point is, what are we doing for the unborn people? At present we're preparing a mess for them. We're making it as difficult as possible."

"I don't agree with you there. I think we're progressing. I grant you all the external ugliness, but look how these cobwebs conceal this fine old wine!"

Hales poured himself out another glass, and continued:

"Where I think my people have it on Europe is that they do believe in and appreciate the good wine under the cobwebs. They're younger, you know. They have more hope, more faith, more belief in themselves. And, by God! look at the kindness and charity and humanitarian movements there are to-day, compared with a hundred years ago. It was probably ugly then, only the ugly things have been destroyed, and it was certainly more cruel. Why, in those days they would hang a young boy for stealing a leg of mutton!"

Arthur thought for a moment, and then said:

"Yes, I believe that's true. But I have a feeling that the commercial system is breeding something more cruel than the hangman's noose of the last century. It is, in any case, a thing which concerns me. I was n't judging only by the people I saw on New Year's Eve. I was thinking of the people I met in business, and what I've heard of politicians, newspapers, and all that sort of thing; the way all these trades, and even the arts, are honeycombed with corruption and false standards."

"Well, there's a lot in that, and I think it's a very big thing you're after. This 'll be mighty interesting to me. My people are coming back again in the fall; I 'll hope to bring them to some theater to see one of your plays."

Arthur had a golden vision of Alice seated in the stalls, looking at the stage, with her lips parted and her eyes sparkling with appreciation of his attempt to "try and help the bad and foolish. "

Leslie raised his glass and said, "Happy days, Gaff!"

And Arthur raised his, and replied, "Happy days, Hales!"

After dinner they visited a pig fair in Montmartre, and continued their discussion of the imponderable. One of Hales's last remarks was:

"If I may say so. Gaff, what I'm afraid of about you is, you 'll go buzzing round the firmament too much. Take my advice and keep your feet on the good old earth while you 've got the chance. Write about yourself and your own experiences."

It flashed upon Arthur that this was a curious corroboration of Mr. Leffbury's advice, when he talked about going to Italy. "Express yourself. Don't be mesmerized by reputation, or by what is termed 'nature.'"

On the following day Hales came with him to the St. Lazare station to see him off, and he was surprised to observe how moved the big Californian was at his departure. He repeated half a dozen times:

"I'm awfully sorry you're going."

And then he seemed to dry up, as though words failed. When the horn went, he wrung Arthur's hand till he almost cried out with pain. The last he saw of him was his tall figure walking rapidly beside the train, and his long arm waving his hat, while his kind face was forcing a smile that was obviously a desperate effort to restrain tears.

"This is a very wonderful thing" Arthur thought as he sank back on the cushions when the train had rumbled out of sight of the platform. And all the way to London he pondered on the strange vicissitudes of affection, which shed her favors in a quite unaccountable manner. Why should Hales, who was quite a stranger to him and, indeed, a foreigner, be so unreasonably drawn to him, and display an affection which he had no recollection of having enjoyed before!

For some time he debated the question whether he shouldn't change his mind and go back to Paris. He could write there as well as in London. But still, perhaps it would be rather mean to Edith.

"Write about yourself and your own experiences."

He arrived at Edith's house in St. John's Wood on the following morning at ten o'clock. The maid showed him through the studio. It all looked very cozy and jolly. The stove was lighted, and there was an easy chair and a Chesterfield, and a thick Turkey carpet on the floor. In the best position for light was an old oak desk, open. On the flap were several scribbling-pads, note-paper, envelopes, stamps, three pecs, a large bottle of ink, and blotting-paper. He hung up his hat and coat with a consciously proprietary air, and strolled to the desk. It was very quiet, an ideal place for writing. He sat for a few moments enjoying the pleasantly attractive atmosphere of the room. Then he took up one of the pens and dipped it in the ink, and drawing a pad toward him, wrote at the head of it:

"Moods: a Tragedy."

The remarkable thing about the five-act tragedy, "Moods," was that Arthur wrote it in six weeks. There was very little else about it that was remarkable, except that it had twenty-seven speaking parts, and the note of tragedy applied to the majority of them.

At about that time Edith, by some means or other, made the acquaintance of that well-known actor, Gregory Brecknock. He used to come occasionally to lunch on Sundays, or to tea in the afternoon. He was an elderly, scholarly-looking man who had had thirty years' experience in playing solid parts in London, without ever having had a "lead." He was very friendly to Arthur, and in due course was prevailed upon to read "Moods. "His opinion was:

"My dear boy, you've some good stuff in this, but it's hopelessly over-weighted. There are far too many ideas and characters, and far too little movement. Ton must come to the theater more, and see how characters are brought on and off, and how you can economize your material."

And so it came about that Arthur became a regular habitué of London theaters for awhile. He went to see everything that was playing. Occasionally Edith accompanied him, but for the most part he went by himself. At the same time he read plays, and studied plays, and talked plays. Gregory Brecknock took him behind the scenes and introduced him to actors. He also took him to "The Old Guys" club, which, as you know, is not far from Adelphi Terrace. It is run mostly by city merchants and lawyers, but has a large sprinkling of "the profession" and is also occasionally graced by the presence of royalty and by some of the most pronounced characters in London. Witty judges and famous pianists, jockeys, prize-fighters and poets—they all look in there on the famous "Old Guys" Saturday nights.

Among all the people he met, Arthur found actors, perhaps, the most attractive class. Their childish vanity and impulsiveness, and above all, their innate kindness of heart, appealed to him. They lived so very much in a world of their own. Their love-affairs were so promiscuous, so desperate, so impersonal, that he found it difficult at times to be certain of domestic relationships. Everybody on the stage was a "darling" or a "dear boy." And at the moment when these expressions were used, they were, indeed, sincerely meant. It was not an artificial atmosphere so much as an ultra-natural one. They were like a lot of children, fascinated by the love of love. The constant call on their emotions kept them in a fluid state. They were most attractive people. When he was introduced to them he liked the way the men at once called him "dear boy" and the friendly, confiding way the women would hold his hand.

He knocked about a lot among these people, and devoutly read his Ibsen. He also studied Shaw and Pinero, and the other modern people, and then at last he settled down again to write "Moods: A Comedy."

At everybody's instigation he made it a comedy, and he reduced the number of characters to eleven, and the acts to three. He struggled hard, moreover, to stick to one simple idea.

The comedy took him much longer to write, nearly three months, and Gregory Brecknock's opinion was that it was "a big improvement, a very big improvement, but still, the way you get your characters on and off the stage, dear boy, won't do at all. And it still wants a lighter touch."

This opinion was generally indorsed by another actor friend called Giles Hobday, who said, moreover, that he would like to show it to a friend who had had a good deal of experience in play-writing. In due course this friend appeared. He was a small, keen-faced man named Klutz. He was more enthusiastic than Arthur had expected. He said he thought something might be done with the play, but he suggested drastic alterations, and he also said: "The title won't do, dear boy. It sounds too gloomy. People want to be jollied along."

Arthur felt very dubious about these alterations. He felt they were going to upset his original idea considerably. At the same time, the bare chance of getting a play accepted and produced, dazzled him. The lure of this world was very strong.

He made another attempt, and rewrote most of it. Klutz thought the result was much better, and promised to show it to a manager's reader.

Nothing more was heard of the play for five weeks, and then it was returned to Arthur with a printed notice of rejection. He showed this to Klutz, and the latter said:

'Ah! I thought that might happen. Let me have it, dear boy. I 've another idea."

He took the play away, and there was another long interval. It was now midsummer, and Arthur thought to himself:

''I'm afraid old Hales and 'his folks' won't see one of my plays in the autumn."

He was working on another play, when a very exciting thing happened. One morning Elutz came bustling in. He was very agitated and mysterious. He said:

"Look here, dear boy, I think I'm on the track of something. Only—er—it's just this. We're all fair and square, aren't we! What I mean to say is, les affaires sont les affaires. I think I see a chance of placing your play, and if I do, I take it you won't have any objection to sharing your royalties with met"

Arthur's heart beat with excitement. He immediately envisaged the glories of a "first night." A crowded house, cheers, calls for the author, a raving press. "Discovery of a new and brilliant playwright!" "A White Hope of the English Stage."

He said as calmly as he could:

"Why, of course not."

"Ah!" said Klutz. "Good! Well, now, it's like this. There's an actress I know, called Flora Beedman. She's a very good actress, and there's a gentleman I know, whose name I'm not at the moment at liberty to divulge, who's anxious to give her a star 'lead.' Do you see what I mean!"

"Yes, quite."

"Well, I 've shown it to her, and she's quite keen. The only thing is, there is n't really a star part for her. Anyway, not enough. Now what she suggests is, you should work up the part of Lady Millworthy and make it the central, dominating figure. It 'll be quite easy. And then, you remember the incident about the muff in the second act? Well, she wants that made more of, too, and what we both think is that the play should be called 'Lady Millworthy's Muff.' That's a good idea, eh?"

Arthur said: "I see."

"Now, if you can weigh in to this, I would n't be surprised but that we can get it put on in the autumn, perhaps at the Comedy, or the Prince of Wales. "

Arthur was trembling with varied emotions. He was both furious and elated. He felt that it was an appalling desecration of the lofty muse at whose shrine he worshipped. He would never be able to convey through the medium of this new development the spirit of the fine purposes which had prompted him to write. At the same time a little voice said: "Here's your chance. Do what you can. You may be able to. You'll be heard, in any case. When you're known, you'll be able to write what you like."

He scratched with his pen on one of Edith's pads, and said:

"Oh, well, I 'll have a shot, if you like."

Arthur did his best to develop the character of Lady Millworthy, and made a good deal of the muff episode. He understood from Klutz that the play was accepted, subject to certain slight alterations which Miss Flora Beedman had commissioned Klutz himself to make, and that it would be produced in London in October, probably at the Comedy.

Hales arrived alone in London in September, and Arthur was able to inform him that his first play was already accepted and would shortly be produced. Hales was wildly delighted. He clapped Arthur fore and aft, and his eyes glowed with pleasure.

"My!" he exclaimed, "that's splendid! Your first play! Well, well, you're a marvel! I have to go over to Paris on Friday, but you just let me know the date of production and I 'll come right over and be there in full war-paint I'm only sorry my people won't be here after all. I had a letter from Alice last Saturday, and there's been some little trouble. They won't be able to get away yet awhile. Now tell me all about this play."

And then, indeed, Arthur felt a little embarrassed. He had to acknowledge that it was not exactly as he intended it to be. He was, in fact, already rather vague about some of it himself, and he felt himself shrinking under the ingenuous cross-examination of his friend. At the earliest opportunity he switched off to something else.

When Hales had returned to Paris, the reality of the approaching production was brought home to Arthur by the notification of a rehearsal to which he was bidden. It seemed too good to be true. He went, and was introduced to Miss Beedman, a large florid woman, not at all the type of person he had conceived as Lady Millworthy. In fact, as the characters appeared one by one, the horror came to him that they were not a bit as he had fancied them. He doubted once or twice whether it really was his play. He certainly recognized sentences occasionally, but the whole thing seemed somehow alien to him. The producer, a swarthy, elderly man, came forward and "dear boyed" him, and said if he had anything to suggest, he would be delighted to hear it. Arthur said no, he didn't think so, and during some unrecognizable scene, slunk out of the theater.

A week before the production Klutz suddenly appeared one morning in a great state of consternation. He came into Arthur's studio and exclaimed:

"I say, dear boy, there's the Tory devil to pay. Gueldersheim's turned rusty. I'm not taking sides one way or the other. I know nothing about it. I 've known Flora some time. She's a good sort. I believe he's using this yarn that's got round just to burke his obligations."

"What yarn?"

"Why, this yam about Flora and young Champneys. I don't believe there's anything in it, not a word of truth. But the old man is furious. He swears he has evidence. And he's queering the whole game. "

"What do you mean? What game?"

"I mean, dear boy, that the play is of. Gueldersheim was putting up the money, and he's backed out of it, all on account of this ridiculous yam about Flora and young Champneys. "

"You mean that they're not going to put on the play?"

"That's exactly the size of it. But now, look here, don't lose hope. I've another idea. You leave it to me again for a bit. "

"No, I'm damned if I do! I'm fed up with your crowd!"

"Now, look here, dear boy, it's not a bit of good cutting up. I'm as sorry as you are; the only thing is to make the best of it. I just ask you to give me one more chance."

Arthur was almost on the verge of tears, and he growled something incoherent. He protested again that he wished to have nothing further to do with Klutz and his crowd. Mr. Klutz was imperturbable, and the interview ended negatively. He got back one copy of the script, but there were other copies about, and also the parts. Three weeks later he received a letter from Mr. Montague Beale, a theatrical agent in Shaftesbury Avenue. It was to the effect that Mr. Beale would be glad of a visit from Mr. Arthur Gaffyn re the rights of his play, "Lady Millworthy's Muff."

This seemed mysterious, but Arthur had heard of Montague Beale, and he knew that he had a good name in the theatrical profession. He was a Jew, and like many others of his race, had the reputation of being as cunning as "a bagful of monkeys" but at the same time being perfectly honest. It was said of him that he never made contracts; his word stood.

Arthur made the suggested visit, and he found a smooth-faced, middle-aged gentleman sucking the stump of a cigar. He nodded and said:

"Good morning, Mr. Gaffyn; I'm pleased to meet you. I 've read your play and I think I can place it."

Arthur said "Really?" in rather inane fashion, and the agent continued:

"I 'll tell you who it's for. It's for Jimmy Cosway. D'you know Jimmy?"

Arthur replied: "Not personally. I 've seen him act, of course."

Jimmy Cosway was at that time a popular actor of light comedy and farce. He was a small man, with a whimsical personality that made people laugh at the very mention of his name.

"My idea is this," said Mr. Beale. "We think there's some good stuff in this play, but we shall want a great deal of alteration. We want the character of the fop, Algernon Gadwood, made more of, and the character of Lady Millworthy subdued. Cosway will play the part of Algernon, and we want to introduce the suggestion of the double meaning in 'Lady Millworthy's Muff.' Do you see? We want Algernon to really be 'Lady Millworthy's Muff,' and then we shall have all the muff episodes to emphasize the point. Jimmy has some very good ideas of 'business' that might be introduced about the muff in the second and third acts. What do you say?"

Arthur mumbled something about not thinking it would make a good farce, and Mr. Beale exclaimed:

"Oh, we won't have it a farce! We 'll keep some of the love element up to concert-pitch, but we 'll have to cut some of those allusions to hypochondria. There's an M. P. who drinks, isn't there? We can't have that. People don't like it. Now Jimmy's producer, Lee Whittle, is a very clever young man. He knows the ropes of the game inside and out. What I suggest is, that he come and talk it over with you."

Arthur thought there could be no harm in talking it over, and he said so. Mr. Beale said: "Good I 'll ring up and make an appointment. "Arthur's interview with Lee Whittle was impressive, and to him unforgettable. Lee Whittle was a young man about thirty years of age, with raven-black hair brushed straight back, and very dark eyes. He had an impressive way of talking and speaking. He came to Arthur's studio and stopped three hours and a half, and he held the floor all the time. He walked up and down, and declaimed in a magnificent voice. Every little sentence was rounded and finished to perfection. He talked Arthur off his feet. He pointed out a hundred and one technical difficulties arising through Arthur's ignorance of stage-craft. And in drawing his attention to the inevitable alteration to these defects, he gradually induced him to introduce the snappy way of piecing it together that, in the opinion of himself, and Jimmy Cosway, and Mr. Beale, the piece demanded. Arthur made desperate attempts to compromise, but so involved did some of it become, that he left much of it in the hands of Whittle to do what he liked with. The interviews, discussions, and alterations went on for three weeks, and then he was given a contract signed by Mr. Beale on behalf of James Cosway and a syndicate.

It was in this way that "Moods: a Tragedy" developed into "Lady Millworthy's Muff: a farcical Comedy." It was produced at the old Cock-Pit Theater in Pall Mall and, as you know, ran for almost two years. When the author watched it on that historic "first night" from the dim recesses of a box, he involuntarily thought of the expression on poor Yardley's face on that morning in the garden at Bradehurst when he looked at his children with the expression of an alchemist who has produced something he cannot account for. The success of the play was never in doubt. Lady Millworthy's muff got the whimsical Algernon into most compromising positions from which he always managed to extricate himself. When, during the third act, an M. P., who in the original play was a hypochondriac, but now was only a libertine of a flippant description, called and discovered Algernon in his wife's boudoir; and when Algernon put on an overcoat, placed the muff on his head, and pretended to be a hussar, saluting the M. P. as he walked out, the house rocked with laughter. But the author thought: "What has all this got to do with a certain night I hung about St. Paul's Cathedral? Thank God I did n't tell Hales about this!"

It is necessary at this point to go back a little and trace the corollary of another progression which concerns the emotions.

Using the evolution of this phase of his professional career, the mind of Arthur might be traced in the analogy of a mariner exploring strange and fascinating waters, endeavoring to concentrate his attention on the compass with a view to avoiding shoals and shallows, and at the same time with vision strangely alert and at times distracted by the new and appealing revelations of fresh vistas of romantic scenes. He experienced, in the first place, a degree of domestic comfort he had never enjoyed before. The oak desk in the studio was the be-all and end-all of his necessary activities. Nothing else intruded. The little room in the annex was fitted up as a bedroom, and in some secret and mysterious way everything which concerned his personal comfort was accomplished silently for him. His clothes were brushed and laid out for him. Clean linen was always to be found in the drawers of the chest. The studio was always kept clean, and dusted, and warm. His breakfast was sent to him on a tray, and very often his lunch, but for dinner he invariably went into the house and shared it with Edith. The reason for having his lunch alone was that if he went into the house for this meal, the three objectionable children were there. In the evening they were in bed.

The change in the character of Edith impressed him in many ways. She was just as managing, but in a gentler, more mothering way. It took the form of asking him if he had a clean handkerchief when he was starting out for the theater, or in seeing that he changed his boots if he had been out in the wet.

She never interfered with his work, but he gradually felt drawn to tell her about it, and ultimately he found it necessary to read everything to her before he sent it to be typed. He began to rely on her in every little way. Sometimes he would become conscious of this reliance, and it would anger him. He would ride the high horse of domineering independence, and do some unnecessarily brusk and thoughtless thing. And then he would feel ashamed of this, and in a rather self-conscious manner make some little atonement.

For long periods she would be to him but a vague, impersonal, protective force. And then suddenly there were intervals when there was something acutely personal about her. He was always a little proud of her when they went about together. She looked a person of importance and distinction when she walked to her seat in the stalls of a theater. She dressed with dignity, and no other woman carried herself so well. He had heard men whisper, "That's a damned fine woman."

The whisper had made him look at her furtively. She was "a damned fine woman" in their sense, and as Arthur knew, "a damned fine woman" in another sense. She had, at moments, that aspect of insolent conscious superiority which is peculiar to certain English women of good birth. It cannot be called vanity, because it is so unerringly sure. A peacock is vain, because it puffs out its feathers and pretends that it is not only beautiful, but superior. But apart from its beauty, a peacock has nothing at all to back up all this pretence. A peacock is one of the biggest fools among fowls. A woman of the type of Edith is not pretending anything; she knows. Her face is simply the index of an innate consciousness of centuries of moral restraint, duty, the exercise of power in a reasonable way, courage in the face of trials and adversities, loyalty to herself and her tradition, self-reliance, a strong and inflexible will, and an intense hatred of what is mean and contemptible.

Arthur found himself wondering about her tentatively. As time went on, the periods when he thought of her impersonally narrowed, and the moments when he thought of her acutely became accentuated. She was, in a way, such a strong foil to himself that she seemed even mysterious.

With his loose grip on all the concrete things of life, and his temperamental moodiness, which carried him along into channels where everything became an affair of experience, either beautiful or ugly, attractive or repulsive, Edith appeared at times an incredible enigma, like an unscalable snow-capped mountain rising from a marsh.

And then little incidents began to happen which made him wonder whether, after all, the mountain was so unscalable, and the very perilousness and hazard of the dubious ascent began to have a strangely attractive fascination for him, even in the realms of imagination.

Why was Edith so peculiarly good to him? Not only good, because she was good to everyone in her sternly puritanic way, but good to him in an almost surrendering way? She revealed aspects of her character, gentle and yielding, which he had not observed her reveal to anyone else, not even to Yardley or the children. When he did anything gracious or successful, there would come to her face an expression of pride in him in a possessive sense. When he did anything wrong, she would look unhappy for the moment, and then would come that brooding, mothering look, as though she must protect him from himself. He believed her to be a clever woman, and one thing about her disturbed him. She made so little comment about his work. He would have to interrogate her for opinions, and she always seemed reserved and diffident about giving them. But for the most part he was always suspecting that beneath those keen fine eyes there lurked the dim reflection of a smile, as though she were humoring him; as though she regarded all these wild hopes and great ideals of his as the harmless playthings of a child she loved.

It would be idle to pretend that the passage of that year marked in him any development toward a less egoistical attitude. On the contrary, he became more self-centered and arbitrary. He was, in effect, "spoiled." And it seemed odd that the spoiling should have been done by the former mistress of Bradehurst! But she was not entirely alone in this. As time went on, Edith seemed disposed to become a more social being. Dinner-parties took place, and little receptions, and snug teas, and always the theatrical and literary element predominated. The tragic affair of Robert Yardley became mellowed, and, indeed, only added a piquancy to the atmosphere of these bohemian gatherings. Nearly all the ladies who came to visit Mrs. Yardley told her that Arthur was "a charming boy." He certainly developed more assurance, and the ability to know how to act in various social positions. He had, as Mr. Leffbury once remarked, "a face the world will love to torture.' He was good-looking in a Latin way, with dark brown hair, rather dreamy eyes, and a pale skin. His figure was slight and elastic, and he had an engaging way of smiling at people who attracted him. Pretty actresses found delight in flirting with him, and in drawing out this impressionable boy. He had a genius for saying the unexpected thing, and very frequently his naivete and impulsiveness would set a room full of sophisticated people in a mood of merriment. He was seldom gay in the boisterous sense, but he had a faculty of disengaging odd and entertaining aspects from the general panorama; and always about him was that restless air of the sentiment being who is searching and is not satisfied.

When he came up against the kind of conditions he would have to cope with for the successful exploitation of his work, he became even more dissatisfied, and yet remained more sensitive to the claim of the inner feelings which had induced him to abandon painting. He saw the tragedy of

"Moods" slip out of his hands and become the thing of furs and furbelows that it was, and he thought:

"Oh, well, let them do what they like. I shall start again!"

And so, indeed, he did. He built on his experience, pointing the structure of simpler ideas with ironic thoughts. Long before the production of "Lady Millworthy's Muff" he had completed another comedy called "One of Us" and he made up his mmd that they should either "take it or leave it. "There should be no tinkering with "One of Us."

He got Gregory Brecknock to read it one day, and the actor said:

"This is very ambitious, Arthur, dear boy, very ambitious. You might get the Stage Society, or one of these extreme stage reform people to put it on for a special matinee, but I'm afraid,—yes, I'm very much afraid that no London manager would look at it."

On that very afternoon a curious little experience happened to him. He went over to the house. Gregory Brecknock was in the drawing-room, talking to Edith. They were laughing as he walked into the room, but they left off suddenly, and an uncomfortable feeling came over him that they had been talking and laughing about him.

Edith stood up and said:

"Will you have some tea, Arthur!"

He observed the proud tilt of her chin as she walked across the room to a tray-stand, and it suddenly rushed upon him that he was jealous. He was jealous of Gregory Brecknock! Why was this actor always loafing around here? Hot on this suspicious terror came the thought:

"Well, after all, what has it to do with met What am I jealous about?"

He had his tea in a rather gloomy silence, and went back to the studio, but all the evening he kept on revolving the fact that he was jealous, and wondering what he was jealous about. He looked at Edith at dinner-time quite furtively, and the man's remark kept recurring to his mind:

"She's a damned fine woman."

He thrust this thought back. It was too ridiculous.

He started to write a third play, and some little studies of London types. He worked consistently for weeks, but at odd moments of the day he would suddenly look up from his writing tablet and ponder. Bound and round his mind would eddy strange little currents of elation, suspicion, wonder. He would brush these aside, but they would recur again.

He developed a habit of going over to the house at unexpected times to ask Edith's opinion about something, or to tell her of his plans. It was early in April when "Lady Millworthy's Muff" was produced, and on that eventful night, also, the slow dance of these dubious emotions reached their apotheosis.

He and Edith occupied a box, and other people in the theater who knew them visited them between the acts. These included Gregory Brecknock, who, moreover, stopped in the box for the whole of two acts at Edith's invitation. There had been a dinner-party before the theater, and everybody was in very high spirits, except the author. Arthur was in a strangely divided mood in which egoism and outrage struggled for supremacy.

After the first act, two young women call the "Person girls" who were friends of Brecknock, came into the box, and they all laughed and joked. Brecknock looked at Arthur's face, and laughed:

"Arthur looks like a boy caught stealing apples in an orchard" he said. "He can't make up his mind whether to bolt, or pick one more."

"It's going to be a huge success," said one of the Person girls. They were all merry, and Edith was unusually for her.

"He's horrified lest he should make some money out of it," she said.

When the lights were lowered previous to the second act, and the orchestra was playing a Hungarian dance of Dvorak's, this idea did, indeed, flash through his mind for an instant. Money! Suppose he did make money! What would he do with it? The trend of his affections switched his mind instantaneously to the bungalow at Bodiesham. He would cultivate the garden, make the place look decent. The curtain went up. The actors were at it again, strutting about, making their points, getting effective exits. He hung back in the box and glanced at Edith. He noted her lips slightly parted, and her eyes shining as she watched the movements of the players. He thought he observed Brecknock also glancing at her, rather than at the stage.

"She's a damned fine woman!"

Something stirred within him. He wanted the play to end. He hated all these people going in and out of canvas doors, and the silly laughter from the auditorium.

Before the last act Brecknock returned to his seat in the dress circle, and they were alone. For some reason or other his mind kept returning to the bungalow at Bodiesham. How cold and bleak it would look there now under the moonlight, with the creepers and grass, like cobwebs, clustering round the white building!

"This isn't the sort of thing I meant to do" he thought at random. "I don't think I'd like to spend money made out of this play on the bungalow."

Suddenly, about half-way through the act, he gripped Edith's arm.

"Come!" he said. "Let's go. I want to go."

He saw the surprised look in her eyes as they shone in the darkness.

"Go?" she whispered.

"Yes, come on! I want to go at once" he answered bruskly.

She obeyed in silence, and he helped her on with her opera-cloak. They went down the passage and out to the foyer, and hailed a cab. They rode home in dead silence, each waiting for the other to speak. When they arrived home the household had retired.

In the dining-room a bright fire was burning, and some light refreshments were placed on the sideboard. Edith was watching him, tremulously observant, and looking a little scared. He strode to the fireplace and lighted a cigarette. He puffed at it for a few seconds, and then threw it away. Suddenly he said:

"Take off your cloak!"

She looked startled, but again she obeyed. She was wearing a black dress of some shiny material that emphasized the glowing splendor of her white skin and the shape of her fine shoulders. At her breast she wore a bunch of lilies-of-the-valley.

Arthur looked at her, and searched her fiercely challenging eyes. They both breathed rapidly, without anything being said. Then he suddenly seized her arm and said hoarsely:

'What does that fellow Brecknock come hanging about for?"

He saw beneath her questioning intentness the flicker of startled surprise, and he knew by that glance that there was nothing in the affair of "that fellow Brecknock." He knew, moreover, that she would be too proud to deny it. He also knew at that instant that he had never really believed it himself. The thing was merely a tool for the medium of his expression of dominance.

"I will have you and break you!"

When before had this phrase occurred to him? She suddenly shook his hand free and started to move in the direction of her cloak, with an insolent toss of her head. In a flash he had thrown his arms round her shoulders from behind and pulled her back. She struggled, but he kissed her neck and cheek, and then twisted her round and faced her.

Her eyes were shining, but the hollows looked dark and sunken, as though she were suffering. She gasped:

"Arthur! Arthur! What are you doing!"

For answer he gripped both her arms and hurt her. He saw her wince with pain, but he still continued doing it. Then, as she shut her eyes, he crushed her to him and kissed her on the lips. He felt her body trembling against his and trying to force him back, as she cried:

"Arthur, I'm eleven yean older than you. Do you hear? I'm eleven years older!"

She kept repeating this parrot-cry desperately, as though it were the first line of her defense, while her lips remained passive to his kisses. Then he said huskily:

"I don't care; I want you. I must have you. I love you."

With ice-ax and alpenstock the explorer was already among the snow-capped peaks. The dizzy heights were scalable, if only one had courage and zeal, and the intense joy of adventure which is the prerogative of youth.

"I am eleven years older than you, Arthur. Oh, my dear!"

Suddenly her right arm was free, and she passed it over his hair and framed his face with the lily curve of it. She looked wildly into his eyes and cried:

"Oh, my dear! Oh! Oh!"

The cry was very near akin to pain as she pressed her lips to his of her own freewill. And then Edith, too, looked like a boy who has been caught stealing apples.

'Oh, what are we doing? Arthur, this is madness. Madness, I tell you!"

She was no longer Edith to him. She was some strange siren he had chased from crag to crag up the slopes of the mountain. They were alone now up there together, and beneath them was all the glory of the world.

"Madness! What is madness?" he cried. "Is the world so very sane? What is it but a place where people go in and out of doors and make each other laugh and cry? If this is madness, then the stars are mad, and the spring flowers trembling in the grass to-night beneath the moon. I never felt so strong, so virile, and so sure as now when I crush you in my arms. Kiss me again!"

She shut her eyes, as though she dare not let him see the passion that rioted within.

"Oh, Arthur, my beautiful, my beautiful!"

And up among the mountain peaks they could hear the god Pan in the valley below, blowing upon his reed the clear sweet notes of an old song he had played from immemorial times.

CHAPTER XVIII

IN SEARCH OF SENTIENT JOYS

Edith became very watchful, and her face still bore the expression of the boy who has been caught stealing apples. Before they started out on that tour of sentient joys, she looked herself squarely in the face and said: "Harden yourself to the knowledge that it won't last." And as a corollary she determined that while it lasted she would get the utmost out of it. They went to Paris, and then on to Switzerland. From Switzerland they journeyed to the Italian lakes, and then to Milan, Verona, and Venice. They stayed at Venice three weeks, and then proceeded to Florence and Sienna. From Sienna they worked their way up the Mediterranean coast to Genoa, and so through Bordighera, Mentoṇe, Nice, and back to Paris.

During this time she studied the temperamental composition of her lover with an almost morbid thoroughness. When he was gay, her heart responded like that of a young girl. When he had moods of depression, she humored him and found the way to restore him to cheerfulness. She knew when to leave him alone, when to rail him, and when to tease him. She would sit for hours in some dim church which did not interest her after the first five minutes, while he mooned all over it and made notes. She would let him go for long walks by himself, while she sat in the hotel and busied herself with her fingers. In the meantime, she took on her shoulders all the unpleasant side of traveling. She bought the railway tickets, looked after the luggage, interviewed hotel managers, selected the rooms, coped with couriers and touts. When the little things went wrong, it was she who kept her head and soothed his peevishness. And she said to herself:

"This is the crowded hour of my life. When the illusion has vanished, a day will come filled with little emptinesses, and he will fall in love."

It was at Bellagio, in the garden of the hotel overlooking the lake, on a seat under a cactus-tree, that she talked to him about her first marriage.

"I was eighteen, and my mother wished it. That is really all. I loved my mother, and I was brought up with an almost Chinese reverence for parentage and duty. I did as I was told. And, in his way, I believe Robert loved me. He was always fond of me to the very end. Do not be deceived. I knew quite well the sort of life he lived. I knew he was what they call 'a man of the world,' which usually means a man who keeps his excesses out of the public gaze. He was a clever num. His people came from Bristol, where they thought a lot of him. It was my idea to go to London. I was ambitious, and so was he. He worked very hard, and I helped him. At least, I did a lot to help his career. We were married for five years before I discovered the thing that was destined to destroy him."

"What was that?" Arthur asked.

"Drink."

"Drink? Do you mean to say Yardley drank, as well as—"

"It began, I believe, in a very usual way. He worked too hard, got tired, and took a 'pick-me-up.' Gradually this developed into the old business of nip, nip, nip. I struggled with him for years, and tried to make him give it up. Again and again he promised, and again and again he broke his promise. Perhaps, if I'd really loved him, I would have been more desperate. But I felt my first duty was to the children. I took them down to Bradehurst. We practically drifted apart, except that for appearance sake he came down sometimes."

"But this is ghastly" Arthur remarked. "I used to like old Yardley."

"I know. So did almost everyone. He was very kind, sympathetic, gentle. The remarkable thing is, it did not affect his brain. If he had lived longer, perhaps it would. But men have told me that he had one of the cleverest and most lucid brains in London. And, for my part, I never knew him to lose his head. He was never once cruel to me, never unkind. As far as I can remember, he never spoke an unkind word to me, or acted against my inclinations. And before I went to Bradehurst, I knew of occasions when he would drink a whole bottle of brandy during the afternoon and evening. Is n't it incredible! I believe there are other men like that. The tragedy is, I could not pity him. I tried hard. I felt withered, frigid, unresponsive. I tried to shut it all out of my mind and to concentrate on the bringing up of the children."

"If you had loved him, you might have saved him" Arthur said suddenly.

"I know. But one can't make oneself love, dear. And when I found out what was happening, every vestige of love in me dried up. I shut him out of my life. As you know, he came down sometimes in the evening, or for week-ends. He had his own room. And I would not allow alcohol in the house. "

The boy thought for a moment, and then he gripped her hand and muttered:

"Hell!"

He did not seem entirely satisfied with Edith's attitude in the matter. He peered down into the waters of the lake reflecting the pale moon. Somewhere in the distance a bell was tinkling.

"It must have been awful for him" he said at last.

She put up her hand and touched his cheek.

"Arthur, you're not angry with me for this? You don't think I ought to hav—"

He could see a tear gathering on the brink of her eye, and he kissed it away.

"It's awfully hard for everyone" he murmured. "Everything's very difficult. The older I grow, the more difficult everything seems. And love—I mean love like ours—is, perhaps, the greatest tyrant of all."

She pressed her cheek against his, and said:

"O Arthur, there's surely nothing greater, nothing finer than this love of ours."

He did not answer. She looked at his eyes, and forced him to speak by the appeal of her glance. And he answered:

"No, no; I know. But I was thinking of that other love at the moment; the love of the big thing, the size of love for the unhappy, the downtrodden."

She gripped his hand and said:

"Do you know when I first loved you J It was on the day of your father's death. I loved you because you were unhappy. I loved you for your baby helplessness, and because I knew you couldn't manage without me. And then I loved you because you hurt me when you were cruel to me. You became a part of me, and I wanted you all the time. O my beautiful!"

It was under the shadow of Santa della Salute in Venice, on a violet night, with the ripples lapping the sides of the gondola, that they spoke of the future. In the distance some full-throated tenor was singing at the serenata, "abominably when you're near, but divinely across a hundred yards of water" as Arthur put it. Edith spoke of his career.

"I want you to express yourself, Arthur, as your friend Mr. Leffbury said. I know exactly what you feel about the play. I'm not going to let you get depressed because you find things not exactly as you dreamed them. There'll be no need to worry about money. You shall do exactly as you like, write what you like, say what you like. No one shall interfere, and if they won't accept your plays as you have written them at first, they 'll have to in the long run. And gradually you 'll find out exactly what you can do, and the best way to do it. I suppose you 'll think it wicked of me, but—"

"What could I think wicked of you?"

"Only that I am ambitious for you. I want you to be a great man, some one talked about and looked up to, a great influence, a force in public life. I know you have it in you."

He had already tasted a little of the sweets of success. He had moved among successful people. And this woman with her quiet power had led him by the hand, and, in her way, had shown him "all the glories of the world."

Intoxicating sounds stole across the water. The mantle of stars gleamed overhead with a special significance for them, as it had gleamed with a special significance in a kindred clime to Troilus and Cressida, and as it was gleaming with a special significance to a pornographic, German, honeymoon couple in a gondola a dozen yards away.

He kissed her chin and murmured:

"I'd like to be something, for your sake. Do you hear? For your sake. Just for you, and because you've made the beauty of this night for me; because you've taught me to love. For my own part, I don't know. As I wander about Italy, I think a lot about old Leffbury and the things he said. What did he mean by, 'Don't be mesmerized by nature'? I went into St. Mark's this afternoon. I didn't like it at first, but it grows on you. It's so damned savage and domineering, such an aristocrat. It lie there on the piazza like some great savage beast, suggesting centuries of murder, piracy, and tyranny, with a splendid bombastic insolence. Then you push aside the great curtain, and go in out of the sun. Directly you get inside, an unaccountable wave of tenderness comes over you. All the cruelty and tyranny seems mellowed, as though something has happened to purify these things. This afternoon there were some women there in their black shawls, and with their market-baskets. They were kneeling in front of the altar of St. Aloysius counting their beads. I felt curiously envious. I knelt down and wished I knew how to pray. I wished I weren't so sophisticated, so 'superior.' I wanted to be absorbed in the Great Thing, whatever it was. And then, when one has that feeling, all these things like careers and success seem so trivial It's only love that matters, love in the big way." They were silent; then she said breathlessly: "Arthur, you love me in the big way?" For answer he kissed her lips.

It was in Sienna that he began to get restless and wanted to return home.

"I am beginning to get the conscious-tourist feeling" he said. "This is no place for pottering about, doing little bits of sketches. One wants to absorb it. It has the face of perpetuity. I am always feeling self-conscious when these native people stare at me. Lazy devils they are for the most part, but they are all doing something. They're part of the scheme. They blend into it. All we tourists who go gaping about open-mouthed,—we're just an excrescence on the thing. Leffbury said,' When you go to Italy, express yourself,' There's a lot in that, for what else is there in Italy to express? When I had been round the cathedral and this extraordinary market-square, and seen those amazing early Siennese masters' paintings, I realized that I had nothing to say about it at all. It is all fixed and finished. I could never say anything in paint more valuable than what Cimabue has said, so why waste one's time? These old boys were successful because in their day they were modems. They did something with the age they lived in. I am a modem. I want to get back to London, with all its sins, and vices, and ugliness, and beauty, and mystery, and do something with that."

And then he added, "I don't know how it is. Italy is very fine, but it's not quite so fine as I expected."

In Rapallo there came to Edith one of the dreaded days, one of the days of "little emptinesses." And she could not account for it Something seemed to have suddenly shifted. There was no quarrel, no outward difference; only the sudden little consciousness of empty moments. The sun shone gloriously on their first vision of the Mediterranean, and the little white villas were spotted about enticingly among the pine hills. Fishing boats drifted lazily in and out of the bay. It was an ideal place for repose, an ideal place for lovers. But something was grimly incomplete. There was a restlessness. Like a good general, Edith acted promptly.

''Let us go on to Genoa" she said.

They arrived in Genoa, and the weather was very hot. There was a lot of trouble with the town customs and some railway officials who wanted to take the luggage away to examine it at their leisure. Edith, with her rather scanty Italian and her best Shropshire-Gaffyn manner, managed to force her way through. But Genoa was not a success. They stayed at a bad hotel that was rather dirty, and there were no mosquito-nets in the bedroom. They slept badly, and the boy was inclined to be quarrelsome.

They cut the sights of Genoa and went straight on.

They arrived at Mentone with a feeling of relief. France was like home. But when they got to their hotel, they found that a bag of Arthur's which contained his sketching things was missing. It had probably never got beyond the notorious officials at Genoa. Arthur was in a state of furious despair, and he cursed the whole Italian nation luxuriously. The next day Edith said she would see what she could do. She sent Arthur for a walk, and then returned to Genoa by herself, from which town she sent him a telegram that she could not get back that night. She was away two days, and then returned with the bag, to find her lover in a state of maudlin apprehension. He kissed her and said he had been a cad, and they had a long and passionate reconciliation. Edith did not give him time to let this cool; they went on to Nice, where he seemed to want to stop for a bit, but like a skilful driver of a horse that has bolted, she drove him on. They were in Paris the next morning, and in London the following day.

Arthur found his studio ready for him, and several letters and statements from Mr. Montague Beale. "Lady Millworthy's Muff" was continuing a great success. Two companies were on the road, and a manager in New York was negotiating for the American rights.

While he had been finding "nothing to express" in Italy, the rolling-stone of "Lady Millworthy's Muff" had been gathering moss for him in England.

CHAPTER XIX

THE FUGITIVE PHILOSOPHER

The impulse which came to Arthur to write "The Fugitive Philosopher" was, to a certain extent, a reactionary impulse from that of writing "Lady Millworthy's Muff." The book was, in effect, a series of essays, which it took him the best part of a year to compile. He came back from Italy full of ideas, despite the fact that he found something lacking in Italy, and the medium of commentary appealed to him at the time as the best one for their expression. It was, moreover, extraordinarily satisfying to receive definite financial offers for another play, and to refuse them. It appealed to his vanity, and it also appealed to another quality in him which was, indeed, the underlying motif of "The Fugitive Philosopher." For the underlying motif of "The Fugitive Philosopher" was to reveal various phases of human life, and to detach from them what was spiritual, and what was material. They were less essays than sketches of various substantive types which moved, or spoke, or came in conflict, and thereby lent point to the discriminating researches of "The Fugitive Philosopher," He was, indeed, a very pleasant, easy-going gentleman, a little vague and somewhat unpractical; and he rode, tilting at these social windmills with a chivalrous inconsequence. He was very, very fugitive, but somehow lovable. He dashed from one point to another, finding beauty in unexpected places, happiness in squalor, love "in the big way" in the breast of a harlot, insincerity in the gaiters of a bishop, solemn nonsense in the pomp of royalty, hollowness in the chink of gold, glimpses of divinity in the heart of the sensualist, joy in suffering, sentimentality in a scheming politician,—and through all things an unerring belief in ultimate good.

These commentaries were undoubtedly the best and most sincere work Arthur ever accomplished. He put the best of himself into them, and some of them appeared separately in the better-class reviews.

In the meantime, life in the house in St. John's Wood moved to the throb of a steady pulse. Arthur, in his way, was happy, and Edith was drawing all the enchantment possible from her "crowded hour." They entertained, and the people who visited them gradually evolved from the theatrical type to a more polyglot species. Soon after their return. Aunt Elizabeth, who had never recovered from the staggering surprise of their marriage, and who only tolerated it on the conviction that "they say that marriages are made in Heaven; Edith ought to know!" visited them.

But by that time the sensation of the thing had been somewhat dwarfed by an even more startling development in her own house, for Eleanor had become engaged to a schoolmaster, a young sandy-haired north-countryman named Burnett.

"They say he's very clever, and will probably soon get an appointment as inspector. Of course they won't get married just yet, dear. But Eleanor's very happy. At least, she ought to be, I'm sure. She's thinner than she used to be. I don't know how it is. They say she drinks too much hot water. It's lowering to the system. He's given her a very pretty emerald ring with two sapphires. It must have cost a good deal."

She turned her attention to Arthur:

"Well, are you going to write another play, Arthur! I must say I was surprised to hear what a success it had been. I can't think how you can have thought of it all. They say you 'll make a lot of money out of it. It seems funny you're making money! I always put you down as one of the Uncle Brian kind. Well, well, dear, I'm very glad for your sake. I expect Edith helped you, didn't she? I nearly died when he put the muff on his head; very funny I call it. They say some of the playwrights make a lot of money. How proud your dear father would have been!"

Hence the fugitive philosopher!

On the proposal of Gregory Brecknock he was elected a member of "The Old Guys" club, and despite the serious call he felt toward the new line of his work, he could not always remain impervious to the appeal of the glamorous life. It was very pleasant occasionally to stroll into "The Old Guys" and to talk and be called "dear boy" by well-known actors, and to drink whisky and exchange views with clever people. And sometimes he would hear people nudge each other and say, "Who is that!" and the answer would be, "That's young Arthur Gaffyn, who wrote Lady Millworthy." Alas I he wished it could have been a more worthy fame. But he promised himself that a day should come when the sufficient answer would be:

"Why, don't you know? That's Gaffyn!"

it was pleasant in "The Old Guys" and it was even pleasanter in certain drawing-rooms when pretty women would come up, take his hand and say:

"Oh, Mr. Gaffyn, I simply loved your play."

And everybody said:

'"Of course you're writing another play. When will it be ready?"

He steadied himself against these allurements, and looked to Edith for support.

"One of Us" was submitted to several managers' readers, but they all rejected it, although one suggested that if certain alterations were made, it might be reconsidered. Arthur refused to do this, and went on with his commentaries. He left "One of Us" in Edith's hands to do what she liked with. She did, indeed, eventually succeed in getting it produced at a special mating by the Prompt Side Club, but it was badly staged and mercilessly slated by the press, who condemned it as dull and "not likely to advance the reputation of the author of 'Lady Millworthy's Muff.'"

Regularly every month he received long letters from Hales, who had returned to California. They were remarkable letters, sometimes covering twenty or thirty pages. They touched on every conceivable subject, and as they were not very legibly written, it is to be regretted that Arthur often skipped a good deal of them. Especially was this true when he talked on philosophy and American politics. Arthur dived among the pages for any news of Hales himself, or of Alice, or her mother, or of their prospective movements. Soon after his marriage he received a characteristic letter from his friend, fall of warm-hearted congratulations and a sentimental effusion on the state of matrimony. He had added, incidentally, that the affair had broken Alice's heart, and that she was trying to kill herself by eating excessively of watermelons. They all, however, sent their love, and a small present was on the way.

The reference to Alice stirred up old half -forgotten longings. He could not exactly define to himself what they were. Only that when the far-flung line of his emotions sought the satisfying hour, he could not find that any moment was so complete, so fine a thing as that moment when he had stood by the child's side in the Luxembourg Gardens and gazed up at the kite. What was it! He could not love the child in the way he loved Edith; she was too young, not to be considered in that way at all. Perhaps there was something about her he envied, that she alone possessed, the stuff of absolute purity and youth. He was still young, but not in the way that she was young. He had been soiled, made cynical, coarsened. He had lost that outlook of the child-mind. If he could only have a child like Alice; but he knew that such a thing was more than unlikely. And he had moments of restless envy. Envy of Alice! She would one day meet a boy like herself, pure, and with the eyes of a child. Ah! What was all this talk of art, and success, and fame? What compensation could it be for the glory of one such moment missed? He was jealous of the youth who would one day love Alice. He knew it was a wild and unreasonable emotion, but it created images and visions which at odd moments crept into his dreams and made "the little emptinesses" that, by a telepathic process, were conveyed to his wife.

More particularly was this the case when the days were fine, and when that first tender warmth heralded spring. He was happiest when the weather was murky and dull. He could have the log-fire burning in his studio, and he could pore over his work. And in the evening there was light, and warmth, and entertainment, and artificial things that satisfied his moods.

In the following August he, and Edith, and the children went down to Devonshire, where they stayed for six weeks at a small house in a fishing village called Freshingley. At this time the eldest girl, whose name was Mildred, was eleven; the second girl, Phyllis, was nine; while the boy, Martin, was eight.

These children, like the majority of children, were at their best at the seaside, and Arthur made a further effort to get on with them. They amused him at times, and he liked to watch them bathing, and shared in their wild joy of revel in the sea and sun. But between them there was always a barrier of distrust. They could not exactly see the point of him, and he felt that they were only polite to him because Edith urged them to be.

They called him "Arthur" and made no attempt to conceal their opinion that he was a rather unnecessary addition to the family. Mildred, who was an extraordinarily quick and intelligent child, gave promise of resembling her mother, but unfortunately she emphasized some of her mother's worst qualities.

As at one time in his life Arthur was prejudiced against a girl, because she was reminiscent of her mother, so it is to be regretted that now he was attacked by shafts of prejudice against a mother, because she was reminiscent of her daughter. He was not by any means aware of this. It was one of these sub-conscious processes which affect us all. He was still convinced that he loved his wife dearly, and that everything was for the best in this best of all possible worlds.

When the moods of restlessness came to him, he persuaded himself that he was out of sorts, or that there was some specific reason for them.

It was not till the last week of their stay in Devonshire that the first canker of real doubt crept into his soul.

One evening he and Edith went for a stroll alone up to the top of Burness Common, which is on the edge of a moor two miles from Freshingley. It was a perfect day, with an almost cloudless sky, and the sun began to set "in the grand manner" as it does occasionally at that time of year.

They sat on a fiat slab of stone which local report described as a relict of the Druids. All around them were low scrub and blackberry bushes, and the air was heavy with the scent of gorse. Little sheep-bells tinkled pleasantly in the near distance, and in the garden of an old cottage a hundred yards away, a man was cutting the lawn.

During the afternoon Arthur had been reading "Paolo and Prancesca" and he wanted to talk about it, but he discovered on the way up that Edith had not read it. He was not particularly surprised at this, but unreasonably disappointed. He talked about the book a little, and about ideals, and then suddenly, when the sun began to set, he felt a great desire for silence. He took her hand and they watched the slow march of the golden light flooding from the west. Everything seemed to become more vivid and significant, and the birds sang above them as if in praise of this wonderful system of gradations that lashed the horizon blood-red, and left the sky overhead the palest topaz; and the bees were making a last desperate effort to snatch the produce of the dying son.

"The time, and the place, and the loved one all to-gether."

The boy sat there with the strings of his heart atoned to this majestic phrase, when Edith said:

"The tints are simply perfect, aren't they?"

It is difficult to know what it is about a word that makes it have the effect of shattering an illusion. A word can, at its best, express but little, yet it can at times give the index to a quality of thought.

Tints! Poor Edith! Perhaps, if she had lived long enough among artists, she would have known that they don't use the word "tint. "It is certain that if she had known the effect the word would have on her irrational beloved, she would not have used it. He started visibly, and then pulled himself together. After all, why should Edith—? At the same time, to talk about "tints" means that you don't appreciate values. "Tints" is a ridiculously trivial word to use in connection with a sunset. Old ladies at sketching classes talk about "tints. "As a word it has no dignity, no majesty, no real beauty; it is a superficial thing. It meant that she di n't feel the sunset in the way he did. And immediately the string became slightly out of tune.

"The time, and the place, and—a vacuum!"

Such are the little things that mark the milestones of our journey, as we go haltingly down the hill when the sun has set

In town once more, the physical effects of the holiday reacted on "The Fugitive Philosopher." He set to work with a willy and drowned the whispers of these unfulfilled longings in the rhetorical outpourings of the gay iconoclast He hammered away at the white-hot metal of his evolutionary ideas, and tried to forge a constructive thesis. He hit out right and left among the social idols, and succeeded in one or two cases in bringing upon himself both opprobrium and praise. An eminent magazine accepted and published three of the commentaries, and one which was called "The Fairway of the Styx" and which described the nugatory movement of a certain press syndicate which, by keeping in mid-channel, never reached either shore, led to a certain amount of discussion. And other people made their appearance at Edith's hospitable board,—critics and editors, and even a well-known publisher.

The great psychological difference between Edith and Arthur centered round that word "ambition." Edith could not help being ambitious in the worldly sense; it was ingrained in her. She could not see the point of doing a thing unless you were a success at it. You should take your place and be recognized as a great exponent of whatever yon were doing. With her keen, practical mind, and her instinct for managing and organizing, she identified herself with Arthur's work, and automatically pushed it forward. Arthur did not know one-tenth of the things she did to get him talked about and famous.

The boy fundamentally had none of this ambition. Or if he had, it was an external thing that he assumed on the nights when he went into "The Old Guys" or similar places. In his heart he despised it in the same way that he despised himself if he drank too much, or made "calves' eyes" at pretty actresses, or lost his temper and behaved cruelly to his wife. All these things he did, and they had their reaction; and then he sighed and "fought his way back. "

But underneath it all was the other thing, the great restlessness, the vague desire for interpretation of the motive of "love in the big way"

One morning he found an envelope on his desk. It was addressed in unknown writing. He opened it and discovered a page cut from a journal called "The Whispering Gallery."

"The Whispering Gallery" was one of those wretched parasites of the press which eke out their miserable existence almost exclusively through innuendo.

There were several pages of short paragraphs which were heralded with the prefix: "Surely It Cannot Be True That—"

One of these ran:

"The author of a successful play now running in London, and who is married to a lady whose first husband died 'in regrettable circumstances,' was expelled from school for stealing!'

CHAPTER XX

AN AFFAIR IN "THE OLD GUYS"

Arthur's first instinct on reading this paragraph was to cry out: "The cads!"

His second instinct was to rush off and fight some one; it was essentially an affair of bloodletting. His third instinct was to show it to Edith; and then he began to reflect. After all, it would do no good to show it to Edith. He had never told her about the affair of the pearl-handled penknife; in fact, he had almost forgotten about it. How incredible it was after all these years! Nearly eleven years, and then suddenly the thing is thrown in one's teeth! How despicable! What good can it do anyone to dish up a thing like that? Who could have done it? One of the boys, probably, who was there at the same time and who was now clinging to the lowest rung of the journalistic ladder,—probably a much bigger blackguard than he was himself I

For of course he was a blackguard. In the light of his present mental outlook it was, in any case, a foolish thing to do. And yet even now he didn't know that he viewed it as a criminal act. He supposed he had a "kink"; it might be called his property kink. "He could n't get the hang of the property business. What, after all, was property? How was it gained? Property was a dead thing, and the gain of it was entirely fortuitous. If property were a symbol of something noble, and if people were rewarded with property for doing fine and noble things, he could understand something of the awe with which it was treated. How did people make money! They either inherited it, or they acquired it by cunning and rapacity, by the exercise of their superior gift of "dealing" with their less nimble-minded fellow-creatures. The simple, reverent person "earned his living" but the huckster, the adventurer, the exploiter, "made money. "He thought of the salesmen at Blinkinshaw's, and of "Lady Millworthy's Muff." It was all nonsense, disgusting. The worst things in life were rewarded with property, and the harder people struggled for property, the more vicious they became. "Carrion crows fighting over a corpse" he thought. And then, "In the end they 'll destroy themselves." He felt a tremendous desire to discuss this with some one, to find some one with whom to share his righteous indignation. Edith? The more he thought of it, the more impossible it seemed to talk about it to Edith. She would n't understand. He could n't explain to her about the penknife. He could almost envisage her slightly startled glance, and her involuntary shrinking back as she said: "But surely, Arthur, you didn't really steal—" His memory reverted to a paragraph he had read in a newspaper the previous week. It was a Sunday paper which reproduced every week a few paragraphs from its edition of ninety years ago. He had read an account of a boy of nineteen being hanged in public at Newgate for stealing three shillings from his master, a cutler in Cheapside. Ninety years ago! It occurred to him at the time as being horrible, but he had not thought of it in connection with himself. Now he did. The penknife was worth at least twenty-five or thirty shillings. At the present moment, if this law still held good, he would be liable to hang! He might have been hanged by the neck in public for stealing a penknife! What was the difference? There was no difference between that boy and himself. The only difference was in the social attitude toward them. In this way, then, people were advancing. Property was, perhaps, less sacred. And so a time would come—If it were less and less of an offense to take property perhaps one day there would come the realization that all property was illusory "objective phenomena."

He became quite elated when this idea occurred to him. An irresistible desire again came to him to talk to some one. He went slowly across into the house. There was a little writing-room on the ground floor where Edith often worked in the morning. She had a desk there, and a lot of files and books. He went in stealthily. She was not there. He glanced at a small pile of letters on the desk, which she had opened and put together neatly. For some reason he felt he must glance at her letters, and he did so. The third one was an envelope identical with the one he had received containing the cutting. He picked it up. It was empty.

So Edith knew; she had taken it away. He looked hurriedly in the waste-basket. There was no sign of "The Whispering Gallery."

He felt strangely alarmed, and yet defiant. Then he heard her coming downstairs. He was conscious at that moment of a somewhat similar feeling to that which had assailed him when he was waiting outside "the Book's" study. He walked deliberately out into the passage.

When Edith saw him she said:

"Hullo, dear; do you want me!"

He looked at her keenly, and answered:

'No. I'm just looking for a thesaurus I left somewhere."

She said:

"Oh, I 'll just have a look for you."

She entered the morning-room, and they both poked about in comers, looking for a book which both knew was not there. He wanted to talk to her, but was tongue-tied. He thought her eyes looked strained, and the pupils seemed smaller, as though she were trying to focus something beyond her normal vision. He said, after a time:

"Perhaps it 's out at the back after all. I 'll have another look."

She said:

"I 'll look in the dining-room."

He followed her there, hoping that the barrier between them might come crashing down, and that he could tell her what he wanted to. They made a ridiculous and abortive search in most of the rooms of the house. Sometimes he came near her, and felt tempted to throw his arms round her and make her weep with him. But just when the temptation was strongest, she would look up at him again with her narrowing eyes.

He went at last, and she followed him over the way.

He found the thesaurus on his own desk where he had been working. At least Edith saw it first, and pointed to it and said:

"Well, you are a funny boy!" and she attempted to smile. But the smile seemed forced and hard. He watched her leave the studio, neither of them speaking.

When the door had shut, he looked at it for a long time, and then buried his head in his hands. He wanted to think the whole thing out clearly. The dominant thought that impressed him was that it was silly, silly and trivial; and yet likely in some way to have fateful consequences. He did n't know what these consequences would be, but he felt that they would assert themselves in some dramatic and uncomfortable way. Perhaps the case would be dished up in the courts. He would have to appear in a libel suit. All sorts of things might happen and be said. But even more disturbing was the effect the paragraph was likely to have upon his relationship with Edith; in fact, the effect it had already had. It was an insuperable barrier. Whether they agreed to say nothing about it, or whether they agreed to discuss it, there would always be that indefinable mental residuum.

His mind went back to his school-boy days when he had visualized himself in a detached way, as a boy hounded through life by the unbreakable verdict of the law, the schoolmasters, the judges, the police, the army and navy, and all the other disciplined forces of society. He felt lonely and wretched. At one time it was as though Edith had detached herself from these forces, and was willing to fight for him tooth and nail. And he knew she would be willing to do this now, in an external sense.

Her opposition would be passive, rather than active. She would fight for him because she would believe it was her duty to do so, and also because she loved him. But it would be a championship vaguely unsatisfying. There were things about him she did not grasp, and things about her he grasped too clearly.

The room seemed dark, and empty, and silent, and he sat there listening to the crackling of the fire.

Suddenly the dark places of his mind were lighted by the inspiring gleam of recollection. It was a spring day, and the little white clouds were scudding before the warm breeze. A child was looking up at the sky and saying:

"People are silly and bad, and they want helping."

Here was, indeed, the ultimate solution. There was no mis-judgment here, no carping criticism, no vague doubts or suspicions. The mere fact that people were silly, meant that they wanted helping. The mere fact that they were bad, meant that they wanted helping. There was no other standard. It was final. You must not hang people for being bad, you must help them. When would these forces of righteousness realize this childish truth? "Love in the big way."

When would they realize that the human soul is more sacred than property! Property! Property l Property l This dead thing that we had made with our hands was now our master. We walked the dear earth, with our hands and feet chained, while the iron God drove us forward with a whip. While we went about our daily work, property was scheming and arranging our future. Nay, more than that, in many a secret chamber in Europe he was whispering and making silent compacts. He was arranging the destruction of unborn children for the satiation of his lust for gold. While we were wanting love and the things of beauty, he was breeding hate, suspicion, jealousy, and envy. He was forging more chains for our feet, more armour for our bodies to wear, more morasses of material difficulties for us to cross. Property made the laws, fixed the customs, ruled the state with a rod of iron, controlled the church, and flung doles of charity in the face of the dangerous poor.

Tick-tick-dot-dot-dash-dash-dash! He thought of that night he passed the newspaper printing plant on New Year's Eve. What was going on behind all this? Plot and counter-plot. What had property in store for the ultimate solution? Was it not more likely that suddenly the heart of man would revolt against the iron God? Then would come the greatest struggle of all.

''For a man to struggle against property" thought Arthur, "is like a naked person with an umbrella fighting a giant in armour and a broad sword. Well, what could he do? The only thing to do would be to run away and breed more men with more umbrellas. And then one day they would return. They would swarm round the man in armour and attack him. A lot of them would be killed, but at last one of them would be able to poke his umbrella into the giant's eye, and then the giant would fall over. And when they had him on the ground they would jump on him, and eventually get hold of his sword, and stick it into him between the joints of his armour.

"Yes" he thought after reflection. "That would be the greatest joy of all, to kill him with his own sword. "

He tried to settle down to work, but it was impossible. He took his hat and went out. He wandered up to the top of Hampstead Heath. A fine rain was falling, but he did not seem conscious of it. He only became intensely aware of large and imposing houses, and automobiles, and policemen. The army of righteousness! He went right across the heath, and then southward. He made his way to Camden Town, and Kentish Town, and passed through districts of congested squalor. The words of "the Book" recurred to him:

"If you will steal, you will do other things. You are the most dangerous type to have in a school; you have ability, and no moral bias."

It was untrue; he had moral bias. It was toward love, which is the only true morality there is. Love, which was as virile in Camden Town as in the mansions on Hampstead Heath. But property would take no account of love, except the love it could buy. Honesty> sobriety, and chastity—these were the virtues that property admired and encouraged. Property had no objection to drinking to excess in his own home, to being brutal and bestial to his wife in the secrecy of his own chamber, to bringing off a brilliant "scoop" in the city by some involved transaction that, performed in a meaner manner, would land him in the police court; but property was very strict when it came to the actions of his dependents.

And so with cynical insolence he drew up a table of moral values. Such and such a fine for drunkenness in public, so many months' imprisonment for interfering with his property, so many thousand pounds for interfering with his wife.

''Think of it" Arthur said to himself. "You can buy an umbrella for ten-and-sixpence, and the virtue of a woman for a similar amount."

Umbrellas kept running through his head that day, probably because it was raining, and he had none.

"You can buy the virtue of any woman who is agreeable for quite a small sum, providing she does not belong to Mr. Property. Then she becomes very, very Expensive. It is exactly the same table, only much more expensive. He has no other way of looking at it than through pounds, shillings, and pence."

In the Euston Road a young girl passed him, with dark rims round her eyes. She passed very slowly, and said something.

He did not stop, but he muttered to himself:

"I could take you, my dear, take you and hurt you terribly. I could even destroy you in an indirect and horrible fashion, and Mr. Property would not mind. You don't come within the iron circle of his rules. Although I have 'no moral bias,' I could love you. Do you understand? I could love you in the big way. I could be your friend and help you, simply because you want help. I think Alice would help you, too. She understands these things. I don't know whether she would call you silly or bad. Silly, I should think, but in any case it would be sufficient that in your heart you were unhappy. Something in her would stretch out to meet something in you."

He found himself near Charing Cross, and he was feeling tired and hungry. He went into a restaurant and ordered some food. While they were bringing it, he recollected that it was Saturday night, the night of "The Old Guys. "

He sat a long time after his meal, thinking and rolling cigarettes. Then he had a whisky and soda, and strolled across to the Adelphi.

When he entered the club he heard the low roar of conversation and the occasional popping of corks. He hung up his hat and coat, and entered the dub-room. There was the same crowd, and the air was thick with tobacco-smoke. A famous Belgian cellist was talking French to a small group of men he did not know. He strolled past them. One or two men nodded to him, and he found Gregory Brecknock talking to two other actors. As he approached them he thought he detected a slight interchange of comment, and the conversation seemed to shift its ground. Their faces looked shiny in the white light, and the skin was drawn tightly across their cheek-bones. Brecknock said in his well-modulated voice:

"Well, dear boy, how's the wife?"

Arthur said:

"All right, thanks."

He stood on the fringe of the group, smoking. The actors continued their conversation, but somehow they did not seem anxious to draw him into it. He wandered away and talked to other men. In the further room Lee Chadde, the comedian, was howling a comic song, and he could hear the roars of laughter greeting the "points." He stood near the doorway and thought to himself:

"Several of these men have seen the paragraph; I can tell by their manner. They look at me and their eyes narrow in the same way Edith's did. There's that old swine, Carraway; he's nearly drunk already. I believe he was whispering about me just now to that other man. He sends companies on tour. He's rolling in money. They say he seduces the girls in his chorus; it's one of the stipulations. They think it's rather 'amusing' here. They call him an 'old character.' They don't mind that about him. At least, it isn't 'they'; it's property. But they look at me like an unclean thing. They're in a perfect terror lest I might go and 'pinch' one of their umbrellas. Well, let them go to blazes! I'm going to have a drink."

He drank several whisky and sodas and felt an insolent indifference to the crowd. He talked to Campbell, the dramatic critic of "The Bird's-eye View" and contradicted him about his opinion on Shaw. He argued with old Wybourg about industrialism, and tweaked a gentleman named Tylor about his melancholy outlook concerning the stage. But all the time there was stirring within him a simmering hatred toward Carraway. His eyes kept roving towards the fat, flabby face of the theatrical manager, and nearly every time he looked, he noticed Carraway glancing furtively in his direction. He was, moreover, whispering to people in thick whispers. Arthur became convinced that Carraway was talking about him and quoting the paragraph.

The old Adam of violence spoke through his veins. It was nearly midnight when one of those unfortunate scenes which are of such rare occurrence in a gentlemen's dub took place in "The Old Guys." Arthur was not exactly drunk, but he had had enough whisky to give him a perverse and ill-proportioned sense of things. He fumbled his way through the crowd till he was right opposite Carraway, and he looked straight at him.

Carraway leered superciliously and suddenly said in his guttural voice:

"Oh, Gaffyn, let me introduce you to my friends, Mr. —"

And then Arthur looked at Carraway insolently from his eyes to his boots, and deliberately turned his back on the three of them. He suddenly felt a heavy nudge in his back, and turning round beheld Carraway's malevolent face thrust close to his. He said with a low growl:

"I'd like to know what the devil you mean by that?"

And Arthur pushed by him and answered:

"Oh, you go to hell!"

And then the preposterous affair rapidly reached its climax. He felt his face suddenly splashed with the contents of a glass, and he turned and slapped the flabby cheeks of Carraway with the full force of his open hand. Then the commotion began. Carraway rushed at him like a bull, but this was the thing Arthur had been looking forward to for nearly two hours. He ducked and brought his left up with a snap to Carraway's jaw, and rejoiced that he had learned something of this game from "old Moll" at Cullington. The fight was not allowed to proceed beyond the exchange of two or three blows before the crowd of men separated them, with cries of: "Hello! What's all this! Steady! Steady!" But to Arthur's delight, he was aware of having got in a really good "left" to Carraway's fat cheek, high up, quite sufficient to result in a pretty useful black eye. The noise became deafening, and two groups surrounded the two men, while the secretary and two older members of the committee were calling out:

"Order, please, gentlemen! No fighting here. Keep them apart. Order! order!"

Arthur found himself rounded up and pushed out of the room, but before he had reached the hall he heard the voice of Carraway bawling out:

"He's a dirty thief!"

In the vestibule of the club, the secretary, who was accompanied by Brecknock, came bustling up and said:

"What's all this about, Gaffyn?"

And Arthur, with the school-boy spirit still strong in him, answered:

"He cheeked me."

There was a great noise of talking all around him, but he thought he heard the secretary mutter:

"Well, well, we shall have to make an inquiry about this."

He went out into the air, feeling strangely calmed. It had been a soothing and satisfactory termination to a restless day. He walked all the way back to St. John's Wood, and did not realize till nearly home that his clothes were almost wet through. He let himself in, and as usual found Edith waiting up for him. She came out into the hall and, he thought, kissed him rather feverishly. Then she put her hand to her head and said:

"I think I 'll go straight up, dear. I have rather a bad head."

He answered quietly:

"Oh. I'm sorry. You shouldn't have waited up. "

She said:

"Why, of course. I could n't go to bed till you came in. You 'll find anything you want in the dining-room."

She started to go slowly up the stairs, when Arthur said:

"I 've been to 'The Old Guys,' I 've handed in my resignation."

He said this, partly because he wanted her to know, and partly because he wanted to see her eyes. She stopped abruptly and looked down at him.

"Have you? Why?"

He answered nonchalantly:

"Oh, I don't know. I think they're rather a lot of bounders."

She looked at him questioningly, and he noticed that her eyes had not altered since the morning, except that they appeared more strained and tired. He said:

"Good-night."

And she answered faintly, and walked hesitatingly up the stairs.

CHAPTER XXI

Whether it is true, dear boy, or it isn't true. If it is true,—well, there's nothing more to "be said. If it isn't true, I'm afraid it's up to you to start a libel action."

Gregory Brecknock walked up and down in Arthur's studio, with short, deliberate steps. He was obviously concerned. Arthur lolled back in his swivel chair, and chewed the -end of a pen. At last he said:

"What do you mean precisely by 'there's nothing more to be said'!"

Brecknock shrugged his shoulders:

"Well, really, dear boy, it simply amounts to the fact that the thing must take its course. The paragraph was produced at the committee-meeting of the club. There isn't the slightest doubt in the mind of any member that it refers to you; although no one, mind you, believes that it is true. The committee simply feels that it is due to the honor of the club, and to the unfortunate publicity that the affair has gained, that you should force 'The Whispering Gallery' to apologize, or sue them for libel. If you do this, Carraway has promised to make an amende honorable, but if you won't, he threatens all sorts of things. He's very annoyed, and his left eye is a perfect gem of colour."

"Well, I 'll tell you; it is true."

''I don't believe it."

"Why not?"

"Why, it's absurd, dear boy. There must have been some sort of silly mistake. People like you don't steal."

"I tell you I stole a penknife. What's that to do with Carraway?"

"That's what Carraway wants to know. He says he made no reference to your stealing anything till you punched him in the eye. And now everybody in London is talking about it."

"I'm not going to apologize, or take out an action for libel, or do anything."

"I'm afraid they'll ask you to resign."

"You can tell them I 've resigned already."

Brecknock did another turn up and down the room, and then he said in an altered voice:

"Come, come, Arthur. I wish you would be reasonable about this. I introduced you to the club, you know. I feel responsible. I'm sure it's all nonsense. Even if there is anything in the statement (boys do do queer things, you know), the suggestion is still libelous. You've made a fool of yourself over this, dear boy. No one would have bothered about the paragraph in 'The Whispering Gallery' if you hadn't made such a scene. The silly rumour would have died in a fortnight. But now you must fight it."

Arthur thought for a moment, and then he answered:

"I suppose you don't think it would matter having Edith dragged into it, too, and the regrettable incident'?"

"That part of the paragraph would not be the subject of libel."

"But it would all come out. No, Gregory, it's all rot. I won't have anything to do with it. Of course I 'll be sorry to leave "The Old Guys," but it won't break my heart."

"But, my dear boy" persisted Brecknock after meditation, "I want to point out to you that if you take this course, the affair won't terminate with your resignation at 'The Old Guys.' Everybody will get to know about it. They 'll believe that the story is true, and they will exaggerate it. You won't be able to belong to any decent club, and you will be boycotted wherever you go. It will ruin your career."

"Career! career!" cried the boy, waxing furious. "What's the good of coming and talking to me like a schoolmaster about careers! The very word stinks. It's what all these fools think about, and nothing else! Careers and personal ambitions; swine with their eyes glued on the ground, rushing down the steep place. Call me a fool if you like, only don't come and howl about careers, as though all one's work was just a means of edging nearer stage-center! Good God! Brecknock, as you stand there, you remind me of 'The Rook.' That's what we called our head-master at Cullington. He talked about my career and about 'the honor of the school.' The honor of the school! Do you hear that? I tell you, all these things, careers, ambition, honor,—are empty terms. How can a thing have honor which hasn't a heart f The words sound like the rattle of dice in a box, and when the player has thrown them on the table, everybody looks to see whether he's lucky, or unlucky; but they don't stop to realize that the dice-box is empty, because in most cases the player has thrown away his all."

The actor shook his head and smiled.

"I don't follow you, Arthur. I'm talking about 'honor,' not 'honors.' I quite agree that what you say holds good with 'honors,' but not with 'honor'."

"What is the difference?"

"I'm not good at definitions. But you know the meaning of honor. It's a big word. It's the kind of behaviour we expect from each other,—chivalry, fair play, and so on."

"I tell you, if you get it down to a fine point, it's just a question of personal vanity. There's no difference between 'honor' and 'honors.' There are crowds of men who are strictly honorable, who wouldn't do a dirty trick to save their lives, and yet who ought to be horsewhipped through the streets of London. And there are crowds of dishonorable men, who play ducks and drakes with the ten commandments, and yet who are of such a quality of soul that the others are not fit to lick their boots."

Gregory Brecknock shrugged his shoulders and sighed.

"Well, if I can't persuade you, I can't" he said, and then he came forward, and shook Arthur's hand.

"You're a rum chap" he added, and took his departure.

After he had gone, Arthur went into the house and interviewed Edith. "I want to go away into the country for a bit" he said. "I can't work here. London is getting on my nerves."

She said:

"Very well. Would you like me to go with you?"

He hesitated, and answered:

"Of course I should like it. I don't want to bother you, though. I'm not very companionable just now."

"Where shall we go? I'd like to go away with you for a change. We can leave the children."

"I should like to go to Bodiesham."

"That would be delightful. I'll make the arrangements."

He went back to the studio and picked up several sheets of manuscript, and put them down again. Words and phrases jumbled through his mind. Careers! Honor and honors! Love I He had been a fool to work up that row with Carraway. If it had not been for that, the affair might have fizzled out. Impulse I A very dangerous person. Impulse, no friend of property. One must always be circumspect, tactful, expedient. A disgusting word, expediency! Expediency was the aurea mediocritas of property. Politicians, editors, publicists, acted invariably through expediency. What a temptation it must be sometimes to act on impulse, to be flagrantly sincere! Sometimes, indeed, the primitive school-boy instinct would assert itself. A member in the House of Commons would call another a "damned liar. "Then property would rap on the desk and say, "Order! order!" The conspiracy of righteousness would re-establish itself.

In the meantime he would go down to Bodiesham and think things out amid the silence of the dunes.

In the afternoon he heard the two eldest children come home from school. The eldest boy was shouting up the stairs, and Edith was calling back in reply. A little later he could vaguely hear the second girl practising scales in a room above.

It suddenly occurred to him:

"What have all these people to do with me? These are Edith's children. They and that part of her life which they represent, which was the finest part of her life, are nothing to me. In a way she loves me, in a passionate, possessive way; and I love her. But she leaves my soul hungry, unsatisfied, empty."

In the evening two people came to dinner, and he proved a morose and unsociable host. When they had gone he said to Edith:

"I hope you won't mind. I 've been thinking about it. But I want to be utterly alone for a little while. After a few weeks at Bodiesham let us meet, and we can go and stay together at Eastbourne, or wherever you like for as long as you like. Only just for the moment—"

Her eyes were watching him intently. He fancied she gave a little involuntary shudder, but she said quite placidly:

"Very well."

He spent the following day getting a few odds and ends together, and late in the afternoon when he was coming out of a shop in Oxford Street, where he had been to get some books, he ran into Levistock. The Yorkshireman looked thinner and more lugubrious than ever. He seized Arthur's hand, and pulled him down a side street.

"The bust has come, Gaffyn," he said.

"What do you mean, Levistock?"

"They 've done the old man in. The place is chaos."

"Do you mean that 'Pa' has left Blinkinshaw's?"

Levistock nodded his head, and spoke agitatedly.

"They rounded him up like a pack of low-bred hounds. It was simply a plot. Henry Waldren and White got hold of James Blinkinshaw and some of the others. There's been a perfect dust-up. About seven of the chaps have been sacked, and Henry and White share Pa's position. Cutting down expenses, you see. And they've sprung it that Pa is too extravagent with his ideas, too idealistic, not keen enough on doing what is wanted by the public. But it would never have come about, if it had n't been for Waldren and White. They don't care one way or the other. They simply wanted his job."

"They betrayed him, in fact?"

"They're swine! They're all swine. The decks are cleared for all the dirty business of grab and take. No one gives a damn. No one has any interest in the firm, except what he can get out of it. It's all dead. Pa began talking one night, and James Blinkinshaw said he was n't going to have a 'serious' business affected by this medieval rot about gilds, and so on. It happened that, at the moment, he had a pull over Fred, because he had just made a lot of money over some hotel deal—nearly quarter of a million, they say. James and Fred had a bally row, but Fred, for once, had to give way. I tell you, it's hell!"

"And what has happened to Pat"

"I don't know. I expect he 'll get a job somewhere else. He took it very well. He seemed a bit dazed and disappointed. He said to me the night before he left, 'I could have done a lot with this place, Levistock. 'I don't believe he cares about himself. He's sick that the big idea didn't come off, sick and disillusioned. He 'll never get such a chance again."

"If you hear where he's gone to, let me know, Levistock."

"All right. I expect I shall hear. What are you doing?"

"Trying to live down 'Lady Millworthy's Muff' and other things."

"Ah! I'm glad you say that. It is drivel. I went to see it. It somehow did n't seem a bit like you."

"I 'll tell you the story of it one day. Good-bye, Levistock."

"Good-bye. "

The news about Blinkinshaw's disturbed Arthur considerably. During the business of packing and preparing for his departure, there kept rumbling at the back of his mind the reflection that nothing can last that exists solely for material ends. Even a business must have some redeeming quality of idealism. There must be character, sacrifice to an idea, a sense of service. All the old business concerns that had survived were like that. They had been started by men of character, and very often handed down to their sons, or others imbued with the same ideals. Directly they came into the clutches of "the claws and talons crowd" they went to pieces. Business was like that, and so were states and communities.

It was the second day of March when he arrived at Bodiesham, and there was no question this time of lacking the "bare necessities." Edith had sent down an old housekeeper and a considerable amount of furniture. He found fires lighted in several of the rooms, and the lawns had been cut and trimmed, but no attempt had been made to interfere with the general character of the bungalow.

He suffered a reaction of remorse on his first night. He felt he had been unkind to Edith, unkind and selfish. He longed for the comfort of her arms and the sanctuary of her protecting presence. He felt tired, and weak, and sorry for himself. The incidents of the last week jumbled together in his mind in a riot of discontent. He felt himself a failure; and everything that he valued was a failure. He, and his father, and Frank Leffbury, and people like themselves were not only not wanted; they were hated. The juggernaut of social progress came pounding across them, anxious to grind them to dust. If they were to live, they must subscribe to the edicts of the great machine. They must do what property required and jettison the rest.

He thought about Edith intently. Why had he experienced that sudden passion to escape from her? It was something to do with his work. He wanted to re-establish himself, "to fight his way back," as Mr. Leffbury had said. His nerves were jangled by the environment of insincerity of which he had become suddenly aware in London. But Edith was not insincere. It was only that she wouldn't quite understand. He wanted to go out on the sand-dunes and be alone, and think about his work clearly, but he had the disconcerting recollection of her reference to "tints." It was wildly unreasonable and selfish, and he was aware of it, and angry with himself for feeling it and giving way to it. He spent a wretched night pitying himself and Edith and the world. The world to which he wanted to give so much, and yet which seemed so anxious to shut him out.

In the morning he rose early and went out on the dunes. A cold breeze was blowing from the north, but he felt comfort in the action of walking and in the contemplation of the open countenance of nature. In the afternoon he painted a clump of sea-holly silhouetted against the black fabric of an old tarred wreck on the shore, and experienced the first thrill of unalloyed pleasure he had enjoyed for many a day.

In the evening the housekeeper cooked him a meal, and afterward he settled down to write.

The month of March proved particularly cold and wet and windy, and his opportunities for finding relief in painting were rare, but he gradually settled down to develop the further disputations of "The Fugitive Philosopher." He revised and polished and furbished that discriminating gentleman until he became a very real and endearing companion. He wrote to Edith regularly, but made no further reference to the idea of meeting her in Eastbourne, and she replied promptly and in loving terms, but gave no hint that she expected him to. It was an unfortunate fact about Edith that she was a very poor letter-writer. She had no gift for expressing herself. Her letters were full of little facts about the house and their friends and the children, and solicitude for his welfare and instructions for the housekeeper; never anything else.

Arthur liked to see her letters lying on the breakfast table, because he knew it meant that she was all right. But he knew so well what they would contain that gradually he began to skim them through. They never had the element of surprise, or expressed any point of view that was not utterly dull.

This was the more regrettable because, in herself, Edith was not essentially dull. A nature so full of ability and resource was ever revealing itself in new lights, but like so many people of her kind, when she sat down to write a letter she became somewhat self-conscious of the fact, and of her lack of the power of expression, and she consequently confined herself to bald statements of little facts, which read as interestingly as an iron-monger's catalogue.

Early in April there came a sudden change in the weather. Arthur went out one day and was aware of that first velvety quality of tenderness in the air which makes one lift up one's heart. "The Fugitive Philosopher" warmed to this happy transition. He wrote entrancingly of the triumph of young life, and even broke into verse of the beauty of "April Among the Sand Dunes."

One day he went through the meadow-lands near Lenby-Wodehurst, and beheld for the first time that year a field of young daffodils. The vision stirred him by its dazzling beauty, but there followed a sudden reaction, a moment of emptiness.

"It is nothing," he thought, "to love this by oneself."

He walked home, thinking of Edith and the daffodils and the mystery of life, little knowing that the inevitable was even at that moment racing through the country to deliver its climax at his door.

For the inevitable on this occasion took the form of a large automobile containing three people, a chauffeur, a very big man, and a dainty woman.

Arthur was just about to have tea when he heard the fearsome thing come snorting up to the gate, and he thought to himself:

"Oh, hell! Here's that wretched Walter!"

He did not go to the door for a few minutes, in fact, not till he heard a voice that he immediately recognized calling out:

"Hello, Gaff! My, isn't this a splendid situation."

CHAPTER XXII

ALICE HEARS THE NIGHTINGALE

Young life was very much to the fore that evening. The climax enveloped our hero with a bewildering intensity. Everything that had ever happened to himself or to the world seemed inconsequential and worthless. All- remorse, foreboding, and regret vanished. He stood there grinning with pleasure, while Leslie kept on calling him "Dear old Gaff" and hitting and punching him till he positively hurt. He could not take his eyes off Alice, and his heart kept saying illogically, "She's entirely different, and she's exactly the same."

His visitors were in a tremendous state of high spirits, and they were all over the bungalow in the space of a few minutes, like children. Leslie, as usual, was the more loquacious, and he explained as he plunged up the stairs:

"Lordy! We did get a turn when we found you weren't at home. Your good wife—My! isn't she a peach!—told us how the land lay. Bit run down by city life, eh? Well, you've struck a quiet enough retreat here, anyway. What a place to work and think! Your old dad built it, did n't he? He must have been a very considerable artist. Look at this timber-roof, Alice. Did you ever see anything like it? Well, we thought we 'd spring a bit of a surprise on you. It was Alice's fault. She had what she called 'wanderlust'; it came on exactly three weeks ago yesterday. She came to me and said, 'Boodles, I want to go a-roaming, or I'll go crazy.' 'All right,' I said. 'In the fall well buzz round Europe.' 'Fall 't she said. 'Nonsense! I want to start to-morrow.' I said it was impossible, but I found our things packed and two seats on the Eastern express booked, and mother fixed it up with some cousins of ours. Whiz! bang! we were in New York in a week, and there we had to lie around for two days, with Alice eating her head off. When we were on the ocean she seemed to breathe for the first time, and was quite agreeable to me during the crossing. We arrived in Liverpool yesterday morning, called at your home last night, and lo and behold! here we are!"

Arthur laughed.

"It's jolly for me. I like people who do things on impulse."

"Dear old Gaff! Now, look here; we've fixed up this old wreck of an automobile and we mean to do some of the rural and cathedral stunts in this island. Is there a hotel nearby where we can rest for two days, and then won't you come with us?"

They were standing in a group in one of the bedrooms upstairs, and the window was open. Under the eaves of his father's house the martins were twittering, telling each other of the mad things of which young life was capable.

Arthur looked at Alice, and said:

"There's no reason why you shouldn't stay here a day or two. There are several beds. It would be ripping. Then we could see. I ought to be working, of course, but it 's awfully nice to have you both."

There was considerable protest at the inconvenience this arrangement might cause, but eventually it was agreed to. Edith's camp-bed was brought into requisition again, and the housekeeper was sent scurrying across to the farm for more eggs and bacon and milk. The chauffeur was sent to Lenby-Wodehurst to put the car up at a garage, and to stop the night where he liked.

While they were having an evening meal, Arthur looked at Alice and said:

"Do you remember the day when we flew a kite in the Luxembourg Gardens?"

And all the time he was thinking to himself:

"It's very curious that I never realized she would one day be a woman. She's very much a woman. She has the poise of womanhood, with all the grave expectancy of a child. Her eyes are limpid and express the wondering vision of a Donatello Madonna.

'Her rapt soul stirring in her eyes'

Who was it said that? She was born for motherhood. She should be the mother of a saint, or perhaps of a sinner whom she would make a saint by her enveloping purity."

He also thought:

"She has her hair up. Now one can see more clearly the delicate shape of her little head. I like the quick way she tilts her chin back and laughs at her brother."

And as these thoughts were racing through his mind, Alice clapped her hands and cried out:

"Will I ever forget the day we flew the kite! And the little fleecy clouds way up above it, and the bearded cabby and the candies we bought at Mouquin's, Mr. Caff! Shall I call him 'Gaff', Boodles? You know we always do at home."

"Yes, you may call him 'Gaff,' but you mustn't call him Arthur. We all know you flirted outrageously with him in Paris, but now that you have your hair up and he's a married man, we 'll have to put a stop to it. Do you know what we call you in Los Angeles, Gaff?

There was a fearful scuffle between brother and sister, but Leslie managed to get out:

"We call you Alice's—"

But he never succeeded in saying exactly what it was of Alice's that Arthur was reputed to represent on the shore of the Pacific Ocean. Alice said it was too bad, and that if he said what it was, she would go right away and have nothing more to do with him. They talked after that about old times, and the modem trend in art, and the careers of some of the men they had known at Monsieur Berthelot's. Leslie asked Arthur a hundred and one questions about his work and his views. And Arthur told the whole story about "Lady Millworthy's Muff" and explained his present ideas. Alice said they were fine, and to his surprise he learned that she had spent the last two years at the California Academy of Science, where she had been making astonishing progress, according to Leslie, in physics and chemistry.

"So that is the way" Arthur thought. "People are silly and bad, and so we will help them through the medium of physics and chemistry."

"To-morrow" he said, "I would like to show you a field of daffodils."

This was received with acclamation, and Alice said excitedly:

"I want to hear a nightingale. Do you know. Gaff, I've never heard a nightingale."

And Leslie added:

"It's a very remarkable thing, Gaff, but in California where we have the very finest scenery in the world and the most beautiful flowers and natural fauna, and where the air is clear and bright, we have virtually no singing birds. While in this little murky swamp of an island, where the air is always damp and the sun shines for about five minutes a fortnight, you have some of the finest songsters in the world. Now is n't that strange?"

Alice said it wasn't strange; it was a very natural compensation, and Arthur remarked:

"Very well. When I 've shown you the daffodils we 'll go in search of the nightingale. There are not many about here. They're not fond of the sea, but we shall hear them further inland. Surrey's a good county."

The following day was warm, with a moist gray sky, and they walked across the dunes to Lenby-Wodehurst. Arthur was in the seventh heaven of happiness. He forgot all about the pearl penknife, "The Old Guys" and his "career"; and alas! it must be acknowledged that he did not think a great deal about his wife. The country around his father's bungalow seemed to have a fresh significance. It surprised him that he had not realized before how beautiful it was,—the gentle slopes of sand with the dark bushes, and the little, definite, pale yellow notes of the young gorse, the low horizon and the great sweep of moving clouds above. It was all moist and sane and loving, and as they neared the meadowland, the gray piles of farm-buildings, and the brown cattle scattered in the green distances, and the young willows growing in a clump by Farmer Ridgway's pond, came into view. Alice had her daffodils. Ah! the joy it was to see her face light up, and the free, splendid way she ran to meet them. She was across a gate and among them, like a mother among her young children from whom she had been separated too long. With little cries of pleasure she gathered them up and held them for the others to see.

And Leslie cried out:

"Well now, did you ever! It's a sight for the gods!"

And Arthur said:

"Is n't it perfectly glorious!"

Leslie was thinking of the daffodils, and Arthur was thinking of the daffodils and Alice, and of the young life that is born on an April morning. They trudged through the moist meadows and penetrated into the coppice near Farmer Cotter's. There Alice found some white violets and primroses, and the hour was very satisfying. Her face was radiant and flushed, and she held them to her bosom.

As Arthur and Leslie climbed over a stile that marked the track on the way to the brick-works, she called out:

"Hi, there, you boys, are you running away from met"

And she suddenly burst into song:

"Oh, never leave me,
Oh, don't deceive me!

How could you treat
A poor maiden so?"

"Do you boys want to go and visit that old brickworks, or what is the idea!"

It was Alice's voice, young and fresh, breaking the spell, but somehow he could not reply. Leslie was saying to him:

"Well, mine host, and what is the proposition now?"

He said "Eh" and looked at them both vaguely. Why have these things the power to come back across the years and jeer at us? Ironic truths! The penknife, the wayward kiss, the sudden yielding to an unforeseen temptation, and lo! something is pushed back, obscured. We are older, wearier, shop-worn. We no longer have the right to look into the eyes of youth. That part of us is damaged. It is only permitted because underneath it all, there is something that is untouched, that we may "fight our way back to." Arthur remembered how, on that morning, the martin had swept in curves above the hedge and had been a symbol to him; as though there were some protecting genius lurking beneath the eaves of his father's house, something that was still sacred to him, a sanctuary that external behaviour could not pollute. Almost mechanically he said:

"I think we had better be returning to the bungalow."

"Well, I could eat something" replied Leslie. Alice laughed, and the day once more resumed its normal loveliness.

They stayed five days in Bodiesham, and then "the old wreck of an automobile" being brought from Lenby-Wodehurst, and the question of whether Arthur would accompany them or not being thought unnecessary of discussion, the three of them started out one morning in search of cathedrals and nightingales and old timbered houses and historical homesteads and rolling country and romance. They went to Winchester and Salisbury and Stratford and Wells and Tewkesbury, and Arthur began to deplore that "the island" was not more thickly populated with cathedrals. He figured it out that in a month they could visit every cathedral in it, and the dream might end.

It was in an old, timbered inn near Winchester that Alice heard the nightingale. They arrived there very late and dined alone in the public room. After dinner they explored the inn, and the insatiable Leslie found in the landlord a most productive source of information. He asked him every conceivable question about the antiquity of the place, the construction of the building, the history of the county; about the landlord's personal life, his ideas, and his religion. And the landlord, who was, indeed, a rare relict of landlordism, was very proud to be thus drawn out, and very proud of his inn and its antiquity, and excessively proud of his own history and of his ideas and his religious views.

Much as Arthur admired this fast-vanishing type of humanity, at the end of an hour he became restlessly aware that in some way the warm splendors of an April night were not being taken the fullest advantage of. He went quickly from the room and explored the upper storeys of the house. There was no balcony, but a small room that was probably used on rare occasions as a private sitting-room had a lattice-window that opened out on to the garden. He stood there for a moment, and then heard a sound that made his heart thrill. He went back on tiptoe to the room where the others were. The landlord was telling Leslie the story of a stuffed pike that adorned a glass case above the fireplace, and Alice was listening a little abstractedly. She looked up and smiled as he came in, but the landlord continued his dissertation. Arthur went up to her, and whispered:

"Come and hear the nightingale."

She stood up with alacrity, and they both went quickly from the room. They did not speak as they crept upstairs, and he led her to the lattice-window in the room above, which was only lighted by the dim reflection of the night sky. They stood side by side and peered out.

The night was still and warm, with the hushed aspect of expectancy. The thin crescent of a pale moon hung idly in the sky, lighted by the glow of myriad stars. The country lay beneath them, formless and mysterious. Deep tones of warm gray and black blended into each other, or vanished mysteriously, broken here and there by vague touches of lighter tone. Trees near at hand took on grotesque forms, and there was the feeling that living things were moving beneath the obscurity. A dog barked in the distance, and then left off.

Alice leaned on the window-sill and looked out. The perfume of spring flowers and the strange complexity of scents which characterize the living land reached them. Down in the garden a cricket chirped, and things rustled in fitful starts and then were silent.

Suddenly it seemed to become stiller. There was nothing but the solemn immensity of the night, the vast illimitable dome of gleaming mystery. And then—

Low down, as if in some hedge, came the first wary notes of the night-bird, as though he was attuning his voice to the mellow symphony of the night. Then came a silence, as though the night were listening, or perhaps an invisible orchestra was recalling the opening phrase away up among the stars where mortals could not hear it.

And then, high up and away—or was it near at hand? one could not tell the place from whence it came—the full beauty of the song broke forth, rich and full and tender, rising and falling, but ever in rhythm with the pulse of darkness. Plaintive and melancholy, but bringing a message of hope and pity, it became less like a song than like the spirit of the night expressing itself in melody in one's heart, something elusive and intangible.

He looked at the girl as she stood there gazing upwards. Her lips were slightly parted and her expression was one of awe and wonder. She did not stir. She seemed to dread lest any movement of her own might break the spell, that a word might bring disenchantment to the splendor of the night.

They were like two worshippers in the dim recesses of a vast cathedral, hushed and reverent, and finding joy in the solemn communion.

And suddenly she slipped her arm confidingly through his and looked at him, and her eyes were shining with tears.

CHAPTER XXIII

LOVE AMONG THS TOMBSTONES

"The old wreck of an automobile" made rapid and sure progress. It lapped up miles of country, like a thirsty carter. And other things more nearly concerning the emotions also made progress toward their predestined end. It was strange that Leslie did not see the danger of this sentimental pilgrimage. He was, perhaps, too happy, too much in love with the genial aspects of friendship and beauty, and the never-ending revelations of this amazing stuff called life.

He would come across his sister and his friend strolling arm in arm through the garden of an inn, and he would say:

"Now then, you two; flirting again?"

But it seemed very natural to him. Alice had been to a co-educational college; young men didn't make her feel self-conscious. Arthur was his friend, and it was a great joy that Alice had taken to him. They were great pals. Besides, there could be no question or anything else. Arthur was married, and that was the end of it. Alice was not quite twenty and Arthur was thirty-two. This, also, gave her the natural right to treat him in a sisterly way, as, for instance, when he discovered them that night in the room of an inn in Hampshire, standing arm in arm, like two children, listening to a nightingale.

"The Babes in the Wood" he called them, although on that night he fully appreciated the nocturne of their mutual enjoyment He talked about the nightingale's song for days, and said it was "really very impressive." He tried to analyse exactly what it was the nightingale did, and why it sang at night, but he found the others somewhat unresponsive in this discussion.

He vaguely wondered once or twice why Arthur didn't ask more about his wife. He could understand that she might not want to make the trip; some women were such home-birds, and she had those three children to occupy her. But he liked Edith; he took to her on the occasion of his visit when he found Arthur away. He told Alice that he considered her "a strong, capable, and very beautiful woman." He admired the way she moved about, and gave them clear, precise information about Arthur's movements and locality. And he liked the way she listened.

"Very few people know how to listen intently and intelligently" he observed.

The arrangement was that they were to spend a month in England, and then to continue their trip for another two months on the continent, visiting France, the Austrian Tyrol, and Italy, and were to return to California in July.

When the last week of the English trip arrived they found themselves in Norfolk. Leslie said:

"Now see here, Gaff, you'd better make your plans and trot along with us to France."

Arthur answered dolefully that he was afraid he would n't be able to arrange it. He must be getting on with his work, and there were all sorts of reasons. And Leslie remarked:

"I know; he's homesick. Poor little boy!"

And then he had a brilliant idea:

"Why not go back and fix it up with the wife, and bring her, too?"

But to this idea, also, there appeared to be vague and dubious objections. As the day of parting began to draw near, a gloom began to creep over the small party. It started with Alice, spread to Arthur, and curiously enough became most pronounced in the impressionable Leslie.

"I'm awfully put out that you won't join us, Gaff" he kept repeating, and he lumbered through the interior of Norwich Cathedral as though he were visiting a mausoleum destined to contain his own bones.

On the night before they returned to London they put up at the village of Heynsham, and after dinner Arthur and Alice went for a casual stroll together through the village. This was according to a habit which had developed during the previous three weeks. There was an old church surrounded by a sea of tombstones which looked very desolate in the moonlight, and their footsteps seemed drawn toward it. They went slowly along a winding path among the tombs till they came to a little stile that led to a deserted-looking road around a coppice. At the stile they rested, and Alice perched herself upon it. Arthur stood beside her and gazed at the tombstones, as though fascinated by their appeal. They were silent for some time, and then Alice said:

"Death is a terrible thing, death and parting. It all seems so cruel."

And Arthur replied:

"It is love alone which makes it cruel."

And he took her hand and held it to his brow, and dared not look at her.

"In the alchemy of nature it seems to me that there are terrible lapses, mistakes. There are so many things that give the illusion of love."

He looked up at her and noticed that she was breathing quickly. Her eyes looked drawn and anxious. She passed her hand through his hair and said:

"Arthur, are you unhappy?"

And he gripped her hand more tightly and kissed it, and muttered with a sob:

"O God!"

She took her hand away, as though staggered by the realization of the immensity of the sudden great forces that were at work beneath these fragmentary words of theirs. She said:

"O Arthur, this is—awful."

They looked into each other's eyes dim with tears, and she gasped breathlessly:

"Arthur, it's no use pretending. You and I—We mustn't go on like this; we simply mustn't. I was a fool to come to Europe. But I don't know how it was; when I was a little girl and you played with me in Paris, I made a sort of niche for you. That's what Leslie meant. They call you my 'saint.' I thought of you, and thought and thought. And suddenly this year I thought of you more desperately. I wanted to see you again. That's why I came. I called it 'wanderlust,' but it was you I wanted to see. It was madness. I knew that you were married but I didn't think about you in that way. I just wanted to see you again, to hear you talk, to know that you were still my saint up there in the niche. And you came down and touched my hand, and we went along the road and heard the nightingale, and things went tearing through my heart. It was all wonderful I And I will go back and dream of these days and nights forever."

He kissed her cheeks which were damp with tears, and he said:

"Alice! Oh, my dear, what is to be done? I am desperate and desolate. When I think of your departure I cannot face the future."

"You will have to face the future, Arthur."

"How is one to tell?" he cried despairingly. "How can youth tell? There are all these other things that have the illusion of love. Youth grasps them and finds too late that they are illusory. A saint? What strange trick of nature is this that, through the fragrant purity of your soul, sees in me a saint! Alice, I am vicious and weak and stained with all the dreary ugliness of the world. I have struggled and given way, fought and been defeated. What makes you see me as a saint?"

She slipped down from the stile and came very near him. Looking into his eyes, she said softly:

"Only this. If I were alone with you to-night, I would trust you with my soul."

He gave a little sob and groped for her hands again. He kissed them and murmured:

"Oh, my dear, my dear!"

"Listen, Arthur" she said again. "I want to help you. All these things you tell me don't count very much. You want believing in. Do you understand! I know you. Deep down you are a saint; you have the sacrificial spirit. All these other things that splash you as they pass, they do not touch you, the real you, the you that lies so deep and silent. Oh, let me look at your dear eyes again!"

She held him apart, and he gave a little cry, as though he wanted to draw her to him. She whispered:

"You 'll think of me, Arthur, not only in the future, but now. You won't make it too difficult for me!"

"No, no," he muttered hoarsely. "It is only that I am jealous of you, I think. J am jealous of the young life in you. I see you here within reach of my arms, and your face is only lighted by the stars. The stars have an unerring way of stating things, and the young life in you is laid bare. That is the difference between us. It is more difficult for you now, and will be more difficult for me in the days to come. For me it is the end, but for you it is the beginning. In some strange way I have cast a spell over you. You think you love me, but the day will come when you will find this to be an illusion, as I found illusion when I was your age. For me there will be no more illusion. I shall grope on, haunted by the vision of 'that other one' who will one day take the place I madly dreamed of. And Alice, much as it tortures me, I'm glad the stars are never wrong. You will be happy, and you will one day come and tell me."

And then she gave a cry and threw her arms round him. "No, no" she sobbed. "I can't let you go like that It isn't true. There will never be anyone else. Arthur, you must n't believe that. Oh, my dear, the world will be all empty and dark without you, empty and dark for ever and ever."

The night was very still, and on the other side of the coppice a peewit uttered his plaintive warning of coming rain. The silhouette of the old church stood out impressively against the night sky, and the air was laden with the perfume of spring blossoms.

Ecstasy, fear, and temptation rioted in the veins of the young man. Visions of dazzling days and nights danced before his eyes. The re-awakening! The dynamic instincts of creative man I Joy and hope surging toward the splendid threshold of the unborn! To live again, to be born again, to look once more through the portals of youth into the realms of everlasting beauty!

The peewit went shrieking across the path, flying very low. To-night the sky was clear; to-morrow would come the rain. And yet—

The child had said "the you that lies so deep and silent."

The affair would not be difficult of accomplishment; he had the power to persuade her. They could simply go off suddenly, leaving a letter for poor old Leslie. He pictured the expression on her brother's face when he read it. It would be terrible. He would either cry, or kill some one. But by the time they met again he would have gotten over it. He would consider it regrettable, but in his inmost heart, "mighty interesting."

It wasn't Leslie who would count in this affair; it was the girl.

He couldn't fool himself, or misread the unerring message of the stars upon her child-face. He could sink low, but he could not sear that "something deep and silent within him" by an everlasting outrage.

He kissed her cheek once more, and felt her lips tremulously quivering against his chin. And then he gripped her arm and said:

"Let us go, then."

She sighed, and they went in silence past the tombstones and back to the inn.

It was getting late, and as they came through the yard at the back she suddenly stopped him. She placed a hand on either side of his cheeks and looked at his eyes, and she said in a whisper:

"I knew that you were my saint"

He looked at her strained eyes, but he could not answer. Something within him seemed to be choking and he wanted to be despairingly alone, to be able to wrestle with his own wretchedness. When they arrived at the inn Alice ran straight upstairs, but Leslie came out of the smoking-room where he had been cross-examining a commercial traveler upon his methods of doing business. He called out:

"Hello, Gaff, I've been looking for you. A telegram came for you just as you went out."

They went along together to the office, Arthur remarking that "it was a gorgeous night." They handed him the telegram and he opened it. It ran:

"Advise return immediately. Mrs. Gaffyn very ill."

It was signed "Beggs" which was the name of the housekeeper.

It is impossible to analyse the complexity of virtuous and vicious impulses which stir in the human heart. At least, if it is not impossible to analyse them, it is impossible to tell which way they will jump when acted upon by some sudden and unexpected phenomena. Does it not seem inconsistent, for instance, that Arthur, who a few minutes previously had been accentuated by an idealistic conception of behaviour, should suddenly experience an almost fiendish wave of hope that some one who was very dear to him, and who had been loyal and passionately loving to him, should die? It was, perhaps, not so much a hope, as a sudden vision that Edith might die, and his mind was more actively engaged with the result of this calamity than with the fact itself. If Edith should die...?

He showed the telegram to Leslie and said:

"I must catch the first train in the morning."

And Leslie said:

"My! This is bad news! Lordy! I am sorry, Gaff, old man. But why wait till the morning? We can dig out the old automobile, and get Raikes to run you up tonight."

It had not occurred to Arthur that this was possible. He said:

"But how will you manage? There's no station here, or anything."

And Leslie put his hand on his shoulder and answered:

"That won't cut any ice, old man. He can come back for us. I 'll go dig him out."

In an hour's time Arthur found himself speeding on the way to London, his mind dazed by varying emotions. The chauffeur was no good in the dark, and lost his way many times, but eventually they arrived in London at half -past five. He drove straight to St. John's Wood. A nurse opened the door. She glanced at him and said:

"She's doing as well as can be expected. She has double pneumonia. It's a serious case."

In the drawing-room he found Aunt Elizabeth sleeping on a sofa. She awakened and kissed him, and said:

"My poor dear! She's very low, Arthur, very low indeed. They say it's touch and go. You can go up and see her, but she won't know you, Arthur. She's unconscious. She's been unconscious for twelve hours. Oh, dear! we 've had a dreadful time. We have two doctors and two nurses night and day. She caught it doing this slumming work in the East End. Got wet through, and sat in her wet clothes all the afternoon helping a mechanic's wife who nearly died giving birth to a child."

"How long has she been ill?"

"Let's see. Friday—Monday—Tuesday night. Nearly ten days. "

"But why did n't they send for me before?"

"Well, you know, my dear, Edith's so funny about that I only heard three days ago when she was getting worse, quite by chance. She said they were n't to bother people, and she kept on giving particular instructions that they were not to send for you. Those were almost her last words before she lost consciousness. And then it grew so serious I told Mrs. Beggs she'd better do so. How did you comet Are your feet wet?"

Arthur went upstairs and beheld his wife lying on her back, breathing desperately. The nurse hovered near the bed. The doctor had called at twelve o'clock and was expected again at six. Everything possible was being done.

Arthur washed himself and then sat in a chair by the fireplace, listening to the terrifying breathing of his wife. His heart was torn by pity and remorse.

It was, indeed, as Aunt Elizabeth said, an affair of touch and go. On the following night the crisis came, and the doctor appeared anxious and summoned his consultant. They spent some time together, and came out of the room looking very grave. Everybody went about the house on tiptoe, and Arthur would not go to bed. He sat there dazed, looking at the others and gripping the arms of his chair in agony. The children were sent across the way to a friend's, and Eleanor called with her husband. She kissed him and cried convulsively. Late in the evening Leslie appeared alone. They had just arrived in town. He said that Alice was resting; she had sent her love. He looked terribly concerned. He wandered about the house, holding his long arms in front of him, as though he were offering himself for any sort of service. He kept patting Arthur's shoulder and saying:

"There, there, dear old man. It'll come out all right! You 'll see!"

He disappeared later, as though he could not stand the strain. Arthur sat on, enduring the agony of the struggle. About dawn he dozed a little, and once the nurse awakened him and said in an awed voice:

"I think you had better go into the next room."

She seemed frightened of his presence and the effect that certain developments might have on him. But he answered like a drunken man:

"'at's all right, nurse."

In the morning he fainted, and they carried him into the next room. When he came to, he noticed a slightly different expression on the nurse's face. She said:

"I think it's going better. I think it's more hopeful."

The doctor came at seven and verified the statement. All day long people came and went, moving softly. In the evening the doctor came to see him, and gave him something in a glass to drink. He touched his shoulder and said:

"It's going to be all right."

Arthur went back in a dazed condition to his wife's bedroom. The breathing was less terrible, but again he sat there through the night.

On the following day the doctor smiled for the first time, and said:

"I think we may say that the crisis has passed."

On the afternoon of that day Arthur slept soundly for the first time in three days. When he awakened at ten o'clock at night he found Aunt Elizabeth in the room.

She said:

"Well, my dear. Thank God! She's beginning to recover consciousness."

Arthur said "Thank God!" and slept again.

About five o'clock he awakened, feeling refreshed. He went into Edith's room. She was sleeping. He sat looking at her. After a time she opened her eyes and gazed at him. She looked at him dreamily, and then closed her eyes and gave her head a little shake, as though dismissing a foolish illusion. He went up to the bed and kissed her brow, but she moved restlessly, as though disturbed by disquieting dreams, and he left the room.

As the days went by a furtive passage of glances took place between them.

With her strong constitution and her determined will, Edith soon seemed to control the vacillating spirits of disease. She lay there without speaking, but alert and conscious, doing the right thing for her body. When Arthur came near her she seemed a little disturbed, as though struggling to control herself more completely. When he kissed her she responded dreamily.

On the fifth day of her recovery he was standing by the fireplace, when she said in a matter-of-fact way:

"You 've come back, then, Arthur."

He came nearer to the bed, and answered:

"Yes, dear."

He wanted to say more, to explain himself more completely, but he doubted whether she were fit to suffer emotion and he did not quite know how much she understood. He added weakly:

"Can I get you anything?"

She shook her head and looked away.

At the end of a fortnight she was sitting up, and Leslie and Alice had gone off to France. He had not seen Alice since the night at Heynsham.

He went back to his work, and it was during that month that he completed the second volume of "The Fugitive Philosopher."

At the end of May the doctor said that Edith must go away and be braced up. The obvious place was Bodiesham. It was furnished and ready, and the housekeeper was still there. He hired a car and they drove down all the way, and for some reason persuaded Aunt Elizabeth to accompany them.

The month of June was glorious, and in the light sea-breezes Edith rapidly regained her strength. Arthur worked and went for walks about the country, and found it peopled with images of Alice. He saw her standing on an elevation among the dunes, the wind blowing strands of hair across her face.

He visited the field where the daffodils had made her cry with delight. They were all dead now, and there was an emptiness in the meadows near Lenby.

Leslie wrote to him and kept him in touch with their movements, but there was no word from his sister. In his heart he followed them to Paris and to Basle, and all through Switzerland and the Tyrol. Her eyes would come between him and the sheets in front of him, and he would think:

"Where is she now? What is she doing? Is she thinking of me? Is she happy? Is she unhappy? Has she already met 'that other one'?

And at night he would sit alone on the veranda of his father's house and dream of her. He would suffer agonies of apprehension lest something terrible had happened to her—an accident amid the Alps, typhoid fever through drinking impure water, a railway smash. And yet, what was it all to him? He would never see her again. She had gone, passed out of his life forever. But he could not face the grim certainty of it. He tried to visualize the joy and happiness that would come to her when she did, indeed, find "that other one." But the vision was more disturbing than the certainty of separation.

He could see her on the steps of another veranda in California, perhaps with children climbing round her knees, and she would start with tremulous joy when she heard the approaching footsteps of that man whom Arthur tried not to hate with unreasonable venom. And on some occasion, in the dim seclusion of the house, she would tell him about Arthur. Then the boy, with the supercilious superiority of youth and possession, would grin and say:

'Toor old chap!"

And he would kiss her pity out of her.

By the end of the month Edith became her normal self, and Aunt Elizabeth returned to town. Edith could walk and work, and she seemed happy and contented again, but anxious to get back to the children, or to have them down there. They did not speak of intimate things. There was a sort of mutual unexpressed understanding between them that somehow the center of their affections had shifted. The difference in their ages seemed more emphasized, and Edith returned to her earlier attitude of mothering indulgence. She never disagreed with him or interfered with any of his inclinations, but her actions seemed more passive and detached. He felt, in a way, a little frightened of her and her calm reserve.

On the third of July there came a cable from Leslie from Bordighera. It read:

''Arriving London eighth. Leaving for States fourteenth."

When Edith read this cable she said:

''Oh, wouldn't it be jolly to ask them to spend their last few days here!"

Arthur looked at her, but her face gave no indication of any feeling other than that of a well-bred hostess suggesting the right thing.

Arthur carried the cablegram crumpled up in his trousers' pocket all day. Occasionally he took it out and looked at it. Early the next morning he sent this reply:

"Wife and I delighted if you will come Bodiesham on eighth till departure."

He lived in a state of fever for the next three days, when another cable said: "Delighted to accept kind invitation."

On the evening of the eighth "the old wreck of an automobile" once more made its appearance in Bodiesham, delivering its two travelers safely at the gate of the bungalow. Leslie started a long apology for not cabling before. It appeared to be Alice's fault. She was like all women, with the obvious exception of Mrs. Gaffyn, he was sure; they simply could not make up their minds. Alice had wanted to go to Oxford and Chester and some other old places they had missed. She was insatiable; she had run him off his feet this trip. The next time he came to Europe he was going to bring a bagful of monkeys with him; they would be more restful. She had nearly killed him climbing inaccessible peaks in the Tyrol; he would be glad to lock her up in the cabin of the steamer; and so on.

When they sat down to dinner they were all extremely garrulous, with the exception of Arthur. Leslie naturally was so, and Alice and Edith adopted it in a wildly defensive sort of manner. Edith surprised him. She appeared to be under the stress of a great and pleasurable excitement in meeting these two. She had travelled a good deal herself, and the recent tour of their guests supplied a topic of conversation that was by no means exhausted when they left on the thirteenth.

Alice was extremely entertaining. With her keen powers of observation, her apt way of expressing things, and her sense of fun, she gave many pungent descriptions of their adventures which kept them all in a genial state of laughter. And Arthur laughed, too. He could not help it, although his heart was aching. She was so young and fresh and buoyant, so redolent of the joyous things of "the young life."

And he kept thinking to himself:

"How beautiful she is! I did not think before about her beauty. I only thought of her as 'my Alice'; all the dear tones of her voice that seem created for me, that mean things only to me. She is blushing now, and I know she thinks she loves me. And so, indeed, she does. But youth will trample on that. She has the inexhaustible fount. Oh, youth is cruel, cruel, cruel! Youth has its own game to play, and will be served. Nothing can stand against youth. Don't be a fool! Don't be a fool!"

After dinner they all sat out on the veranda, and there was no opportunity of talking to Alice alone. She would give him quick little pleading glances, and sometimes an expression would come to her face, a little pucker of the brow, a strained look like that which came to her in Heynsham churchyard when she said:

"O Arthur, this is—awfuL"

It was not till the following afternoon that he secured a few words alone with her. They all walked across the dunes to the sea, and Alice and Arthur soon took the lead. When they were a hundred yards ahead, he whispered:

"Well?"

And the tones of her voice attuned to his as she answered:

"Oh, my dear, it's been dreadful. I wanted you horribly. But you mustn't talk to me now, or I shall cry, or do something awful. We ought not to have come. It's only going to make it worse. "

"Why didn't you write to me, Alice!"

"I was frightened. I wrote to you several times, and tore up the letters. It seemed so mean. I could only write to you in one way, and I'd no right to."

"You received mine?"

"Oh, yes. I couldn't have lived without them, but I was terrified lest Leslie should see them. I read him little bits, and then burnt them. If he were not such an innocent babe, he could have told everything by my manner. But O Arthur, you ought not to have written me like that. Your letters went right through me. You ought not to write to me, but you must. I shall give you an address in Los Angeles where you must write me often and tell me everything, every little thing about yourself. Your letters will be the only thing I have."

"And you will write to me?"

"Yes; only let me write to your club, or somewhere. It's frightfully wicked, but I can't lose you altogether.

Do you know what you are! You 're just my unsatisfied longing! I used to long for you in Italy, and in Switzerland. I longed for you in the morning and the afternoon and the night, especially at night when I was tired. I used to think how much more beautiful everything would have been if you had been there to share it When we saw anything particularly beautiful I thought of you at once, and then I longed and longed, and I knew it was no good. I used to cry at night sometimes, and then scold myself. Do you think I'm terribly wicked!"

He glanced at her fair face as she frowned perplexedly at the vision of the sea. And he smiled grimly and answered:

"Yes. You're a terrible adventuress!"

She shook her head and whispered:

"You mustn't laugh at me, Arthur. It is wicked, you know. I sometimes wonder and wonder what there can be about me that you find to love. You're so wonderful and clever. You have everything, and I'm just a child."

And he said hoarsely:

"If you talk like that, I shall suddenly take hold of you and kiss you in front of the others. Oh, you darling!"

She blushed, but her eyes shone.

"For heaven's sake! don't do anything mad, dear."

As they came round a slope and upon the foreshore, she suddenly clutched his arm and cried excitedly:

"Look! look!"

Two yachts were manoeuvering within half a mile of the shore. They looked splendid scudding before the windy their white sails striking a note of gaiety upon the luminous expanse of sparkling water.

"That is what I envy," Arthur thought as he observed her eyes reflecting the sudden vision. "She has the genius of youth. She can destroy in a flash the solemn bickerings of regret. She is the medium of nature. Nature will play upon her in this way until the impressions and visions increase and increase, and then there will be nothing left of the old regret. She will rise, a new and beautiful phoenix from the ashes of this miserable romance. What troubles me is that, blindly as I love her, I cannot help envying her. Why should I envy her? I have had my youth."

They sat on the shore and threw pebbles, and Edith and Leslie joined them. Leslie was giving Edith a concise precis of the manner of conducting the tomato industry in Southern California, an industry in which he and some of his family apparently had a commercial interest. When he observed the yachts, his mind immediately flew to the American Cup Races, and he said that over in the States "Sir Thomas Lipton was held to be a good sportsman, and everybody wanted him to win."

Despite his affection for him, there were moments when Arthur felt that Leslie was an unconscionable bore. He would give slow and deliberate dissertations on all sorts of subjects, expecting the others to be as interested as he; and in the meantime the precious moments were slipping by.

Li this respect he had to acknowledge that Edith behaved extremely well. She seemed to go out of her way to take him off their hands, and during th3 next two days they found several opportunities for roaming off together.

During the evening of the following day, just before dinner, they went up into the pine-wood behind the house and were lost to sight. They sat upon the moss-grown stump of an old tree, very close together, and he kissed her hands. After a silence she whispered:

"Tell me. What are you thinking of?'

And he groaned:

"I'm counting the hours. There are seventy-three left, and then—"

She pinched the tips of his fingers and said:

"Arthur, dear, you simply mustn't look at it like that. We 'll be back some day very soon; you see if we don't. And now, tell me about your work. What are you going to dot"

"Oh, grub along and do things that nobody wants."

"That isn't true; you know that people want them. You are one of the rare ones; you have the power of creation. It's the most precious gift in the world. Think of all you can do to help. More and more people want help. You must dip into yourself and produce the things that help them."

"Like that wretched play that will never stop running."

"O fugitive philosopher, how can you say that! You know that what matters is that you are true to yourself. I'm going to work hard, too. When I get through this physics business I'm going to take up medicine. It's all we can do, Arthur—just push along and help people. I can help a little bit in my material way with medicines and advice. I think I ought to have a good bedside manner, don't you? But you—you can help so much more. You can help spiritually. You can help to shape things, give form and thought and poignancy to the most matter-of-fact existences; show people how to think and live and appreciate beauty. What does it matter if some of them jeer at you, or trample on your work! What matters is that those for whom your message is intended will know you by your work. Do you ever walk along a crowded street and look at the faces, and suddenly you look into one pair of eyes, and you don't quite know what happens, but you are conscious that in some way life is a finer thing than it was before! Those who have the great secret know each other in a crowd."

He looked at this strange child who talked so wisely, and used such simple phrases, and he said:

"With you; yes, yes, with you."

He could n't exactly formulate what he wanted to say, but he stroked her hand and managed to add in a low voice:

"You Tl always believe in me, Alice. I know that. It will help me to go on. It is only through the eyes of women that men accomplish things of beauty, and yours are the most beautiful eyes in the world. Yours are the eyes that Shelley must have dreamed of and Leonardo painted, but which Napoleon would not have understood. Strange! As I talk to you, I seem to realize the cleavage—creation and destruction. The world has so far been ruled by the destroyers, by the old, by the tyrant, but the days of youth is dawning."

They were silent, and then he continued dreamily:

''I promise you I will go on. I shall always think of you. Perhaps when I am no longer dazzled by the contact of your presence, you will help me the more. You make me feel strong and virile. It's a big thing to feel, this great glow of life passing all around one, and to know that, for good or evil, one influences it. I sometimes think of the million, million unborn children whose happiness we hold in the hollow of our hands. Yes, yes, one can do that, be an influence, help to shape things."

"Oh, Arthur, I shall be so happy if you'll promise me that."

He pressed her hand and rose. As they came through the wood she smiled and said:

"Even if you're not a saint, it would be so easy to make you one. You just want a little managing. I think I would throw you in the deep and make you strike out for yourself."

CHAPTER XXV

THE DUST OF THE SEA

When the day of parting dawned, the elements adapted themselves to the gloom of this event in a portentous manner, for it rained heavily and a cold wind blew from the east. In the morning they all went out for a walk in mackintoshes. The two younger members managed to scramble ahead of the others and to carry on a breathless and scrappy dialogue with the rain beating their faces.

"Only five hours more!"

"Five hours and seventeen minutes!"

"I will spare you the seventeen minutes to pack and dress. For the rest, you must keep near me and let me gaze at you."

"Arthur, you're simply shameless."

"Why?"

"It's the way you look at me. Surely the others can read your eyes."

"What does it matter? People never begrudge a meal to a man who is just going to be executed."

"But you're not going to be executed. You're only going to be left behind."

"I love you."

"And you made a promise."

"Which I shall keep. Only, while we walk along like this for the last time, I want to keep on whispering, 'Alice, I love you.' I want to impress you on the air. When you have gone I shall come out here sometimes for walks alone with you. I want the sea and the sand and the gorse and these slabs of stone to bear witness; then when I whisper, 'Alice, I love you,' they will understand and be sympathetic."

"And as I walk the deck of the steamer, I will accompany you. I will look at the sea and I will think, 'It's the same dear sea that he is looking at, and he loves me.' There! Are you satisfied?"

"For one of the precious moments, yes. You are a darling!"

"When will you write to me?"

"I will write to-night; you will get a letter on the steamer at Liverpool. And then you will not hear for three weeks. "

"You have not told me where to write you."

"Oh, write to 'The Old Guys Club, Adelphi.' No; I had forgotten; not there. I will send you an address to-night."

"You are going to work and win out. I shall be so proud of you."

"Anything I do will be because of you."

"And no one will ever know. I suppose there are thousands of people like that, who have some dear and wonderful secret that helps them on, and the world never knows."

"They're calling us to go back to lunch."

"And to waste another of the hours."

"Not quite; I can sit opposite you at lunch and watch you."

'Like an open book. Or rather, like an open newspaper with flaming headlines: 'I Love You. Romantic Affair in South England.'"

The rain stung their faces and the keen air braced their nerves. They were both young, and they laughed in the face of their impending doom.

At lunch-time Leslie said:

"Well now, if you good people would only come over to our side, we'd give you the time of your lives. You'd just love California, Mrs. Gaffyn; the scenery is wonderful and the climate makes you want to jump around like a cat. Why not come over and spend a summer with us?"

Edith smiled and said:

"It would be delightful; it's very kind of you to suggest it. I'm afraid—you see, I have the children to consider. "Then she paused, and added:

"I don't see why Arthur should n't go."

Arthur glanced at his wife and a curious little wave of fear swept over him. He could not account for it; he could not foresee any reason for fear of any sort. It was like a subconscious warning of some impending calamity that he had no reason to expect, and yet which chilled him with its insidious touch.

Leslie said:

"Why, yes, I'm sorry; I suppose that is so. Well, if Arthur would come along, we'd look out for him."

But he seemed a little doubtful whether he ought to persuade Arthur to make such a journey without his wife. He switched off again into the glories of California, its eucalyptus trees, its flowers and fruit and people and social life, till Alice pulled him up with:

"In fact, everything except nightingales."

And then Arthur looked at her, and his eyes proclaimed the flaming headlines. The car came for them at five o'clock, and Arthur went with them as far as Lenby-Wodehurst, where they took the train.

The departure was like a dream. They huddled together silently in the car, and Leslie shared their grief. He did not even seem to notice that they sat holding each other's hands and looking out of the window. When they arrived at the station there was little time for weeping. As in a glass darkly, Arthur saw Leslie bustling about calling out to porters, and Alice standing wrapped up in her rain-proof cloak, with the collar touching the little pink lobes of her ears. And he could see only her eyes through a mist and feel the tremulous pressure of her hands. As the train came thundering in, Leslie gripped his hand and said to Alice:

"Kiss him good-by."

She did so, and he stood there in a trance, with the magic of that kiss tingling his cheeks and the vision of those eyes that burnt him with their longing. Then she whispered:

"I am going to be so proud of you."

A clatter and roar, the shriek of a whistle, and the dream vanished. But still he stood there, with the rain tempestuously striving to wash away the imprint of that kiss. He laughed softly at the foolhardy effort of the gods. No violent onslaught by any combination of these cunning devices of nature should ever rob him of the memory of that tender caress.

He walked out of the station and through the muddy streets of Lenby. At the comer of Steed's meadow he called at a cottage where an old farm laborer named Hilton lived by himself. He was an old man who had lived in the cottage for twenty-two years, and Arthur knew him well. He came to the door, and Arthur said:

"Good evening, Mr. Hilton. Will you do me a favor! I may shut up the bungalow and travel about. In any case, I want to know if you will mind my letters having addressed to you here? I will call for them; or if I am away, I will leave a covering envelope for you to forward them. I will pay you for this."

Old Hilton looked at him meditatively and said:

"That 'll be all right, sir."

Arthur proffered him half a crown, but he shook his head:

"There be no call for that, sir. Thank 'e kindly. I'm always pleased to oblige folk."

Arthur said:

"It's very kind of you, Mr. Hilton. Good night."

"Good night, sir."

He walked across the meadows and came out upon the dunes. It was getting dark and the sea was roaring dully. He walked toward it, as though he had an urgent message; and so, indeed, he had. He stood upon a little hillock and murmured:

"Alice, Alice!"

Gulls went shrieking overhead, and the murmur of the sea struck a note of perpetuity.

He stood there a long time, aware of the vibrant forces of Nature around him and curiously intent on his own place in this setting.

"No one has ever been able to think these things out properly" he mused at length. He felt strangely incomplete, as though a great part of him had been cut away and the other part was trying to find itself. It was at present being blown about, with its face washed by the salt rain.

"That's what we all came from" according to Darwin" he reflected at random. "The dust of the sea!"

He tried to think about "the dust of the sea" but another phrase seemed more pertinent and elbowed its way to the fore.

"They who have the great secret know each other in a crowd."

Yes, it was very evident; he would have to start all over again, grimly and earnestly. He had made a terrible blunder. He had fallen in love with a young girl with whom he had no right to fall in love. She had gobbled him up, as it were, body and soul, and there was only this little part of him left. What was he to do with it? The salient features of the case were two. First, she would get over it; she would get over it quite quickly and fall in love with some one else. Of that he was perfectly certain. The second feature was that he wouldn't get over it. For him it was the end, except for that one little part of him which stood gasping on the sand. And concerning that he had made a definite promise. He had promised her that he would go on. That was the most important thing in the world, the thing to cling to,—his promise to her. For that was the little part of her that he could always keep.

His case was so desperate that he had come down here to try and find himself. If it had not been for his promise, this little part of him might easily be thrown away. It could go oat now, for instance, straight into those breakers, and beyond them to where the current was very strong, bearing down the channel eastward.

But no, he couldn't do that; for Alice still held him by some peculiar power, although at that moment she was racing away from him in a train forever. Therefore he would have to make a tremendous effort. He would have to key up this little part of him into a living and interested force. Alice had said, "You have the power to help spiritually, to shape things."

Yes, this very living agony would help him in that. From the ashes of his grief he would be able to raise up images that, after waiting, they who passed him in the crowd would understand. And of those others who came after, they would know him less by what he did than by the love that he imparted. He experienced a moment of tranquillity.

"There will always be the sense of incompleteness that robs the full hour of its splendor, but there will be moments of calm when I shall find within myself the power to help others. A great impersonal love. There is consolation in the very thought of it."

He turned his footsteps in the direction of the pavilion.

"I must concentrate on what I am going to do for her sake," he thought. "I must struggle to keep my mind attuned to the appeal that springs perpetually from the memory of her image. It will be terrible and cruel, the more terrible because now I can only see all in rigid perspective. Alice vanishing forever, and then the narrow way of my life that will begin again when I enter the pavilion. Edith will be waiting for me. She will probably be knitting or sewing. She will look up and say, 'Did you get your feet wet, Arthur?' and then I shall change my boots and wash, and get a book and sit down. And then we shall start our life again. In a few days we shall go to London. I shall resume my work, and she will be immersed in bringing up those children. And so it will go on. One will accomplish a certain amount of work, and then one will grow old, and eventually one will die, and—God! One will have never known the complete hour."

The rain blew in more tempestuous gusts. It was getting dark and the pavilion looked a little ghostlike, with its white profile somewhat blurred against the dark line of fir-trees. In the L-shaped room with the veranda on the first floor, where they principally lived, a vague lit was burning.

"Edith has not lighted the large lamp" he thought.

He plodded up the wet paths to the front door and let himself in. He heard the housekeeper in the kitchen moving about near the range. He took off his hat and mackintosh, changed his boots and went upstairs.

The bungalow seemed curiously silent. He went quietly into the sitting-room. He could not see his wife at first, for she was round the angle of the room. But as he went forward he was conscious of her sitting by the small lamp. For some reason or other he did not go straight to her, but drifted to the window. He felt a little impatient and irritable. He wanted her to say:

"Well, Arthur, did you get your feet wet?"

And then he could resume their normal companionship again, and the big struggle would commence. He was anxious to begin the big struggle.

He stood looking out of the window and noticing the fantastic shapes of shrub and trees in the half-light. Suddenly it dawned upon him that Edith had not spoken.

He looked across at her and to his surprise observed that, although she was sitting near the lamp, she was not sewing, or knitting, or reading. She was apparently just sitting there, with her hands on her knees.

The light from the small lamp seemed to be flickering a little uncertainly. And then it was that he was again assailed by the chilling gusts of fear he had experienced earlier in the day. What had happened? What was going to happen! Nothing could be more terrible than the misery he was enduring, and yet something seemed to tell him that it might be more feral, more wildly unreasonable.

He was trying to raise himself above his sorrow, to assert the little part of him that remained, but this instant mood of tragedy that seemed to haunt the hollow spaces of the bungalow was thrusting out its arms to pull him back.

He passed his hand across his brow, and said faintly:

"Can you see? Don't you want the big lamp?"

Edith did not answer. He walked across the room and looked at her, and then she jumped up and seemed to slink back against the wall. And when she looked at him her eyes were sunk in the dark hollows of her face. He stood gazing at her and listening to the wind moaning round the bungalow. When at last she spoke, her voice sounded high, crueller than the wind, a disconnected thing blown from some land where the sun never shines. She said: "Well, you didn't go off with her, then?" The unexpectedness of this statement lashed the strings of his heart. For a moment his whole power of volition stopped. The spectrum of his moral vision was broken into a discordant jumble of coloured lights. It was neither what he expected nor desired, and yet it did suddenly release one ray of dazzling beauty—Alice racing on her way to London and Liverpool, but still accessible!

But he knew that he could never adjust the impulses of this bright vision to the demands of concrete action. It was not for his own sake, or for Edith's sake, that he had let Alice go.

At the same time he was intensely aware of an outraged sense. It was not his idea of the way to begin the big struggle. In all these years of their married life Edith had not once crossed him, had never been angry with him, had humored him as a mother does a spoilt son. And suddenly she turns and rends him with these terrible tones of her voice, at the very instant when he has resolved to be true and loyal to her, when he is going to make amends. And she was saying other things, cruel and bitter things, things that seemed so cruel and bitter that it required an effort to understand them. "You fool! do you think I could n't see?" And then something terrible and common-fibered: "You, with your stupid ideas that I've put up with all this time I All this high falutin' nonsense about ideals; and then you go and make love to the first young girl you meet I Oh, I knew it would come. I'm not a fool."

Suddenly she flung herself on a chair and buried her face in her hands and sobbed.

"Oh, go! go!" she cried. "What is the good of pretending, you and If—"

He saw her shoulders heaving, and in the dim light her hair looked bedraggled and almost white. The reflection came to him that the days were coming when her hair would be truly white and she would sob alone in the darkness.

The moment when that common-fibered something in her had jarred upon him gradually became diffused in a wondering pity. This woman had given him her all, her love, her health, her strength, and her life. And now for the first time she had flung her dignity to the winds and was grovelling at his feet. She was a raw, naked bit of herself, as he was, crying out for some light in the darkness. She was crying shamelessly:

"I know you love her. I want you to love her. I knew this would come, Arthur. I gambled on it. I have no right to stand in your way. Listen!"

She suddenly stood up and swayed in his direction. She nervelessly seized the lapels of his coat, and said:

"They don't sail from Liverpool till to-morrow. You still have time. Go away with them. Go and live in America. Start your career again. In a year or two marry her, and write and tell me you are happy."

The monstrous offer of sacrifice came quivering from her lips, the bitter renunciation of age to the bowels of youth. The cleavage between their mental attitudes never seemed more definitely declaimed. Despite her moral superiority, her sane and healthy outlook, he saw her at that moment a thing of commoner clay than himself. She had taken him when he was Alice's age, snatched the best years of his life, aware of what would happen, and then through cold-blooded reasoning bowed to the bitter inevitability. He had given up Alice because Alice was intangible, a delicate spring flower belonging to the spring, the predestined mate of some other virginal blossom; and he could almost hear her whisper:

"I am going to be so proud of you!"

She was racing away now to where the sun shines on lake and river and brilliant flowers, and where "the young life" may find itself. And he was standing grimly in this dark bungalow on the threshold of "the big struggle."

What more profitable beginning could be made than here in the dark places of this woman's heart cowering before him? To set aside all blame and regret, to look pity between the eyes and give it your all because it needs it?

Suddenly he seized her shoulders, as he had that night when he first asserted his power over her. Almost brutally he crushed her to him and kissed her.

"Edith, I won't have this! Do you understand? We are all assailed by these things at times. Who isn't? But you are my wife. We've got to win through. I'm not going away. I'm going to stay here with you. Do you hear what I say? We've got to help each other. Bliss me; give me your lips!"

"No, no!"

When at last she hung helpless in his arms, their usual relationship was somewhat reversed. It was he who fetched the Chesterfield and made her put up her feet, and then he lighted the fire and the large lamp. He ordered the housekeeper to cook the supper, and afterward read to her and talked quite calmly of their future plans. And when at night he had supplied her with hot water-bottles and the other comforts a convalescent values, he lay awake listening to her regular breathing.

The rain and wind had somewhat abated, and the martins were silent under the eaves of his father's house.

CHAPTER XXVI

KICKING THE SHAVINGS UNDER YOUR FEET

In a small room at the top of a narrow building in Notting Hill, an elderly, bearded man was poring over a drawing-board. The building was owned by Messrs. Tonks & Aiken, a firm of decorators and builders in a moderate way of business. In truth, Aiken was no more, but Tonks was an ambitious young man from Lancashire, with unlimited "ideas" and very limited capital. He was very proud of this little business, and particularly proud of the fact that in the top room he kept a real designer of his own. There was considerable romance about this designer, for he had been, and still was, in Tonks's opinion, the greatest designer in England. That he had been reduced to the position of working for Tonks was due, in the first place, to the strange debacle that had occurred in the decorating world a few years previously. The firm of Blinkinshaw & Bepstow had "sacked" nearly everybody, and other firms, finding that there was no need to keep up the high standard which this firm had established, had "managed"—that is to say, they had abandoned the attempt to try and produce anything except what the public wanted.

In the second place, this Mr. Leffbury, the designer, was known as a very "difficult" man. He had worked for all sorts of people. He would n't work for anybody he didn't like, and he wouldn't do anything he didn't like. Consequently, Tonks was rather proud that he worked for him, and not only worked for him, but worked for precisely one-eighth the salary that he used to receive from the princely firm of Blinkinshaw & Bepstow. Tonks flattered himself that he understood Mr. Leffbury, and so, to a very large extent, he did. He called him "Pa" and left everything that concerned his own work entirely in his hands. When he produced idealistic schemes of decoration that no client would look at, Mr. Tonks just grinned and debited them in his books against the jobs that were successful.

On this particular afternoon it was nearly dark, and he had come up from the shop to the first floor. He called up the staircase:

"Hello! I say, Pa!"

And a voice came back:

"Yes, what is it?"

"Can you see a young feller named Gaffyn?"

"Eh?"

"There's a young feller named Gaffyn wants to see you. Shall I send him up r'

Mr. Leffbury came out on to the staircase and scratched his chin.

"Gaffyn, eh? Oh, yes, I remember. Send him up, will you? I'd like to see him."

As his visitor entered he called out cheerily:

"Hello, Arthur, how are you? I'm glad to see you. Have a cigarette."

It was ten years since they had met, and during that time Mr. Leffbury had only occasionally thought about the young man. He was, indeed, a man of curiously impersonal friendships. He tried, though not always successfully, to treat everybody alike. Was he not a protagonist of some hare-brained scheme of the brotherhood of man? His work brought him into contact with hundreds of people, and he took them as they came and tried to find the good in them. But he retained a vivid recollection of the visit which he had paid one afternoon to South Kensington Museum with the boy, and the strange association of him with Italy and Donatello. As he glanced at him now he thought:

"Good Lord! I was right about him. He has been tortured by something. He looks like an idealist struggling with the claims of sense; one of those primitive saints painted by Cimabue. How thin and worn he looks!" Arthur perched himself on a high stool, and said:

"Hello, Pa! it's nice to see you again."

He was affected by the way Mr. Leffbury had aged. His beard was almost white and the hair on the top of his head was exceedingly sparse, but his eyes retained his keen and interested glance.

Somewhere at the back was the pleasant hum of a steam fret-saw, and a boy was whistling in the yard below. The little room was warmed by a gas-stove that throbbed gently, and on the buff-coloured walls were drawings in various stages of completion. He was aware of an odd sense of jealousy of this little, bearded man. What was his secret of happiness! The room seemed like a sanctuary from distressing thought; it had the placid air of concentration in absorbing work,

Mr. Leffbury said:

"Excuse me while I wash in this paneling, or else the colour will run. You're married, are n't you!"

"Yes."

"Children?"

"No."

Mr. Leffbury sighed and proceeded with his watercolour wash. Once he glanced above his spectacles, and the thought raced through his mind:

"Backed by some silly love-affair."

Hot upon this there came disturbing visions of his own youth.

A sunlit garden of Highgate; a girl in a large straw hat, looking up at him quickly from under its shadow. Something of an aristocrat; no "game" for an humble draftsman. She was the daughter of a client, but she had found something in him which, she had said, "made life a finer, bigger thing that it was before." She was smiling, and from across the garden stole the sound of an organ droning in the church. Her father was moving on the gravel path, and he could hear the pleading tones of her voice: "Prank, Frank, nothing will ever be the same again." A thrush was talking in his garrulous way up in the cedar tree. For the rest, no one was allowed to share these memories that stirred in the heart of Frank Leffbury and he resented any intrusion that threatened to disturb them.

So for a time they remained silent, each unreasonably jealous of the other. When the elder man had finished the wash, he held the drawing to the stove in order to make it dry more quickly, and said:

"Well, what have you been doing all these years, Arthur?"

"Oh, writing mostly; I'm working for the 'Resurgent.' I belong to a society called 'the Morgeson Society.'"

"What's that?"

"It's a society run by a man named Morgeson, who's very wealthy. The idea is to discover children of unusual talent among the poor in the East End, and then to help them."

"Ah, ha! I see! 'The general excellence of society, eh?'"

"Something of the sort. We 've already discovered two perfectly amazing Jewish children in Shadwell—musicians. We've sent one to Brussels and the other to Prague to be educated. We found a little girl in Nine Elms. She's ten, but she has an extraordinary memory. We're negotiating now about her training. The Morgeson Society unearthed about twenty-five children last year. They're all astounding. There's a mine of talent in the East End that goes to pot every year because no one looks after it."

Mr. Leffbury looked at the younger man and said:

"And so you're very happy?"

Arthur looked a little gloomily at his hands resting on his knees, and he answered:

"It's interesting work."

Mr. Leffbury thought:

"And you're as miserable as the deuce."

Out loud he said:

"How old are you, Arthur?"

"I'm thirty-five."

"As much as that? Lord! how time flies!"

Mr. Leffbury had not recovered from his spasm of jealousy, and he felt resentful over this sudden intrusion into his placid retreat, bringing with it associations of youth and passion, dreams of Italy and its dear regrets, and the realization of his own age and his crusted calm. He said a little boisterously:

"Do you hear that steam-saw, Gaffyn? I 've arrived at the stage when I must have the drone of the working world around me. I like the sound of saws and planes. I love the smell of size and paint. To be bothered by people asking questions all day, to have problems to solve, to walk among men in blouses and kick the shavings under my feet and give instructions to the little potbellied foreman in his shirt-sleeves, with his bowler hat jammed right down over his eyes—that 's my idea of happiness.'

And Arthur thought:

"Why does he say this to me! Besides, he's lying a little; not altogether, but he's keeping something back. I don't believe he's happy at all."

He gazed mutely at a large section of a cap washed in umber, hanging on the wall, and said suddenly:

"Where are all your dreams. Pa, that you had at Blinkinshaw's?'

The older man looked up at him quickly, as though about to make an angry retort, and then he sighed instead and wiped his brushes on a rag.

"I'm not working any more to-night" he said. "Come and have a bit of dinner with me. There's a shabby little Italian restaurant near here. The food is poisonous, but it's the best there is, and one can get a tolerable flask of Chianti."

Arthur made no reply, but he suggested acquiescence by his deliberate manner of rising and putting on his hat. They turned up the collars of their coats, for the night was damp and windy, and sauntered out into the street.

They entered the cheerless restaurant with its red plush seats and mirrors, and managed to secure a seat in the comer. They were each consumed with their own inner emotions and were a little self-conscious of the other. The difference in their ages was too great to allow of any particular intimacy, and they looked upon each other as merely a means for introspective discoveries. It was Arthur who broke the silence. He said:

"You must forgive me mentioning Blinkinshaw's, Pa, but yesterday I saw an appalling sight. I met that chap 'Henry.' He was shuffling along a side street in Bloomsbury. His clothes were frayed and his toes were positively sticking out of his boots. His face was blotchy and puffy, and his eyes bloodshot. He cadged sixpence from me, and darted into a 'pub' with it, like a rabbit bolting down a hole. I knew he drank, even in my time, but I never realized how it could destroy a man. He's little older than I am. I could not help thinking of him on the night when I came to see you first. He was such a gorgeous creature. "

Mr. Leffbury broke a roll and nibbled the end.

"Well," he answered, "that is where one of my 'Blinkinshaw dreams' vanished,—into the bar of a pub. You seem, to an extent, Arthur, to have given up the role of artist for that of reformer. My experience tells me that we reformers have more to fear from the people we want to reform than from outside opposition. The older I grow, the more I realize that man must be thrust back on himself. There is no outside help for him. He has to save his own soul."

"So that is why you walk about the workshops and kick the shavings under your feet!"

The older man looked at the younger a little dubiously and answered:

"I 've thought about all these things that torture you, Gaffyn, and I tell you there's only one solution—love and work. In combination I mean; work is no good without love, and love without work is a destroyer."

He watched the younger man's face, and a perverse mood came to him to probe the tumult of his youth. Between them lay a dubious concoction described as "calves' brains." He took up the silver-plated spoon and fork and served Arthur with a portion. Then he drank a glass of Chianti in little sips and looking across the table, said:

"This love question is the most illusory thing in nature. A young man and a young woman meet, and finding a lot in common which corresponds to the physical attraction which they have for each other, they weave a senseless myth that they are special people, specially designed for each other; that they will live in this way to the end of their lives, and that afterward they will be united eternally in some fantastic union. It's absolutely ridiculous. Either would have been equally competent to have loved some one else. Love is too big a thing to box up like that. There is a universal love which sways the magic of creation. It is only that these two have drawn a little of it to themselves, and embellished it with all the mysterious glamor which surrounds sexual attraction."

He studied the look of gloom which clouded the young man's face, and added:

"We eat up each other in time, in the same way that you and I now devour the brains of a young calf who had the same illusions in some damp meadow."

Arthur pushed the plate from him and muttered:

"Why do you torture me like this?"

Mr. Leffbury suddenly became earnest:

"Because I wish to God it was you who ruled the world! When I say you, I mean youth and impulse and love. It must come to that, for the old, who own, rule, and govern the world, have worked without love in their hearts. In the trouble that is coming—and there is very big trouble coming to humanity—it won't be the young who are to blame, or even the weak or the sensual. It will be the old, who have worked without love. Was n't it you and I who talked about the work-box? What wonderful things we've made out of the work-box, Gaffyn! Things to save time, to increase comfort, to 'speed up' humanity, to create luxury! And what does it all amount to? Work without love. Do you remember the old punishment, now abolished,—the punishment of abortive labor? A man was made to carry bricks across a yard, and then carry them back again, and so on all day. In time it drove him mad. What does this prove? That even the vile have a soul, the instinct of service. Man cannot work without love. But these chartered libertines of righteousness, these old men whispering in their secret chambers and pulling the wires, are simply carrying bricks from one end of the yard to the other and back again. One day they will go mad, and then they will drive the young before them like cattle to the slaughter. For that is the peculiar form that this madness will take, a sort of perverted sense, a joy in destroying what is young and splendid. Do you know, when you came into my room just now and I said something cruel and unreasonable to you,—do you know why I did it? Because I was suddenly jealous of you, of your youth. And I am quite a nice old man, as old men go. But you see it everywhere; the old coveting the things of youth and wanting to destroy the young. And the old have the power. They have the instruments, the accumulated symbols of coined labor of dead centuries, with which to wreak their perverted vengeance. The young, you see, have to be 'educated,' and that is where the old men get their biggest pull. They can teach what they like, print what they like, inculcate any doctrine they like. The young find themselves 'baptized' before they're conscious, wearing stiff collars and reading the newspapers before they've had time to think. The young never get a chance, not a dog's chance. They're tied hand and foot and pushed into the maelstrom. The only hope for the world is when the young shall rule it."

The younger man looked down and fumbled with the bread by the side of his plate. He suddenly said:

"Impulse—is impulse right, Pat I have particular cause to know. You have spoken of impulse. I want to think about it clearly."

The older man was about to reply when he observed his companion look up at him with a strained and anxious look. His lips were trembling and he was obviously anxious to impart some confession. He looked down again, and Mr. Leffbury remained silent. And then in a low voice Arthur said:

"Three months ago I left my wife. I am alone, and there are all sorts of impulses—"

CHAPTER XXVII

THE SENSUALIST

"'Let us go across to my rooms; I live not far I from here with my sister. I think she's out 'to-night; in any case, she won't disturb us. We can have a smoke and chat, and if you feel in the moody you can tell me all about it."

There was a mild squabble over the bill, each wanting to pay, out eventually the matter was settled by a division.

When they were at last ensconced in two easy chairs on either side of Mr. Leffbury's fire, that gentleman continued:

"An impulse has, in any case, the virtue of being a free action, untrammeled by self -consciousness or tradition. A good impulse is a permanent good, and a bad impulse is only a transient evil. For instance, an impulse may strike a blow, but will never wage war. It has the gift of recovery; it isn't vindictive or calculating. That is why impulsive people are invariably naive and lovable. It's these long-headed, calculating people who cause all the trouble. Roll yourself another cigarette."

Arthur fumbled with the tobacco-pouch and succeeded in making himself a somewhat billowy-shaped cigarette. Then he said:

"Perhaps you're right; bat I must ask your opinion whether I should act on impulse now. I married my wife on impulse, and she married me on calculation, I should say. To that end, impulse has proved wrong."

"And calculation has proved criminal. You say your wife was eight years older than you. What is this but the old covetous of the young and anxious to destroy it? She knew what she was doing. And so the affair has proved a failure?"

"Not at first; it seemed all right. And then one day I fell in love. She was an American girl; this was seven years ago. "

"Ah! a girl of your own age?"

"No; the same tragedy repeated itself. She was much younger than I. If she had been my age, I think I should have acted on impulse."

"And you, too, wanted to destroy the young, and you forswore it?"

Arthur struck a second match to light his unsuccessful-looking cigarette.

"In a way, I suppose. It didn't seem playing the game. She was so young and splendid. I loved her in a fantastic manner. Oh, it is all very difficult, Pa. I hate these people who are always shouting their slogans about the 'will to do this, that, and the other.' I am like an astronomer with the will to study the stars, who is condemned to live in a basement Sometimes one can peer up and get a peep over the area-steps of some pale star above the housetops. It is just enough to make one reckless; one wants to grasp the whole firmament. It was something like that I felt about her. She was my one star, the thing that proved there was a sky above. I loved her desperately, and yet she made me want to worship her from afar. And so I conquered my impulse. Was I wrong?"

Mr. Leffbury puffed solemnly at his pipe.

"Tell me," he said. "What was the cause of the estrangement with your wife? Had it to do with that?"

"No, curiously enough, it hadn't. We had that out and settled it. The trouble was caused by a pearl-handled penknife."

"What on earth do you mean?"

"When I was a boy, I stole a penknife at school. I was dismissed for it; I never thought any more of it. But eleven years after, when I was becoming a little known, the affair was dished up by innuendo—

you know, in one of those filthy rags, that do these things. But I wouldn't move in the matter. I made rather a fool of myself, and was hounded out of a club I belonged to. My wife knew of it, but wouldn't say anything. It caused a serious breach between us, however, one of those strained, unexpressed things. I became aware of her looking at me in a queer, furtive manner, as though I were an unclean thing. I thought it had blown over, but suddenly up it came again. You see the imputation had never been denied; in fact, it was undeniable. And then it became twisted and exaggerated. I went on with my work, but I found that people cut me and publishers boycotted me. I believe some story went around that I had been doing some dirty business in the city—running a bucket-shop or something! It became quite interesting. I believe it would really have amused me, if it hadn't been for the effect it had on my wife. We ignored the matter at first, but eventually it couldn't be ignored and I told her the whole story. She behaved in the most womanly manner, and forgave me and sympathized with me, as you may imagine, but her eyes! Good God! into her eyes there came that look, like a thick veil between us. With her training and her tradition it was impossible not to feel the cleavage. She fled to the opposing camp, and my heart hardened against her. I felt very much alone in my struggle with her. The combat was unequal. She had everything and everyone on her side, and she was a woman of action, while I could only review the battle in a detached way, like a spectator. The pawns we fought with were the marshaled array of little things.' Oh, those little things! How much more important a part they play in the struggle than the big things. I learned to put up with the children; Martin, the boy, is quite a nice chap. There was never the suggestion of a quarrel; it was only just the way she looked at me in odd moments, her frigid patronage, little worrying ways of fussing over purely material things, a certain narrowness of outlook. And then, beneath it all, despite her somewhat insolent sense of moral superiority, a 'common-fibered' something. How can I explain it?

''She seemed to fall away from me, to be a different person. She became less my wife than a symbol of those forces of which you spoke. Pa; forces I felt myself to be just outside. Honestly, this civilization of ours beats me; I give it up! I feel like a child in an engine-room. I see the wheels going round and great cranks turning, but they mean nothing to me; I want to be out in the sun. It was at this time that I joined the staff of 'The Resurgent.' You 've heard of it? It has been described in the respectable press as 'a magazine run by madmen for madmen'; you know what that means—anyone who won't sell his soul is a madman.

"The thing surged on, working up to little climaxes and then dying down. The tragedy was not helped by the fact that I had not the ability to be cruel. When these little climaxes came she used to cry, and swear she loved me. And I pitied her intensely. I was tied to her by all these years of companionship, a time marked by many hours of tenderness and passion. I believe in her hard, aristocratic way she loves me still. My love for her is dead, but I cannot kill my pity. I sometimes pray for the power to be cruel. Our separation has worked by drifting methods. For longer and longer periods I went down and stayed at my father's bungalow at Bodiesham. I found it a sort of sanctuary, as though it were still haunted by his gentle, distinguished presence. I can work there. As you know, I made some progress. 'The Fugitive Philosopher' was well reviewed. I have done other stuff that has called forth some meed of sympathy from unexpected quarters. A child said to me, 'They who have the great secret know each other in a crowd.' That's true enough. Pa. We have to turn to children for wisdom and love, eh? Heavens I have you any whisky?"

Mr. Leffbury produced a tantalus from a cupboard, and set out two glasses and a siphon. When the concoction was mixed, Arthur drank half his tumbler rapidly, and continued:

"I suppose in time I shall become like Henry, Pa, and shuffle down back streets, with my toes sticking out of my boots."

He laughed a little wildly and rested his feet on the fender.

"I know what they say of me—I'm a sensualist. And it's true; I am a sensualist. But my idea of a sensualist differs from theirs. Do you know what I mean by a sensualist? I mean a man who has the whole world at his feet, and then doesn't take it. That is the maximum appeal to sense that a man can enjoy. Who was that old fool? Nero! He fiddled while Rome burnt. My heart goes out to that man. My only dread is that he fiddled badly, scraped like a rich amateur. But if he fiddled well! Here was an idealist for you! The one man who realized that spirit is more important than matter, that it is better to make divine music than to save property. Why shouldn't Rome burn?

"I am a sensualist because my life has been concerned with qualities and textures, rather than with substances. Well, why not? I have helped to shape things a little, haven't It What else do any of us dot We're not finished products, any of us; we're tendencies. We're just the sentient nerves connecting the dead with the great unborn. The dead are clamorous, calling to us to carry on the things they fought for, but the unborn are more insistent. They touch our hearts with the knowledge that they will reap our sowing. Life is quality, not quantity. Sometimes these fools will seize a segment of clay and round off the edges, and call it a general, or an admiral, or a judge, and shove it into a wall at Westminster and speak of 'Glory' and 'Honor.' Do you know why they do it? They do it because they're afraid of the dead and afraid of the unborn. They have to keep on pinching themselves to show that they're alive. It gives them confidence to see a tombstone and to bring in acts of Parliament. Oh, the pompous drivel! They will spend a century discussing whether Shakespeare's father was a publican or a butcher, and will write tedious books to prove that another man wrote his plays, but they won't understand that the only thing that matters a damn is themselves in relation to the spirit of the plays.

'Shakespeare was a sensualist. He got up in the morning and drank beer for breakfast, and the beauty of the sunrise would make him cry. What better biography could anyone desire than that? If there is a God, the sensualist must be very dear to him, for he interprets so many of His inventions, like a skilled musician playing the works of a composer."

"One night I was alone in the bungalow at Bodiesham. I was suffering terribly, when, for some reason or other, I started thinking about Christ. It's a strange thing. I was then thirty-four, and I think it was the first time I had thought about Christ seriously. At school I attended two services daily in His honor. Why is it that we always have His teachings dinned into us till we hate them, at an age when we have not the imagination to grasp them? I detested the Christian religion, with its dull dogma and its dreary service in the ugly chapel. But on that night I was so wretched I groped for consolations. And on a sudden I thought of that bearded Jew who was crucified at Calvary because of His convictions. And I thought the story through, and wished I had not heard it before. I should like to have come across it suddenly for the first time that night. I should have liked to have had it told me by an Arab storyteller, his body swaying in the moonlight under the white wall of a Syrian mosque. Or even more than that, I should like to have written the story myself, to have had it come to me in a dream. For when you come to think of it, it's the most wonderful story in the world. With its background of olive groves and violet nights and Eastern music, and against this that amazing full-blooded man who was not afraid to hate the Scribes and Pharisees, and who took a stout whip of thongs and drove the money-changers out of the temple with lusty blows. Here was a sensualist after one's own heart. That was the one thing He could not stand—the moneychangers in the temple I And when they heckled Him, He answered them in parables—a splendid, artistic touch!— and parables that will live forever. He was the one man who was not afraid to let himself go, and they killed Him for it and shoved thorns and nails in His flesh, and so He pointed the salvation of the world in terms of physical sensation. And after he died the money-changers went back to the temple, and they've been there ever since. But what I like is His insistence on the great divergence between sin and the sinner. He hated one and loved the other. He shut no one out. He raised the Magdalen from the dust, and did n't ask questions when the afflicted were brought to Him. And then that wonderful incident at the end, when the thief who was crucified with Him turned to Him. I like to think of that thief, not as a muscular hooligan of the highway, but as some little whining Jew of a property receiver, a man whose life wouldn't bear looking into. Think how he would have suffered! The sickening terrors of fear and remorse and contrition, his hopelessness and utter isolation! And then the ghastly pain as he looked down at his bleeding limbs, the limbs that perhaps' only his mother had loved in her idolatrous way! Floods of self-pity swamp him, and suddenly, as the sweating horrors of death close in, he looks up and into the eyes of a God who says: "'To-day shalt thou be with me in Paradise. "'It's the most wonderful story in the world! It's getting late. Pa, and you have n't given me your opinion about my impulse."

Mr. Leffbury watched the young man's face intently. In the little room, lighted by a cold incandescent gaslight, he listened to the voice of the young man of whom he had been envious. He answered in a low voice:

"Arthur, when you move about in the crowd I hope you will always find one pair of eyes that knows your 'secret.' I would help you if I could. What is this impulse now you want me to adjudicate upon? Your relationship with your wife, as far as I can judge, has gone beyond impulse. Is it the other woman, the girl?"

Arthur nodded:

"Next week she is coming back to Europe. The thought of it tortures me. I am a riot of impulse. I love her wildly, desperately. What am I to dot"

"What is the difference in your ages?"

"Twelve years."

"Does she still love you?"

"How can I tell? We have been sending lovers' notes to each other. It is six years since we met. She is a child, impressionable, happy. It may have been an illusion on her part. The young forget. There is romance in writing loving letters. How can I trust her youth? She says things that send my spirits raging up to the skies, and at other times things that fill me with foreboding and doubt. She talks of people I have never seen, speaks affectionately of youths who go with her to picnics and dances. It is all a wild jumble in my brain. How can one trust the written word? She has the genius of love. How can I detach her love for me from the ocean of love which is her natural birthright? What am I to do?"

The older man thought for a moment, and then he said kindly:

"Your impulses won't lead you far astray, if you keep them worthy of your secret. The secret which you and I believe in, Arthur, and those others who will know us in the crowd, is that that world which we believe in, that world that shall one day evolve from these chaotic happenings, is the world you have pictured to me—a child in the Luxembourg Gardens gazing up at a kite."

CHAPTER XXVIII

12B Bue de la Grande Armée,
St Germain.

To Frank Leffbury, Esq.:

My dear Pa,

I wanted to escape from civilization, so I came to Paris. You may understand this paradox better than most people. It is, indeed, not a paradox at all, but a very obvious platitude. Paris presents more "escapes" than any city I know. You may think from this that I am leading a wild life, becoming a sort of "Henry." Alas! this is anything but true. I am far too unhappy, too distracted to face the reaction from these doubtful pleasures. I only find relief by probing about and looking into faces more unhappy than my own. I promised you I would tell you the outcome of my adventures, and so I leave this letter to explain itself. My pen runs on, but I feel a queer, detached person looking over my shoulder, if you can understand what I mean. Have you ever seriously contemplated self-destruction? I have, and I failed, not through lack of courage, but because I reached the point when I realized that self-destruction wouldn't be any solution at all. One has to hug one's dear remorse all through one's life, go to bed with it, get up with it, follow it through the work-a-day world until it becomes one's companion, learn to love it like a piece of old furniture that has been in the family for generations. Nature, who overdoes everything, is particularly prodigal when it comes to questions of sexual attraction. The thing is ridiculously overdone. I am told that barely one twentieth of nature's production attain to maturity. Perhaps it is her inverted way of expressing the fact that quality is more important than quantity. She does n't give a damn for all this wastage, as long as the best survives. I do not understand this popular belief that human life is sacred. Why is it sacred? Because we don't understand it? But what do we understand? Nothing, except the impulses of our own hearts. I believe in the sanctity of an idea, but not of a person. Otherwise we might lay ourselves out to produce millions and millions of healthy policemen, shall we say? Fancy the world entirely populated and overcrowded with healthy policemen and dairy girls. Heavens I it would be better to produce one sickly Heine writing from 'his mattress grave."

I am writing all this down as it comes into my head, because I want to forget all about you. I want to set down just what I have gone through and how it has affected me. I want to dig it out of myself. You will realize, then, that this is a selfish letter, written more for my own benefit than for yours. But it will help me enormously to give it to some one, and so you must pay the price of having too sympathetic a heart.

When I beheld my beloved again—it was in the vestibule of a hotel—she seemed to me more wondrous than ever, more intensely my own. She was the complement to the shattered fragment of me that had roamed the earth these many years. She was more and more of a woman, with the brooding motherliness of her kind. As I touched her little fingers, that sacro-sensuous message swept through my heart. I don't know whether it is sacred or profane, but the message seemed to be: "You will be the mother of my children. "

I could hardly speak to her, she seemed so rare and wonderful a thing. There were a whole lot of them there, apart from her brother; all young people, buoyant and gay, and full of lively purposes. I was introduced sketchily. I did n't get the hang of who they all were, or what they were doing, except that they were going on a tour round Europe. They talked prodigiously—you know what these Americans are!—but I liked them for their simplicity and youth, and their keen way of lying in wait for impressions. If I had any misgivings, it only took the form that my heart's desire was more of an assured woman, her attitude more mothering and consciously friendly. She called me "old man" and "dear old Arthur" terms the significance of which I did not grasp till afterward.

So crowded were the white-hot arrangements of this joyous party—they left the following night for Paris—that I did not get an opportunity of seeing her alone. I dined with them, and her face was flushed and excited with what I believed to be the joy of seeing me again. I was to meet them a fortnight later in Switzerland, and take the Italian trip with them.

But just before my time for departure a cable came from her brother to say that sickness had broken out in the party. He advised me not to come and said he was writing. I suffered an agony of suspense awaiting his letter, dreading some terrible news about my dear one. But when the letter came it said that one of the girls and one of the young men had developed typhoid fever through drinking impure water. They were very ill, and the party was upset Alice and another girl had constituted themselves nurses. He would let me know later how things went.

It was three weeks before I heard again. Then the brother wrote once more. The invalids were getting on well, but the boy, who had the ridiculous name of "Cinders"—I think it was a nickname— had been very ill. He and the girl were staying on at Lausanne, and Alice and the other girl were going to remain and look after them, while the rest of the party were leaving for Florence. Would I join them there? Then I began to suffer paroxysms of misgiving. Why had Alice not even sent me a card! Why should I go to Florence? What was Florence to me or I to Florence that I should worship her while Alice was nursing some boy in Lausanne? I became restless and distraught. A dozen times I packed my things and prepared to start for Lausanne, and a dozen times I changed my mind. Perhaps, after all, she did not want me to go? She had not written.

And then her letter came. It was a long and loving letter, full of regrets for not having written before, crowded with details of the tedious "Cinder's" illness, and embellished with endearing terms; but there was no hint that she expected me at Lausanne! For the first time I began to suspect the "dear old man" attitude.

I was consumed with jealousy and doubt I replied post-haste, not daring to express my doubts, but hinting desperately at my desire for her and my anxiety to see her again immediately.

Again three weeks went by, and then came another letter like the last. They were staying at Lausanne—they had learned to love the place—until September, and then they would be coming back through London.

I had no misgivings then. I heard the slow music of this dance of tragic circumstances drawing nearer and nearer, and across the fair prospect of my newly awakened life there fell the shadow of the dancers swaying slowly to its gentle rhythm.

I lived in a sort of trance for weeks. I wrote to her every day. Sometimes I tore the letters up, sometimes I sent them. I bullied myself into an obeisance of a kind. I said, "You fool, is n't this what you predicted! What else could you expect?"

Work was out of the question. I was living alone in rooms at Chelsea at the time. I used to wander about the streets at night and think: "Is she asleep? Is she awake? Is she thinking of met That other one, has he really comet Is it possible that anyone could love her as I love her?" And then I would break away in despair and mutter, "I can't go on! I can't go on!" In the morning I would try and write calmly to her. There was a stimulus for writing calmly, for if I considered the letter calm enough, I sent it, but if it was too violent, I kicked myself into tearing it up.

She wrote me two more letters before the month of September came. They were very similar to the others, kind, affectionate, but marred by an undercurrent of pity. God! how little a thing pity is when we die for love!

I began to dread the day when she would come. I was frightened; I felt insecure in my grip upon myself. The strain of those months was telling upon me terribly.

It was in this mood that I came to Paris. It was on the way; she would have to pass through it. I was, indeed, starting for Lausanne. But here I hardened my heart. In the agonizing crisis that came to me, I realized for the first time that it would be possible to be cruel. I knew that I could leave my wife utterly and finally. She would get over it and "settle down"—a disgusting term I—but for me everything else was finished.

And now I am in a fever of despair. I wander about the streets desperately, and at night I do not sleep. Again and again I have visions of the tragedy that is upon me. Do you know what will happen, Pa? I can see it all as vividly as this pen I hold in my hand. A letter will drop into the box. Her dear writing. Listen; this is what she will say:

"I have some wonderful news for you. I am in a dream. It is all too beautiful to be true. You were right, Arthur dear, in your prediction concerning me. I want you to forgive me and to share my happiness. Will you come and see me to-morrow at—and I will tell you everything.

Yes, yes, I know she will ask me to 'share her happiness.' God! And then I shall laugh in a silly, hysterical way, laugh and cry and rage, and then everything will be dark and silent.

Of course I shall go. I shall go the next day to the flat, or hotel, or whatever it is. I shall go to "share her happiness" and to offer her my hand. I can see it all quite clearly and I rehearse my part by day and night.

I can see the little room with the Chesterfield before the fire. The maid announces me. And then as I enter, Alice, with a little cry of pleasure, comes forward to meet me. She "old man's" me unmercifully. I observe the cosy security of the room, the crumpled cushions on the Chesterfield, Alice with one of the strands of her beautiful hair dishevelled, her eyes deep and a little tired, as though she had been disturbed in a dream, and a boy in a gray suit who rises and grins at me in a friendly, patronizing way. She will say:

"Dear old Arthur, I'm ever so glad to see you!"

And on her face will be the strained glance of pity.

Everything is finished and inevitable. I cannot speak. I stand there gazing foolishly at her gold-brown hair and that incriminating curl I love so dearly. In all my life I have never suffered as I suffer at that moment. She never seems so much my own, my very own. All the dear lines of her little body, and the wistful poise of her small head. O God! I had made them mine. Everything about her is mine. I have stamped it on my heart and carried it about with me in a thousand earthly fragments. And now she stands before me with the eyes of a lover, languorously happy, as though the horrors of sense have become exalted and she finds in them some divine elation.

I cannot believe that I must not take her in my arms. It is the supreme moment I am to awaken in her, when I see bewilderment pass to the yielding ecstasy of love.

I do not know how long I stand there, but my eyes are trying to convey:

"Alice, Alice, it is I. You and I, dear. Surely there can be no other. You cannot have forgotten. Those hours we loved cannot be forgotten or destroyed. This is some mad dream, this other thing. If I were alone with you, surely I could reawaken—If I could press my cheek against yours, as I did that night when you said you could not let me go, surely I could draw you back to me. It must be so. Oh, my dear, my dear."

Again and again I rehearse this scene. But she smiles and speaks to me again in her warm voice, and I turn and shake the boy's hand. I can see him, too, quite clearly. There is nothing wrong with him. He is real enough, one of her own people. I can see the clear gray eye, the strong and purposeful chin. Yes, yes, I must "share her happiness."

We talk inanely about Swiss hotels, or the way of making omelettes at Mont St. Michel, or something equally ridiculous, and then I stand up and congratulate them, and pass out of their lives. For I know I have not the strength to be "an old pal."

"Dear old Arthur,"

But she will not leave me alone with her pity. She tells the boy to wait while she walks with me to the end of the street. And the boy grins, with the conscious superiority of his unassailable position.

In the street she presses my arm.

"Arthur dear, I'm so sorry."

And I keep on repeating:

"I'm glad for you. I hope you'll be happy."

The tears are in her beautiful eyes as she says:

"You 'll never do anything foolish, Arthur!"

"No, no, I won't do anything foolish."

And then like a fool, I give a sob, perhaps, and the tears are streaming down her cheeks, but I manage to say:

I 'm all right. I 'm all right. I'm sorry. Alice."

We are at some crowded comer and I mount a bus. I am struck by the fact that people are laughing and talking, and boys are selling newspapers. Why on earth should people want newspapers? What news can there be when love is shut out?

From the top of a bus I look back and see her standing waving to me. She looks so fragile and slight, so alone amid the ugly turmoil of the corner, I cannot get it out of my head that I ought not to go back and look after her. My Alice! My dear!

Then, with a swerve, we pass into the obscurity of the night. I have been through all this a hundred times to-day.

If you have any pity, Pa, leave your muddy drawings for a day and come and see
Your disconsolate disciple,
ARTHUR GAFFYN.

CHAPTER XXIX

MR. LEFFBURY REPLIES TO ANOTHER LETTER

Nottingdale.

My dear Arthur:

Why are you always destined to make a fool of me! I am very busy to-day (a music-room for some blasted lady of title. Tonks and I are getting a move on. I am now his pupil), and yet I left off early and came home. I went to my desk and took out an old sandalwood box. There are certain things in it I am not going to tell you about them; you don't deserve it. The white lilac is in bloom in the garden of the square here, and on my table are these yerba huena letters of yours. There is too much yerba huena about them altogether. By the way, I did read your "Fugitive Philosopher" and I must concede that you are something of a philosopher, or in any case, you are the most unreasonable person I have ever met, which amounts to very much the same thing. Perhaps, in my life, I have tried to be too static a philosopher. I have always wanted to know everything, to have all knowledge at my finger-tips and to weld the result into some cosmic understanding. Tour desire seems to be to know nothing, to feel your way through the maze, and to be always peeping over the edge. You are, indeed, something of a cheat. I had great hopes, in my position of father-confessor, of observing you find your way out by some fine spiritual evolution. But you must needs meet the old trouble with the usual moon-calf remedy. I am disgusted with you, but I add to my store of knowledge. I discover that, after all, all philosophy is fugitive. It is as fluid as the Gulf Stream and equally as debatable a warmer of humanity.

When you wrote me that preposterous letter from Paris—was it only last summer!—and I left my work and went over and found you with a fever in some vile-smelling rooms, my philosophy was of a fixed and rigid order. I was really rather pleased with it; and I enjoyed my visit immensely. Heavens! how I worked and dived within myself. I did not realize that philosophy could be so good a friend to man. Indeed, all that can be said is that in trying to help you, I helped myself.

Don't you remember 'kicking the shavings under one's feet'? Didn't I demonstrate to you the joy of things purely intellectual; the love of work, the love of one's fellow-man, the consciousness of being in touch with the great heart of humanity stretching out toward God? I will acknowledge now that I started talking to you with my tongue in my cheek, because I pitied you, but so persuasive and eloquent did I become, that gradually I began to believe that what I said was true. I was tremendously pleased with myself. I think I left you in worse case than I found you, certainly more argumentative and irrational, but I returned to London with peace in my own heart. For days I could think of nothing but what a satisfactory person I was. I had been haunted by the eyes of youth at a magic casement, expectant for the satisfying hour. And lo! the magic casement had become a dark tower of troubled gloom, and you had drawn me into it, and I had done my duty. I had pointed out to you the illusion of these sentimental periods. The satisfying hour is only found within. I was pleased that I had pointed this out to you. And I was wise enough to withdraw another remark I had made. "No," I said. "The world has not one tenth the power of torturing you that you have of torturing yourself. A child like you can no more escape from his temperament than a leopard can escape from his spots."

So pleased was I with this postulate that I wrote it down, I remember. And I promised myself to help you. I would weave around you a delicate web of this shifting philosophy, that would have to be adapted to moods and seasons. And suddenly you cut the Gordian knot of my placid self-satisfaction with your outrageous telegram:

"I went to Lausanne. There was no other."

Was ever a man made to cut so ridiculous a figure! Fool and renegade! Because a girl who has been intelligently educated calls you "old man" your Latin blood becomes suspicious. You see the dancing elf of friendship when you are yearning for the warm breasts of Hebe! In your fevered anxiety it does not occur to you that a girl who has had years of training in physics and medicine would naturally nurse any fellow-being in a crisis ! Because her letters are sane and healthy, and are not couched in the same outrageously sentimental strain as your own, your imagination riots with scenes that are more vivid than reality. Indeed, with such as you there is no point of difference. As I see you, your only hope lies in this woman. She may make some sort of man of you, if she only makes you her slave. I note with satisfaction that you went to Lausanne; Lausanne did not come to you. Odd's Bodikin! I really believe you expected her to! You seemed to accept it as your natural prerogative that a girl like this would run after you, an officially married man into the bargain. I rejoice that she made you go to Lausanne. In fact, I have a confession to make concerning this girl. I have written to her and I have had a reply—one of the nicest letters I have ever had in my life. Among other things she said this: "You bet your sweet life. Pa Leffbury, I won't spoil him. There has been a conspiracy to spoil him all through. I'm going to make him prance like a two-year-old."

There is great hope for this child.

So loose and inconsequent is your grip on concrete things that if I were holding a watching brief for humanity, I'm not sure that I should not dismiss you altogether, but for the fact that you have the salutary effect of disturbing me. In fact, you are the most disturbing thing in life, its kind of moral genius, with an infinite capacity for suffering and enjoying.

Some there are who have a faculty for pushing their way about in a crowd. Others can only look on from a window, but so profoundly does the spectacle move them that they are driven to express their vision of it. And so, if their expression is sincere enough, they may eventually become more active agents than the pusher in the street below. To this end I would, perhaps, justify you.

At any moment the magic casement may light up and become a place of revelation. And who shall say from what obscure comer these things we desire so much may not come? You are all visions. A wooden box, an empty room, a shut door, dumb ghost-ridden things,—these are the realities which move you. The history of a race, the precision of science, the phenomena of social progress, mean nothing to you at all. You are just outside them. You are as apposite to the functionary of society as a haunting scheme of colour, or that recurring theme in Schubert's Impromptu would be to the steel frame of a New York building.

Even when you send me an extravagant message from Las Palmas:

"I have found the great solution, Pa Leffbury. Every hour is a satisfying hour."

I rage against the tawdry apothegm, but I am haunted by the vision of you. The "great solution!" Fiddlesticks!

"Every hour a satisfying hour!"

Yes, yes, I dare say! And every duck is a swan, and no one has ever been in love before, and the "great solution" is once more this calf-love affected by the moon.

I promise you you will suffer again intensely, despite your "solution" for the simple reason that others will suffer and you are only the "sensitive nerve." This Alice of yours will have a bilious attack, or she will have children, or you will see a poor child with a scrofulous neck, and behold, the magic casement will again become a place of torment. You will rage and weep, and be a source of irritation to others, as you are to me, but neither they nor I will be able to dismiss you.

It is good for us all to be disturbed sometimes in this game of hunt-the-thimble. For isn't it really all rather like that? We're primarily time-devourers. We hate time, and invent things to destroy it. Everyone is glad to find it is later than they expected. We are glad when it is near the end of the day or the week. We are glad when winter is over, and the spring, and half -past six, and the term, and the summer, and even the holiday—just as though we were secretly hunting for something. We're like a lot of greedy children with a pudding in which some one is reported to have put a lucky sixpence. So anxious are we to get at the sixpence that we tear the pudding to pieces bit by bit. It is not till we begin to get old that we are apt to ask ourselves whether the chance of a lucky sixpence is worth the destruction of the whole pudding.

You with your satisfying hours!

Do you imagine that your description of California moves me in the slightest? You would find equal delights in Bayswater or Canning Town in your present mood. Of course I know the madrons tree; it is simply the Greek arbutus. But what are tamales? And what is an adobe house? And an oyster loaf f And what, in God's name, is a high-ball? It is useless to ask me to share these joys with you. I am as much a slave to my "shavings" as you are to the eyes of your mistress.

I am, in fact, angry with you, angry and a little jealous; and for the reason that you have the faculty of escaping "just outside. "However we may circumscribe you, you will always be there dancing about, like a will-o'-the-wisp, just outside the circle. The schoolmaster will say you are "a detrimental," the politician "an anti-social" the churchman will give you up as a hopeless case; and yet I must concede this point to you, that if they cannot encompass you, it is they who are "just outside. "They do not, in truth, know their job, and that is the only quality I can bring myself to reverence in any man.

I went to St. Anne's in Soho on Wednesday night and heard Bach's "Passion" music. It is evergreen, and gave me great comfort. To-night I have discovered a new and interesting blend of tobacco. I am honoring you by smoking it as I write. No, I shall never come and see you, but I feel better for writing this letter, calmer and more of a static philosopher, and I will always be pleased to put you right upon these hoary theses that you are so apt to evolve. Upon one I will put you right at once. It is not the old who rule the world. It never was and never will be. It is the young. Whatever we may do to them, they triumph. It is their game all through. People talk of a world-calamity, but I promise you there is only one conceivable world-calamity —that humanity should lose the faculty to fall in love. It isn't the old or even the wise who keep us all agog, but youth with his disturbing visions. You never sent me back that copy of Kant's "Critique of Pure Reason" which I lent you. I don't suppose you ever will, or that you will ever read it, you young devil! Ah, well! I have bullied you enough to-night.

Your friend,

Frank Leffbury.

STACY AUMONIER – A SHORT BIOGRAPHY

Stacy Aumonier was born at Hampstead Road near Regent's Park, London on 31st March 1877.

He came from a family with a strong and sustained tradition in the visual arts; sculptors and painters.

In 1890 the teenage Aumonier attended Cranleigh School in Surrey. Although he would later write critically about English public schools (with articles for the London Evening Standard and New York Times) in how they tried to impose conformity on students, records indicate that he integrated well into Cranleigh. Aumonier was a passionate cricket player, belonged to the Literary and Debating Society, and, in his final year, became a prefect.

On leaving school it seemed the family tradition of the visual arts would be his career path. In particular his early talents were that of a landscape painter. He exhibited paintings at the Royal Academy in 1902 and 1903, and 1908. An exhibition of his work would later be held at the Goupil Gallery in London in 19ll.

In 1907 he married the international concert pianist, Gertrude Peppercorn, at West Horsley in Surrey. She herself was the daughter of a landscape painter (Arthur Douglas Peppercorn, occasionally cited as 'the English Corot'.) A son, Timothy, was born in 1921.

A year after his marriage, Aumonier began a brief career in a second branch of the arts at which he enjoyed outstanding success—as a stage performer writing and performing his own sketches.

The Observer newspaper commented that "...the stage lost in him a real and rare genius, he could walk out alone before any audience, from the simplest to the most sophisticated, and make it laugh or cry at will."

In 1915, Aumonier published a short story 'The Friends' which was well received (and voted one of the best short stories of 1915 by the Boston Magazine, Transcript).

Despite his age being 40 in 1917 he was called up for service in World War I. He began as a private in the Army Pay Corps, and then transferred as a draughtsman in the Ministry of National Service.

By now he had four books published—two novels and two books of short stories—and his occupation is recorded with the Army Medical Board as 'author.'

In the mid-1920s, Aumonier received the shattering diagnosis that he had contracted tuberculosis. In the last few years of his life, he would spend long spells in various sanatoria, some better than others. In a letter to his friend, Rebecca West, written shortly before his death, he described the debilitating conditions in a sanatorium in Norfolk during the winter of 1927, where the dampness was so severe that a newspaper left beside the bed would feel "sodden to the touch in the morning."

Shortly before his death, Stacy Aumonier sought treatment in Switzerland, but died of the disease in Clinique La Prairie at Clarens beside Lake Geneva on 21st December 1928. He was 55.

Whilst Aumonier's works are now slowly coming back into circulation at the time of his death his works were extremely popular and his loss was a profound tragedy for literary society.

The chief fiction critic of The Observer, Gerald Gould wrote: "His gifts were almost fantastically various; they embraced all the arts; but it was the charm and generosity of his personality which made him—what he unquestionably was—one of the most popular men of his generation." It went on: "The things he wrote will be remembered when the company of his friends (no man had more friends, or more devoted and admiring) are with him in the grave; but just now, to those who knew him, the thing most vividly present is the charm and wisdom of the man they knew."

Of his general appearance and manner Gerald Cumberland gives us this interesting set of observations: "A distinguished man, this—distinguished both in mind and appearance. Self-conscious. Perhaps. Why not? His hair is worn a trifle long, and it is arranged so that his fine forehead, broad and high, may be fully revealed. Round his neck is a very high collar and a modern stock. When in repose, his face has a look of shy eagerness; his quick eyes glance here and there gathering a thousand impressions to be stored up in his brain. It is the face of a man extremely sensitive to external stimulus; one feels that his brain works not only rapidly, but with great accuracy. And at heart, he takes himself and his work seriously, though he likes on occasion to pretend that he is only a philanderer."

In literary terms Aumonier was amongst the best short story writers these shores have produced.

The Nobel Prize winning author John Galsworthy called him "A real master of the short story. The first essential in a short-story writer is the power of interesting sentence by sentence. Aumonier had this power in prime degree. You do not have to 'get into' his stories. He is especially notable for investing his figures with the breadth of life within a few sentences." Galsworthy asserted that Aumonier "is never heavy, never boring, never really trivial; interested himself, he keeps us interested. At the back of his tales, there is belief in life and a philosophy of life, and of how many short story writers can that be said? ...He follows no fashion and no school. He is always himself. And can't he write? Ah! Far better than far more pretentious writers. Nothing escapes his eye, but he describes without affectation or redundancy, and you sense in him a feeling for beauty that is never obtruded. He gets values right, and that is to say nearly everything. The easeful fidelity of his style has militated against his reputation in these somewhat posturing times. But his shade may rest in peace, for in this volume, at least he will outlive nearly all the writers of his day." In summing his up Galsworthy suggested that, through his stories, he would "outlive all the writers of his day."

James Hilton (author of Goodbye, Mr Chips and Lost Horizon) said "I think his very best works ought to be included in any anthology of the best short stories ever written." He cited 'The Octave of Jealously' as his favourite short story for the March 1939 edition of Good Housekeeping saying it was a "bitterly brilliant tale."

Rebecca West said of his writing in 1922 that his ability to blend reality with the imaginary was "the envy of all artists."

More than 87 short stories in more than 25 magazines, and in 6 volumes published during Aumonier's lifetime.

Among more than 20 other magazines, his work appeared in Argosy Magazine, John O' London's Weekly, The Strand Magazine and The Saturday Evening Post, as well as being anthologized, and adapted for film and television.

Short Story Collections

The Golden Windmill & Other Stories (1921)
The Friends & Other Stories (1917)
Miss Bracegirdle & Other Stories (1923)

Novels

Olga Bardel (1916)
Three Bars Interval (1917)
Just Outside (1917)
The Querrils (1919)
One After Another (1920)
Heartbeat (1922)

Other Works

A volume of 14 Character Studies: Odd Fish (1923)

A volume of 15 Essays: Essays of Today and Yesterday (1926)